# THE PARIS VENDETTA

# THE
# PARIS
# VENDETTA

## SHAN SERAFIN

THE MYSTERIOUS PRESS
NEW YORK

THE PARIS VENDETTA

Mysterious Press
An Imprint of Penzler Publishers
58 Warren Street
New York, N.Y. 10007

Copyright © 2024 by Shan Serafin

First Mysterious Press edition

Interior design by Maria Fernandez

Library of Congress Control Number: 2023923317

ISBN: 978-1-61316-527-0
eBook ISBN: 978-1-61316-528-7

10 9 8 7 6 5 4 3 2 1

Printed in the United States of America
Distributed by W. W. Norton & Company

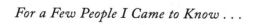

*For a Few People I Came to Know . . .*

# PROLOGUE

L et's try this again. Let's look at it from the beginning, doing the math, the physics, the science, the *art* of launching my chair backward—literally up and backward—to get airborne—shoving myself off the floor as hard as possible to generate the momentum needed to flip over—somehow avoiding a concussion in the process—land on the ground, crack the strut, free my hands, free my legs, then roll to my knees so I could get up and bull-rush him. Bull-rush, right? That's a thing? To topple him. To blitz him. Which would stun him, right? Which would give me, what, about two and a half seconds to scramble and yank the knife out of his hands?

If he had a knife.

He had a wrench, a large plumber's wrench. I saw that much. I wouldn't know what to do with a wrench—obviously wrest it from his grip—but if I could get a knife, if I could get a *knife*, I could immobilize him, then undo this rope, then undo this clamp, then undo this nightmare that's got me stuck here, trapped in a basement, somewhere in Paris—somewhere underneath it—where every single aspect seems stolen straight from the depths of hell—a bare bulb hanging from the ceiling, a rusted door, the wet air, the barren walls—an unimaginably harsh location where this guy asked me his one question, literally his one question, his only question in the past five hours, before saying absolutely nothing else.

"Where is she?"

He said it with a slight accent—Eastern bloc, or maybe Scandinavian, maybe German—and I'd replay those words in my head repeatedly, pathologically, over and over again, analyzing all the implications, over and over, chopping up my thoughts into a thousand fragments, trying to find some way to answer the unanswerable. Where is she? I tried every response. I tried everything I could to convey to him what I had. Theories. Assumptions. Guesses. Verbiage. Excuses. Where is she? I'd offer an answer. I'd wait again. I'd answer again. I'd wait. Talk. Wait. Panic. Talk. Panic more. Stop. Wait again. Talk again. Over and over. No solution came. No progress was made. Instead, after an eternity, I'd arrived at the sickening sensation that he was now standing behind me, on the verge of an exponentially increasing explosion of violence.

Where was she?

I had no idea. The only thing I knew was that something sinister was smoldering back there inside this unknown man and a limit had been reached and an amount of time had run out and the slow footsteps I was now hearing behind me were the footsteps of an adversary who was approaching me to speak up after hours and hours of saying nothing, after a full day of watching me fail to oblige him, bending toward the back of my neck to utter five horrific words, which he hardly raised his voice to deliver. "You . . . now have . . . sixty seconds."

# CHAPTER 1

Jennifer Graham. In the hotel lobby. This was five days earlier. There were two women in this equation and Jenn was one of the two. She and I were walking quickly through the conference crowd, smiling as if the evening were proceeding along quite smoothly, as if everyone had been gushing over our hard work, which, in my unsolicited opinion, wasn't far from the truth.

"You can't pretend it doesn't exist," she said to me. "You can't pretend the problem isn't real. You have to own it. You have to live it, breathe it, embrace it. Confidently. With open arms. Understand? Open arms. You go up to the microphone, you look the crowd in the eye, you stand tall, confident, you sound expensive, you make a slightly-offensive-but-not-offensive joke, avoid big words, then convincingly laugh at the pressure after fully *acknowledging* the pressure. You own it, then assure them that the 'it' doesn't exist."

"Okay."

"I'm telling you exactly what needs to be said so that you and I—so everyone—the entire team—takes a step closer to actually making this work."

"Okay."

"You disagree?"

"No."

"What part do you disagree with?"

"None of it."

"What part do you disagree with?"

"Just . . ."

"Adam."

"Everything. Literally everything you just said."

"God, I knew it."

"I'll do whatever you want. I'll say whatever you want, but don't ask me three times if I disagree with you, because I can't fend off that kind of Jennifer-ness. No, I don't think sales is about putting your weakest foot forward and calling it your best foot."

"It's about owning it. We own it. 'We as a firm have seen the issue at hand, Mr. Client, and we can assure you the issue is irrelevant.'"

"Or 'We as a firm have a bunch of martinis ready for you, Mr. Client, so without further ado . . . drink your body weight.'"

"No."

"Yes."

"No."

"They're literally going to be asking about the delay, *wondering* about it."

"Drunk people don't wonder stuff. They relate to you. They look over and say, 'Wow, I really relate to you, you relatable fuck.' First rule of sales: it's a business of relationships."

"You can't solve problems with a martini."

"Second rule of sales: you can solve problems with a martini. And I get it. I get it, I get it. We're the hosts, I get it. We had a logistical delay, which, small as it may seem—a shrewd European banker is going to question whether we're competently handling large European contracts. I get it. But I promise you, tonight of all nights, right now, they are upstairs at the bar, waiting for nothing *but* the bar."

"Why are you fighting me?"

"Why are *you* fighting *you*? I said a hundred times you can do the opening words."

"You're who they like."

"No."

"You're giving the opening words because they like you, Adam. Because everyone likes you. Because tonight you will say the right thing and you will *believe* in saying it. That's my point."

"I already said I'd do it."

She stopped in her tracks, stopping both of us, right in the middle of the lobby, so she could get in front of me and win her case. We were both insanely jet-lagged and thouroughly overworked.

"Look around. What do you see?"

"The . . . lobby?"

"What do you see?"

"The . . .?" I genuinely didn't know what she was doing.

"I'll just give you the answer. You see a hotel full of corporate people casually wondering why there's a security check for our event."

I love Jenn. I've loved her since the Tuesday morning we first met eight years ago. She's more than a best friend. She's the best part of me. She's all anyone should ever aspire to be.

"You know what I see, Jenn?"

"You don't get a turn."

"I see Paris."

"No."

"Through the windows, I see Paris. I see the streets, the cobblestone, a sensuous lamp, a neat bridge, elderly people making out. You know what this town is known for? Everything good and expensive. Paris outshines all other cities like an embroidered quilt among Burger King napkins. That's what's here."

"You don't actually think that."

"Doesn't matter what I think. What matters is that everyone at this convention thinks it. They think it, they love it, there's a slight mystique every time they answer the question: 'Hey, Earl, where ya goin' next week?' 'Business trip in Paris, Alan.' 'Paris!? You total fucken' asshole.' Because everyone loves coming here because it's a brochure on sex, and, yes, actually, I do believe it makes other cities into a Burger King napkin. This is night three of five. These people have been doing banking math all week so I really don't think the terrace lounge party—Let's repeat those holy words—Terrace—Lounge—Party—is the place where they go to hear another apology about another glitch."

"It's not a glitch. It's an unplanned security check as a result of issues here at our event, which will make them wonder if our firm is ready to handle a four-point-eight-billion dollar loan, which is a hesitancy that Evan, our CEO, *your* CEO, said to avoid yet now we can't even send these people up an elevator without a rectal exam."

I took her hand in mine. "You're an event planner, the best of the best. You live and die by the words 'a nice evening,' and I love you for this unrequitedly, and I will do what you tell me to do out of this unrequited love. You win."

"Did you even hear one word I said!?"

"No."

We'd arrived at the back of the line of people waiting for the elevator, queued up with their ID badges out for the hotel staff. They'd announced a technical issue, which Jenn felt would be regarded by our guests, the people around us—clients, associates, bankers, brokers—as a security breach. I disagreed with her until now—until I saw that the hotel staff weren't the ones checking ID badges. It was the French police. The gendarmerie. All jokes aside, it'd taken fifteen minutes before they'd gotten to Jenn and me, and in that time, the line had doubled behind us and had begun to look quite serious.

"Madame . . . uh . . . Jennifer?" said the officer, reading her badge.

"Yes," she said.

He looked at her. Looked at her ID. Looked at her. Checked a list of names. "*Merci*, thank you, you can go." He let her through. "Mister . . . uh . . . Adam?"

"Yes," I said.

He did the same. Looked at me. Looked at my ID. Looked at the list. Looked back at me. "You are Mr. Adam?"

"Yeah. Adam Macias."

He kept studying my badge.

I tried to be casual. "Is there . . . a . . . ?"

Whatever result he was seeing on his portable scanner had flagged something because he then uttered the sentence no foreigner wants to hear from someone with a weapon. "You . . . will . . . uh . . . come with me?"

"Sorry?"

"You . . . uh . . . You will come with me?" He pointed to the side area. He wanted to talk to me apart from the main crowd, privately, already turning to lead the way toward wherever we were going, already a few steps ahead of us so that Jenn and I had to hurry to follow him.

"Why would police need to talk to you?" she whispered to me.

"Why would police need to talk to you?" she whispered.

"It's fine."

"How is it fine?"

"I don't know."

"Your ID was flagged."

"Yeah."

"How is it fine?"

"Because . . ."

"Because . . . ? You're not worried?"

"Not fully."

"But a little bit."

"No."

"Adam."

"I'm mostly sure it's fine."

"Mostly?"

"Yeah. I'm a hundred-percent . . . mostly sure."

# CHAPTER 2

They led me to the far side of the lobby with Jenn following alongside. I could feel the back of my neck getting warm. I could feel the people behind me staring—watching a guy get pulled out of line. *Oh, they're pulling someone out.* Watching me get escorted away. *Oh, it was him.* Making various comments about skin tone without mentioning skin tone. *I knew it'd be him.* The main cop leaned over to his colleagues and murmured some unintelligible French. *"Dites aux autres que la porte est dans l'angle mort,"* he said.

I couldn't take my eyes of the automatic weapons. French police carry very serious machine guns.

The main cop turned to me. "Uh . . . It's okay for you we are talking for a moment?"

I fired a regular gun once. It was at a gun range and scared the hell out of me. The first shot was the real shock—felt like the thing was gonna fly out of my hands—and that was just a pistol.

"Sure," I said.

"Uh, Mr. . . . Is it Macias?" said the sergeant. "This is Spanish, no?"

"He's American," said Jenn. "With an American passport."

"Can I ask you to tell me your recent activity, Mr. Macias?"

"Activity?"

"Why?" said Jenn.

"We need him to tell us what he was doing for the time prior to now. Mr. Macias, did you scan the service elevator? With your badge?"

"My badge?"

The officer pointed toward the back area of the hotel. "The east door. It, uh . . . It connect you this. You are using this badge for this?"

"Yes . . . uh . . . I think . . . Yes."

"You are in France for business?" he said to me.

"Yes. The conference."

"You are not here for other business?"

"Sorry?"

"You are not here for other business? This is, uh, not an official question."

"Then he doesn't have to answer it," said Jenn.

"It's fine," I told him, hardly interested in whatever legal rights I wasn't being afforded by whatever constitution this guy wasn't following. "I'm not here for anything other than business."

"You activate service elevator?"

"Yes."

"Why you are doing this?"

"For a young woman."

"Who?"

"Who? I don't know."

"This woman . . . She is asking you . . . to use it?"

"Yes."

"She is who?"

"I don't know. She seemed to be a guest."

"What is she . . . uh . . . How? You are describing her for me."

"She's tall. Maybe five-ten. She's, um, European. But maybe Eastern bloc. Blue eyes. Short blond-ish hair. She looks . . . uh . . . good. Y'know?"

"No."

"Like a model. Like, I mean, like, she's not the kind of girl you see often." Jenn was right next to me, hearing all this. "She had an accent. And a mark. A mark around her neck."

"Of where?"

"Sorry?"

"Where? Where this is?"

They had me show them where. They actually had me lead them all the way across the lobby, out of the main area, over to the service elevator. You can imagine how cooperative I'm trying to be, not letting myself make any fast moves, still preoccupied with the machine guns. I led our little group across the main atrium of the hotel with the entire crowd staring. I swear, if I'd pointed at, like, a chandelier, everyone would look up and cower from it.

"This was a sexual type of conversation?" asked the cop. We'd arrived at the rather secluded area where I met her. "You are acquainted to this girl before this moment?"

"No."

"And she stands where exactly?"

"Roughly . . . uh . . ." I put myself in the spot in question, a patch of carpet near the stairwell door, using my hands to position an imaginary version of her by her imaginary hips.

The main cop looked around, then stared at one particular corner of the hallway. "This is a position where the camera would not to see her, no?" He wasn't just asking me. He was asking the general posse around him—his assistant, the hotel manager, the other machine-gun guys.

"*Oui, inspecteur*," said the manager, rattling off no words I could understand. "*L'autre coin a une caméra mais l'un d'eux serait trop obstruée.*"

"This girl," the detective said to me, "she, uh, tells to you things. How it was? You show us." He motioned to the ground. "Show me your step. Position. Step. What she is doing in front of you?"

"She did, uh, nothing at first. And then she became . . . uh . . ." I had to think of it and think of it fast. I had to figure out how to tell them what happened but alter it slightly so that I wasn't actually lying. Because you can't lie. These guys would know a lie. But you also can't, you absolutely can't, under any circumstances, tell the truth. Not about this. Not with this firm. Not with our shit. "She stood . . ." I started to say, "uh . . . there . . . and she did . . . uh . . . she did exactly what girls like her do . . . She, yeah . . . She did exactly what girls like her do . . ."

# CHAPTER 3

"Me?" I pointed to myself with enough self-doubt, self-deprecation, and self-directed uncertainty to emasculate my confidence long before the following encounter would do its share. "You mean . . . me?" I'd turned around to face the most genetically improbable female I'd ever seen. This was forty-five minutes ago. This was her coming up to me. A five-ten beautifully built, breathtakingly exotic aesthetic masterpiece of a human.

"Yeah, hi," she said for a second or third time. "Hi. Sorry . . . but . . . um . . . Is it . . . um . . .?" She was pointing at something, hesitating with her words as she spoke, trying to hide her accent and smiling to cover the shyness. "You are part of the conference?"

"Uh, yeah, the . . . the . . . here in the hotel."

"You are . . . uh . . . uh . . . participant?"

"A participant? I am." You daydream about moments like this. Relentlessly. You begin in grade school—daydreaming, wishing, hoping, planning, rehearsing, growing older, growing weaker, hoping, losing hope, losing hair, gaining weight, yet still always daydreaming, that a moment like this, with a female this unworldly, could unfold in front of you. "I'm actually part of the event."

"Do you know what time they stop serving drinks?"

"I think probably eleven. If this were LA, they'd stop serving at one thirty because the law in LA says two. I'm from LA. But here in Paris it's . . . I think they don't stop. Or maybe they stop at four, or, I don't know. I mean, I grew up in Venice Beach, which is low income but it's also trendy in a way." What was I even saying?

She was taller than me, and when I talk to taller females, I fidget. She exuded a bold sensuality just doing nothing other than nonchalantly standing there—her black-lace choker hinting at some kind of submission-domination game where no one's sure whose role is whose. Her eyes were audibly gorgeous, and you could barely look at them yet barely look away. She carried a little gift bag that said "La Radiance" on it, with a jar of oil inside nestled on a clump of tissue, and you're trying not to stare at her legs but they're everywhere. Every time she switches body positions, even slightly shifting her foot forward or to the side, every part of you floods with need.

"I think everything is normal tonight except the elevators are restricted now because the hotel had a complaint. Your necklace." I pointed to it. It was partially hiding what looked like a bad rope burn. "It's, uh, really chic."

"Do you know if this is the other elevator?"

"This . . . is . . . probably . . . maybe the service one." I looked over at the panel, at the electronic scanning pad for it. "If you're going to the terrace, they want us to take the main elevator because this one is for equipment. Sorry about mentioning the necklace thing. I wasn't saying it was bad—your scar. Your scar's great. I mean, not great. I mean, it's cool. It's cool to have a scar . . ." I couldn't have sounded dumber. "Scars are where life happened, y'know?"

"Is there any way you could call it?" She gestured toward the elevator panel. She meant for me to scan the door with my conference ID badge.

"Oh, totally." I hurried over to do it. "You're going to the event? Sure, totally."

"Will you be up there?"

"Yeah! Should be fun. The view will be great, don't you think?"

"No."

"No?"

"Paris is better from the streets."

"Oh, yeah?"

"Thank you."

"Yeah. Okay." I stepped back as she stepped past me. "This is, like, day three of the conference for us. We get maybe one final day to go throw stuff off the Eiffel Tower or whatever. They keep us busy. Hahaha. So . . . uh . . ."

She left.

# CHAPTER 4

"**A**nd that was it," I said to the cop. "She went upstairs and that was it. She mentioned some details indicating she was a conference guest, so I assumed she was a guest, so when she asked to go up, I let her up."

The cop and his men stood there, letting my report continue to tumble out of my mouth, sizing it up, sizing me up, then after a moment, the main guy spoke. "And that was it?"

They seemed to be waiting for more and I didn't have more. I could feel my temperature rise another degree. I'd just given them the only version of the evening that could sidestep the complications involved, telling it in just the right way to make myself seem the way I needed to seem.

"That was it," I said.

"Officer," said Jenn. "Can I ask you what tip you're responding to?" She stepped into the middle of our group.

"This is a response to a tip, right?" she said. "All this security? Did you get a phone call? I'm asking you this because I'm part of the conference staff, so whatever you're working on, it's relevant to me." She could see his confusion, or at least the confusion he pretended to have, and she was unfazed. "*Votre réponse c'etait pour quoi exactement?* Let me just tell you there is nothing remarkable happening at the event. We'd know because we're part of the conference staff and we've seen nothing, and he's the host of the event on the terrace, which actually won't start without him, which means things will get more chaotic for you, for you as police, if you prevent him from helping things stay organized because the guests are going to get upset and start wandering around the building and it'll be increasingly difficult for *you* to get *your* work done without him up there fixing it."

She stood her ground. She was forcing him to take a good, long look at her conviction. She might've even stepped *toward* him a millimeter, a negotiation tactic, subconsciously causing him to wonder just how much she'd be worth arguing with if he chose to oppose her. She's an ice-cold glacier of determination when she wants to be. And she always wants to be.

"Okay," he said, and waved us through. He was done with both of us, done with me, done with her, done with the story, just like that, no fanfare, already engaged in a new conversation with a different cop while the hotel manager handed us back our passports. The other two officers stepped aside to let us walk directly to the elevator line of conference members as Jenn then led us *past* them to take me to the far door, bypassing the wait entirely, to have us go all the way up the ten-story building on foot.

"I'll do it," I said to her about halfway up, ready to clear the air.

"What?"

"I'll do it. I'll do whatever speech you want. I'll make the announcement. I'll believe each word I say."

"Great," she mumbled, continuing to walk.

"That's it?"

"What?"

"Just 'Great'?"

"Yeah. Great. Cool. Thanks."

"I don't need a thanks."

"Okay."

"I thought you'd . . . y'know . . . gloat."

"No."

"I'm sorry about the mess."

"With the cops? No. You did what you had to do."

"It's tough trying to understand a foreign language, let alone with guns around. I'm surprised they were polite but I'm sorry it hung us up. What do you mean I did what I had to do?"

"Try to keep yourself to three drinks upstairs, okay? Go slow. You'll be fine if you go slow."

"What do you mean I did what I had to do?"

"With the cops."

"What?"

"You lied."

"I *lied*?"

"It's okay. I get it. Hence, me saying, 'You did what you had to do.'"

"What makes you think I lied?"

"About what you and the girl talked about."

"Seriously?"

"I know you. It's fine. Can we please focus on the event? We're three flights away."

"You're upset I talked to that girl."

"No."

"That I spent valuable minutes flirting with some high-class prostitute instead of being ready to get in the line I *should've known* based on Jenn Logic would be increasing in length."

"She wasn't high class."

"For the record, she came up to me."

"I'm sure she did."

"She asked about the seminar. She saw my ID. She came up. She seemed to know the conference schedule. That's the thing."

"Your tie looks off."

"I can't tell who's who when someone just comes up to me."

"Fix your tie."

"So if you're upset—"

"Adam."

"I'm just saying there's—"

"Yes, I'm upset! Okay?!" She got right up in my face to start fixing my tie, yanking it out to redo the knot from scratch, tugging hard with each point she made. "Yes, I'm upset you talked to some girl and made us late, okay? There. However . . . I'm not letting that interfere with my focus right now because I want this deal so bad it hurts my lower colon, because if we pull this off, we'll get *multiple* nations back to financial health, which is a miracle, which is professionally *admirable*, which would thereby justify why I put up with years and years of defending our sad-shit company against the sad-shit illegal sex shit we keep drowning ourselves in. So, no, I'm not shocked some hooker got confused by a door-knob and needed you to rescue her. I'm shocked about being late, that's all. I want to close this contract. I want our names on that little plaque in the corporate hallway that nobody looks at. I don't *care* if nobody looks at it—*I* don't even look at it—but I want our names there. That's all. So can you please just go make a Pulitzer Prize–winning speech?" She finished a full Windsor knot. She stepped back.

She made a slight adjustment.

"You look good," she said. She smiled. Genuinely. "You're the best account manager we have. Use your instincts. I don't care what you say, actually. Just be you." She took my hand without waiting for my retort and led us up the final flight of stairs to the top landing where we'd caught up to the small number of conference attendees who'd chosen the same exhausting route we did, who were slower than us, who were joking about how out of breath they were, how badly they needed a drink—trading hellos with us as we all then clustered at the doorway where a hostess was letting people through one-by-one, and when it was my turn to step out into the wonderful fresh air of the Parisian twilight, I heard several women yelling in the distance, which was obviously the squealing joy of people scooting around on a dance floor to Europop, because I was hearing several men squeal too, which made the whole thing feel like it was on the verge of perfection until I understood that these people weren't actually shouting for joy. Something at the far end of the terrace had gone disturbingly wrong and they were reacting to it. There was a man who'd caught fire. Evan Goldman, our CEO. He was covered in flames, literally burning alive, his body being singed right in front of us.

# CHAPTER 5

You're so stunned by the instant introduction of unexpected information that your brain doesn't immediately accept what's in front of you. You realize you've been perceiving new details for several seconds without fully registering any of them. In addition to the pockets of people freaking out, there was a cackling laughter that echoed across the area, sounding almost like a demented animal. This was the final discovery in my chain of discoveries—that this laughter wasn't laughter. It was the bloodcurdling cry of our chief executive, Evan Goldman, screaming in pain—literally sizzling alive in front of all of us and crying out with a depth of agony you wouldn't believe biologically possible. Our boss, the most influential man in the building—and this week, arguably in Paris—was rolling around on the patio while apparently no one had the means to help him. The well-dressed crowd stood frozen as more and more screams came from more and more people. "Do something!" was shouted in different languages, and I soon realized that Jenn was no longer next to me. In fact, Jenn was nowhere to be seen.

"Jennifer!" I called out.

Most of us were riveted in place, especially the people around me, who were too far removed from the spectacle to take initiative. There had to be about sixty of us standing there, idly. Evan was on the other side of the crowd from us under one of the bungalows, in a position slightly elevated by a wood platform, so I could catch glimpses of him if I moved a bit. Several men were whapping Evan with jackets and couch pillows and torn curtains and whatever else they could find—one lady throwing a pitcher of water on him.

"*Il ne marche pas!*"

"*Plus fort!*"

"*Je dit IL NE MARCHE PAS!*"

It wasn't working, and they were shouting that it wasn't working as the dull, blue flame that covered his body refused to go out. A few other people had joined the rescue effort. God, the noise this guy made—that's what you can't get out of your head. The visual itself was mesmerizing but his unholy cries of pain were enough to make you nauseous. All of us wanted to converge and help him somehow, but other than the half-dozen people surrounding him, nobody else moved *because* nobody else moved. Jenn had grabbed a fire extinguisher—that's what she went to do. I don't know where she found it—no one else had the wherewithal—but over the tops of everyone's heads she could just barely be seen as her brunette updo zigzagged its way toward the bungalows to deliver a huge plume of whiteness on Evan. She was dousing the guy when the entire situation got ten times more surreal—the wooden frame of the bungalow had caught fire. It'd been draped in silk sheets, and we now had giant streaks of orange flames slapping upward at the sky and converting to dark, black, disturbingly fast-rising pillars of smoke. The yelling turned to shrieking and before I could move, having been wedged in the doorway of one of the only two stairwells, I was pummeled by the surge of a crowd in panic.

"Jenn!" I called out.

I did my best to stay on the terrace and keep track of her, to give myself a chance to find my way toward her, but at a certain point in the turmoil, at the tipping point in the balance of mob dynamics, I couldn't rightfully stand my ground without blocking everyone. So I turned around and headed downstairs within the swell of the crowd, descending a full flight before exiting the stairwell to circle back up to the roof by some other means. It was shortsighted on my part. The floor just below the roof was becoming a chaotic mess in its own right. Several patrons had shouted there was a fire above them and thus sent the restaurant into a frenzy.

Jenn was now officially separated from me.

I descended all the way down to the ground floor where I was rushed forward through the front doors past an increasingly agitated population of people. The hotel staff were being aided by those police already present along with additional police, lots of them now, who'd pulled up out front. Fire trucks were arriving. Ambulances were arriving. Emergency lights were lighting up the massive stretch between the Concorde and the d'Orsay. Your sense of the passage of time is shot to hell. You see things and hear things but don't quite remember them merely seconds after they happen. I had a warped hyperawareness imbibing the visuals around me, noting sounds, noting particular voices from way across the crowd, while retaining none of it. I couldn't keep track of what I was doing or what I'd just done, waiting within the growing throng of spectators, cordoned off from the area. I wandered back and forth among them, looking for Jenn, calling for Jenn, trying to see her face in the ranks of anyone who passed. The police would know, right? That's what I told myself. They'd have some record of her. But they were overwhelmed, and even in trying to talk to some of the paramedics, hoping to run a name by them—"Uh, Jennifer Graham"—just to see if a description got me anywhere—"she's half Asian, about five-seven, age thirty-eight"—our conversation went nowhere. I waited. I let the clock tick. I tried to pick out the most amenable-looking officer I could approach but the math of it had kicked in. You spend your work weeks calculating percentages, using actuarial statistics to convince people of things. With five fire trucks, one fire boat, six police vans, at least three ambulances, and a crowd of several hundred people, the chances of this havoc involving zero additional fatalities had to be zero. People were going to get hurt. I looked back up toward the top of the roof. It was *still* on fire. I could see the smoke but the angle was too steep to discern much else. An hour had elapsed down here and it was time for me to pose the question, the question I didn't want in my head but which was forming on its own. What were the odds Jenn Graham *didn't* make it out of the building?

# CHAPTER 6

Another two hours went by with me sitting down on the street curb. Some of the conference participants had left by this time, probably heading back to the other hotels—the locations across the river, the slightly-cheaper-but-still-insanely-expensive rooms that most of us had checked into for the week. I remained where I was on the sidewalk, hoping to get at least *some* news of Jenn. I'd tried calling the reception desk at her hotel—no news. I'd called her room—nothing. I'd called her cell phone fifteen different times and was about to try a sixteenth when I saw Trevor.

"Macias!" He spotted me from across the crowd and came over.

"Yo."

"Yo, man, you good?"

"Pffff. Not really. You?"

"I'm all right."

Trevor Manning. One of the key members of my team.

"This is nuts, right?" he said. "This is a zoo."

"Where were you guys?"

"Us?"

"Yeah."

"Across the street."

"Have you seen Jenn?"

"Jenn? No. We're all over on the far side. Right by the benches." He pointed to the other side of the parking lot where several of the more social participants were circled around, chatting. This was his handiwork—the organizing of it. This was what he did. Schmooze. Lead a pack. He was the portrait of modern commercial banking. Aggressive. Young. Fit. Tall. Carefully disheveled hair. Bleached teeth. Never resembling anything but a tennis ad. "Everyone's over there. Dustin. Me. Monica. The Deutsche-Z guys. Plus, those two chicks from London. Let's go, man." He wanted me to get up.

"I gotta hang by the ambulances." I stayed where I was.

"For what?"

"To make sure she's out."

"Who?"

"Jenn. I gotta make sure."

"Dude, she's out."

"No."

"She has to be."

"How do you know? You saw her?"

"Everyone's out. It's been three hours."

"That doesn't mean anything."

"Dude, don't be a rag. You're not sitting here, are you? Just, like . . .?" He tried again to coax me up off the curb. "Let's go, man. I met up with the Deutsche guys and they wanna hit a couple bars on the Champs-Élysées. We're gonna grab drinks and see who wants what. Let's go."

"Drinks?"

"Yeah."

"Now?!"

"That's the word from the top."

"Now?! They said go out? In the middle of a crisis?!"

"It's not a crisis."

"Evan was on fire."

"His status is unknown. Calm down with that."

"I was *there*."

"We don't know anything about—"

"I was *there*."

"And you talked to a doctor? You saw a report? No, right? No. And until we confirm anything, we don't dramatize it."

"Oh my God, I'm not even—"

"Look, look, look, I get it, dude. I get it. I'm the same. This looks serious. But the directive from LA, from Head Office, is we keep everyone chill until anything's confirmed. We're the only people who do this shit. You and me. No one else. We handle it. And they literally said, 'Don't exaggerate anything. Handle it.' So are you in or are you in?"

"No."

"My German sucks, man."

"I don't know German."

"I get it, trust me, but most of the conference people weren't up there when it went down and they don't *know* what went down. Gerald becomes acting Number Two and he's saying don't exaggerate it. He's saying don't spread rumors—if you need to go to a hospital to get checked out, go. Otherwise, confirmations by nine a.m. because we're in Europe to work."

"Trev." I wasn't sure I was going to tell anyone. "I'm gonna get talked to by the police."

"For what?"

"I don't know, man. I got pulled aside by three cops before this all got started. It's nothing big but after this shit . . ." I pointed to the commotion in front of us. "I can't be sure."

"What're you talking about?"

"I got flagged by the cops for some breach thing. They pulled me aside before the event because they were checking IDs, and when they checked mine, it was flagged for scanning a service lift."

"So what? Why'd you use a service lift?"

"I didn't. I scanned it for some random-ass girl and they tracked it on a log sheet."

"C'mon, that's not a thing."

"They're gonna ask questions how he got burned."

"*If* he got burned."

"Trev—"

"You don't know what happened yet. None of us knows. That's my point. We have real-world issues. BNP, Suisse, Deutsche, those guys were already on the fence. The final twenty-four hours before inking a deal is everything. Everything. You're the one who taught me that. They came out tonight to cut loose, but trust me, if you give 'em a reason to panic, they'll go full Nuremberg on you. The word from corporate—"

"Fuck corporate. Fuck 'em with a dead cat. I'm not gonna go lock down commitments after I watched a guy get scorched alive. I *know* they're telling us back off, saying he's hurt or the sky's falling or yeah, yeah, all that, but I'm telling you, in twelve hours this shit's gonna get real."

"Of *course* it is. That's why they want to us to make progress now. That's the entire reason. We had a shrinking window to begin with. Now that window's shutting."

He made sense.

"We can overreact to this or we can help them calm down and make some money," he said. I didn't want him to be right but he made his case. "You're the one guy who can call the biggest fish."

"Barely."

"Barely's all it takes. You can make that call."

I started to get up.

"You're gonna come?!" he said.

"No. I'm going to go check hospitals."

"C'mon."

"I'm going to find Jenn."

"Fuck you."

"Fuck me. Agreed."

He stood there a moment, then laughed, then offered his hand. "You're a good man, Macias." We leaned in to hug and shake hands frat-boy style. That's what Trevor embodied—the unending, optimistic adolescence of Wall Street. "You're a hero in some weird alternate universe." He patted me on the shoulder. "Just not this one. Go find Jenn."

# CHAPTER 7

S imply put they didn't care. The people at the top didn't even see it as a safety issue—the fire. They'd eventually show the necessary concern—publicly stating just the right amount of sorrow at just the right time with well-worded, classy statements of nothing—but any internal usage of the word "crisis" only applied to that which directly threatened the enactment of our multinational European economic stimulus package, and I had to own up to this. This was what you signed up for, man. This was the industry. Your best friend ran into the burning corner of a building to save someone and your management isn't even bothering to make sure she's okay—but you knew how this business works. You knew, and that's why you second-guess your own criticism of it. Gimme a couple endless hours sitting on a street curb followed by three more hours waiting in a swivel chair in a temp office, and I find gaping holes in my own logic. *You're paid to do what they say, man. If you don't like it, don't cash a paycheck.* Don't act like you're not what you yourself built. Indeed, it's this sort of self-doubt that hits you at 3:15 a.m. while alone at your workstation. I took a taxi straight to the main branch of our Paris location. I sat at one of the generic desks they'd assigned us, logging in to my terminal, making a half-dozen calls to various hospitals, also calling the front desk of the hotel she was checked in at, describing her, pleading with whoever would listen:

"She might be in her room incoherent, sir. She might need you to break protocol and then let me know her medical status regardless of whether or not she requested that you check on her." I sat back and closed my eyes to try to ease the sting, tilting my head against the chair, hoping to improve my vision, then drifted to sleep, exhausted by the unfairness of it. This was the exact moral dilemma Jenn herself ranted about daily. Daily. Yes, we hate this job, Adam, but we show up precisely *because* we hate it. So we can fix it. From within. Which, in her eyes, included closing this week's deal, which was what everyone in the department was on edge about, not just in regard to the complications of the week, but something we fretted over for months, for a year, bickering, disagreeing, panicking, all while constantly reading about ourselves in the news. That was the not-so-minor detail that would unravel this whole thing. I checked my phone again. Nothing from Jenn. I had a bunch of missed calls at this point, including one from a French number. Four digits. The time was 7:05 a.m. I'd managed to half nap, half stew for several hours. Congratulations, you lazy ass. I sat up and started to check my voicemails. "Adam, hi. It's Eduardo Costas of Banco Madrid. I hope you are okay. I hope everyone is okay. I'm wanting to perhaps, yes, receive some update on the, uh, situation . . . and . . . uh . . . Yes, thank you." He was one of the higher-producing reps we had. "Hi, Adam, it's Charlotte Leeds, HSBC. Hope this message finds you in good health. What a night, I must say, hahaha. I do hope we are all safe. I'd heard the rather severe news but, uh, I'd love to know that you yourself are okay and that, um, we can discuss any next steps. When, of course, it's appropriate, of course. And so, yes, please do let me know." Then, "Good morning. It's Franz Müller from BEM. Please call me at your earliest convenience."

I pressed stop.

I pulled up my web browser. I wasn't surprised at the number of calls but there was something about the tone. In each of them. The gravity. What exactly did these people just find out? My news feed defaults to headlines from every major city on the globe. I did a quick search for our name, expecting to have to sift through numerous articles before finding anything, except that, no, yeah, wow. We were a major head-line. Our firm. Everywhere. "CEO of Euro Bank Severely Burned," "CEO Evan Goldman Placed in ICU," "Bank Exec Maimed," "Evan Goldman Third-Degree Burns." The top story in every business sec-tion of almost every market. Tokyo. London. Beijing. And those were just the cities that were awake. Half the world was still in bed, yet to spin their own versions of it. Third-degree?! The *AP* wire reported he was scorched head to toe, likely to die by the end of today. Whatever hours of life he still had were replete with pain. Some sources even had him gone already. So that was why everyone was calling in the early hours, hoping to sort it out, pretending not to worry about their own revenue. Trevor's intel was right. I picked up the phone and dialed the only number that mattered.

"Service," said the voice at the other end.

"Hi, this is Adam Macias of Euro Mutual calling for Nikos Dimopolous."

"You've reached his answering service, sir."

"When would he, uh, get a message?"

"Unfortunately, I have no info on that, sir. This is just a service."

"Right. I just need him to know . . ." This was big. I purposefully started this call before I was ready for it so that I could avoid stuttering through it. "I just need to him to know . . . Nikos . . . to know . . . that we are going strong. Everything is going strong. Going ahead as planned."

"Okay. 'Strong.' 'Going ahead as planned.' This was Adam Mancini, Euro Mutual?"

"Macias."

I had no real hope of getting a return call from Nikos. No one did. Nikos Dimopolous didn't want any part of this, yet based on dollar value alone, his name topped my call list, his name *was* my call list, and covering that list was the only reason I existed. Second below him was a guy named Franz Müller, whose firm represented six-hundred-forty million of the overall four-point-eight-billion needed. He probably phoned the world this morning, knowing Franz, but the fact that I was someone he personally just called meant I might have some traction with him. I was barely valuable to the overall equation—a highly replaceable cog in a massive machine—but I happened to have a working relationship with several of the bigger names. Not that I was a best friend or respected comrade to any of them. Outside of Nikos, I was more like an affable nephew. I dialed Franz.

*"Guten Morgen."*

"Franz?"

"Adam?"

"Hello, sir."

"You're alive!"

"Hahaha, yes. Alive. And I'm assuming you are too. I'm assuming I'm not communicating with, like, a vaporous apparition."

"I might enjoy the cheap travel but, no, I'm still solid matter."

"You sound good."

"Is that so?" He had a thick German accent but considered himself fluent in English. Good natured for the most part. "Thank you for the exaggeration."

"No, I knew you'd be okay. I know you're big on mountain biking and you swim too, right? Avid, right? So you have the stamina to handle things."

"Well, I was on the east side of the roof."

"Wow. But you're okay?"

"I feel okay."

"Good. Okay, then, Franz, I'll get to the point. You called me because you're unsure where we're at."

"Well. I'm—"

"You called because you wonder if my firm has the resources, or, let's say, intestinal fortitude, to plunge forward in the midst of an apparent setback like the one we had."

"Well, I don't want to seem too—"

"You're expecting me to tell you just how logistically impossible it is to proceed and just how much leniency I'll need from you and the other banks."

"Well—"

"You expect me to ask for your understanding."

"It—"

"Franz, I'm about to tell you the exact opposite . . . Fuck understanding. I'm about to tell you the only fact that's relevant: let's fucken' make money."

"Oh . . . uh . . . okay."

# CHAPTER 8

In my worn-out bag of sales tricks, this one was the oldest. None of my teammates liked it, certainly not the aggressive types, certainly not Trevor Manning. The odds of it backfiring were way too high unless you fully sold it, and selling it meant enduring *scathing* humility. You take your enemy's best punch. You absorb it. You own it. You wear it. You leave him with nothing else to take you down. You make sure he's stunned by how confidently you do all that and then you close the hell out of him. "You're absolutely right to doubt us, Franz. I'd doubt us too, if I'd earned the right to sit where you sit. What happened last night was a major letdown, and we let you down, and we're beside ourselves with embarrassment about the lack of professionalism in allowing it to take place, and we're going to make it up to everyone by streamlining the rest of the process."

"Streamlining?"

"Streamlining."

"Making it . . . ?"

"Making it up to you."

"So it's going ahead?"

"Amsterdam is going ahead."

"Wow."

"Yes."

"Uh, I was simply—"

"We're in Europe to make money, Franz. A lot. We are. You are. No shame in that. We're here to ink the deal and something as temporary as a couple flickers on a roof isn't going to distract us."

"Okay, but I'm reading about certain things in—"

"We're greedy, Franz, and excuse me for being crass in the face of mortality, I'm aware of how callous I sound, but let that serve as testament to my point. I'm hardly qualified to talk to someone of your stature with this much bravado, so if I'm doing it, if *I'm* doing it, I'm doing it because for the first time in our three-year business relationship, Franz, I, Adam, happen to know a fact with more certainty than you, which is the fact that we're about to make a sickening amount of money and not one single thing can derail it, and I know deep down you're wondering just how full of shit I am and you're gonna mentally scroll through each encounter we had in the past three years, realizing this is totally unlike little Adam, which, based on the sheer percentages involved, should tell you just *how much* money we're about to make. So today I'm the asshole who speaks the unspeakable. This is bigger than Evan Goldman—sorry for his temporary discomfort. This is our greed and our greed happens—just happens, *just* happens—to benefit you."

"Uh . . . Wow."

"To the tune of three point one percent concessional, word from our COO is Amsterdam is on."

We traded byes and hung up. I had to believe it was literally the only thing he needed to hear. Focusing on a hospitalization was the traditional tact to show here, and I didn't show an ounce of it. All the months and months of being the lamb in the suit in the corner of the room, yessing this guy to death, needed to pay off right here. He had to hear me say it with a conviction that couldn't be doubted. Trevor's intel was right. In the heat of the moment these guys didn't want a moral pause. They didn't want to confirm our health is okay. You could hear him hide his glee. He just wanted his hand held while we whispered how obscene his commission was going to be. Within a minute I had the same exact call with the banker from Madrid—Eduardo. Almost word for word, same speech. "You're wondering if we're going ahead, my friend." Same circumlocution. Same pause. Same bullshit-initial-twenty-seconds of feigned humanitarian concern before transitioning to what his own morals wouldn't let him be the first to say out loud. Are we closing this deal? Eduardo, we're about to make Eduardo a staggering amount of money. I started to dial the fourth name on my list when an incoming call came. My phone rang with the same strange four-digit number that'd rung me earlier. I picked it up out of habit, out of reflex.

"Hello?"

"Monsieur Adam?"

"This is him." I'd clicked over to a lady with a heavy French accent.

"I'm sorry to bother you, Monsieur Adam. This is Detective Élodie Michel with the BRI unit of the Paris Police Department. I spoke with your receptionist, and he said you might be at your desk. Can we talk?"

Talk? She'd caught me on my outbound line. I'd answered it before realizing I shouldn't have. I went blank. "S-sure. Go ahead."

"Not on the phone. I'd like to have you come in to the prefecture."

"Right now?"

"When can you come in?"

"Come in? You mean . . . ?"

"To the station."

"Uh, the . . ." My throat went dry. I tried to clear it without sounding like I needed to but I think she could hear the guilt. "Uh, may I ask what this is regarding?" She'd called me at work via a transferred line, which meant she'd talked to at least one other person in the building, on my team, in my company, referencing my name. That was very, very far from a good thing.

"I hope your health is recovering, Monsieur Adam. I'd like to ask if you know of any reason why someone might attack your company."

"Attack it?"

"Was there anyone who threatened any colleagues?"

"No."

"Your company is being investigated for past activities, Monsieur Adam, is that correct? Who is your direct supervisor?"

"My . . .?"

"Maybe there is some personal information that could be relevant to this case."

"You mean here in Paris or—?"

"Does your company have any concerns about being investigated?"

"Investigated? No."

"No?"

"I mean, not that I know of."

"Why would someone attack Mr. Goldman? Why was your ID badge used to scan the south service elevator?"

"I don't—My badge?"

"Why was your badge used to scan it? It's true, no?"

"It's true."

"Why?"

"There was a girl. And, um . . . she was lost."

"What does that mean?"

"She needed to use the lift and, uh . . . and, uh, I actually said all this yesterday to another offi—"

"Unfortunately, we don't have any confirmation of, uh, Ms. . . . uh Ms. . . ." She rifled through whatever file she had in front of her. "What did you say her name was?"

"I don't know her name. I'm sorry, I don't understand how this is . . . uh . . . is . . ." My phone was now ringing on two different incoming lines. I could see a random coworker looking over at me from across the large office. "Actually, I—"

"Do you know how Monsieur Goldman was burned?"

"Uh . . ."

"Monsieur Goldman's face and torso had been coated with a flammable gelatin several minutes prior to his catching fire. The gel remained ignited despite attempts to smother the flames. It was compounded by the fact that propane tanks were nearby, which I'd like to know if you—"

My incoming line beeped right over her voice. A long beep.

"Detective?" I said.

"—or anywhere in the—"

"Sorry, what?"

"—persons. You didn't hear me?"

"No, but, so sorry, can please you hold?" I didn't wait for a yes. I clicked on the new connection, having no idea who I'd be greeting but in no position to risk ignoring the potential revenue. "Hello?"

"Adam?"

"This is him."

"Hey, man." It was a Mediterranean voice.

"Hey."

"How's things?"

"Great."

"Yeah? Cool. Haha."

"Sorry . . . Who . . . ? Who is this?"

"Hahahaha. Nikos."

"Nikos?!"

"Yeah."

"Nikos!"

"What up, man!"

"Holy shit."

"Yeah, you good?"

"Yeah, yeah, no, wow, what's up, man!"

"What's goin' on!"

I couldn't believe he called me. He had a giddy, friendly, upbeat energy, which I couldn't help reciprocate. I was now on the phone with six billion dollars. "Nothing's going on, man! You got a quick minute?"

# CHAPTER 9

Nikos Dimopolous. We'd met twice—both occasions coming well before he was relevant to the financial world. His jet-setting dad had controlled all the money; his older, better-looking, better-dressed, better-represented-in-the-press, better-loved brother stood alone in line as the sole heir to the fortune. That brother and that dad died six months ago in a mountain-road accident and, just like that, overnight, Nikos became the tenth-richest kid in the country. He had no idea how to handle such a massive inundation of wealth and attention. At this point he trusted zero people around him, yet for whatever intangible reason, those two dinky occasions where I chatted him up at two random parties, random events in New York and Dublin, made me a confidant in his eyes.

"That's good," he said.

"Yeah," I said. "And you? How's Athens?"

"Me? I'm good. Athens is good."

"Good."

"Yeah."

"So you heard the news?"

"No."

"You didn't?"

"No. The news about . . . ?"

"My little company."

"What's going on? You okay?"

"Well, uh . . . Well . . . A challenging situation . . . and, um, yeah, I'll just be real, man . . . It's fucked. Our CEO was burned last night in a fire at an event and now his life's on the line, and . . . and . . . it's real. Yeah. I'm calling you because I'm supposed to assure you that this all means absolutely nothing . . . but . . . um . . . um . . . but . . ."

"Wow, that's serious."

"Yeah, I just want to be honest. A lot of people are going to come at you from a lot of different angles." I took a deep breath. Very few times in life had I been staring down the barrel of this many decimal points. "I'm not saying I have any idea what it's like to be in your position, but it won't be easy to figure out who wants what."

"But you're gonna be all right?"

"Me? Personally? I'm great. I mean . . ."

"I'm just asking because of what you told me about banking."

"Yeah."

"How you like it clean."

"Wait, you mean *New Year's Eve*? You remember all that?"

"Yeah, totally. We talked money. We talked about your dad."

"Holy shit, you have a *memory*."

"Yeah, it was a trip. I asked you why you did banking and you said because it was clean."

"Clean. Christ."

"No, yeah, you were saying, 'Not literally clean, but morally.' Wearing a tie and being part of a system where everything lines up in nice columns, with no room for unfairness. Everyone has strict rules."

"That's embarrassing you remember that."

"Nah."

I had no idea he was listening that night. He had it almost verbatim and we were both six drinks deep.

"You said it took you years to realize how wrong you were."

"Twelve years," I said. "Then one day you start finally seeing the reality and you're, like, damn, literally *nothing* in banking is fair. Even the US dollar itself is a parlor trick. In fact, 'fair' isn't even in the equation. Which in a way is the sales pitch I'm using with a guy like you. 'Hey, this is a low-risk, high-reward situation, because it's rigged in your favor.' You're gonna get hollered at from all sorts of slick people. Your lawyers, your accountants, your generals or whatever the fuck Greece has. Generals? And everyone's going to want a tiny piece of your pie."

"Yeah, yeah, I know. I don't sleep at night. Ever since this all started . . ."

Neither of us said anything for a moment. He seemed to be genuinely struck by the reality of his situation. He was nobody until his father's death left him in charge of a multibillion-dollar estate that he has no idea how to manage, no idea how to protect, no idea how to shield from the talons of the vultures who're circling.

"I'm sorry, man."

"No. 'Poor little rich kid.'"

"No, no, no, man, fuck that. What you told me at that party . . . That stuff about your brother . . ."

"Yeah."

"Look, I'm not even trying to come close to knowing what you're going through. I'm sure it's, pfffff, it's insane, but bottom line, we both had some intense shit with our childhood so . . . uh . . . so . . ."

"It sucks, dude . . . I miss him but . . ." He went quiet again.

At first I wasn't sure if the line went dead or not. I didn't want to make it awkward by interrupting the moment with an oafish *Nikos, you still there?*, so I stayed quiet, sitting on the line, wondering what exactly I was letting this conversation become. The jet lag and the smoke and the indignation I felt about last night—I was basically talking this guy *out* of the deal. "No matter what this whole conference thing's about," I told him, "no matter how different our backgrounds are . . . I just want you to know . . . You're a good son and fuck anyone who says different."

"Thanks, man. seriously, thanks for all the stuff you said. We should hang out again."

"For sure."

"This thing's in Amsterdam, right?"

"What thing? The conference?"

"Yeah."

"You wanna meet there? I thought you hate this stuff."

"Yeah, but I should go."

"Really?"

"Yeah. To hang out, hell yeah. I mean, I gotta warn you I don't know much about debt finance and all that. I hate the stuff but I know it's necessary for my country and all that, but yeah."

"Okay."

"That must sound stupid."

"No! It sounds like the mind of a quiet, thoughtful motherfucker who's real enough to know what he doesn't know, which puts him fifty steps ahead of the next guy. You'll go far, my brother."

And he was in.

We agreed on the details, we said bye, we hung up. I sat back in well-earned satisfaction. It was a major victory, and within several minutes of logging it into the system, I looked up to find the COO coming over to my cubicle to personally congratulate me. I sat up, realizing his eyes were already on me and no one else. I knew the phone call was unorthodox and I knew he'd be the one guy who'd praise it. When you close a whale, you get a handshake. I had my humble aw-shucks speech ready to go along with the essential credit to the big man himself. Without your great guidance, sir . . .

"Adam," he said.

"Yessir."

"Thanks for the great work this morning."

"Oh, well, uh, I appreciate you saying that, sir. Thank you."

"Unfortunately, based on recent events this company needs to terminate your employment."

"Sorry?"

"Effective immediately." He turned to the security guard, who'd accompanied him, who I didn't even see until now.

People were watching.

"Please escort Mr. Macias out of the building along with his personal belongings."

"What for?" I said.

"You're terminated for violation of company codes of conduct as per the guidelines agreement. The security personnel will ensure you take your belongings and leave all company property on your desk."

"Why?!"

# CHAPTER 10

They'd waited until I'd closed my confirmations. Seven total. They could've canned me an hour ago when the detective first called. They could've even done it last night—based on what scant justification they were giving me now—but, no, they knew what I'd accomplish for them if they simply dragged their feet for sixty smart minutes before taking any action. I'd called two-thirds of my top-ten clients and booked seven out of seven. Monster numbers in a business of monsters.

"Thank you, Adam," said the COO, turning to leave before I could conjure up a single worthwhile thing to say back to him.

I sat there at the desk, unsure how to move. I had almost nothing to carry out the door. I forced myself to get up and begin the march out of the building, passing Trevor, who stood in his temp cubicle, holding himself back from approaching me as if I were covered in contagion. You could hardly blame the guy. Within minutes I was out on the sidewalk. On the streets. In Paris. I tried Jenn again. I called and texted her. Left a message. Basic words. I had to say something without putting her in a tricky position. On a company phone, who knows how many people hear these messages? "Hey, it's Adam. Are you good? Send me some sort of rant so I know you're good. Miss your rants." I crossed the street, then turned around to stare at the building

I'd just left. It looked impenetrable. For most people, a job is a job. But me? No. I didn't have a healthy psychological distance from a career. I had an obsession. There was still soot in my hair, and these clothes smelled atrocious. I got talked to last night by a foreign cop. This was a bad time to be overseas for a job and not *have* that job. I tried to envision Jenn in my same position. What would she do? I trusted her, admired her, envied how well she handled anything thrown her way. I dug into my pants pocket and found a clump of my own business cards, next to a pen, next to my designer sunglasses, which I put over my bloodshot eyes. That girl from last night could definitely tell the police I wasn't part of this mess. That was my thought process: the girl helps me. The girl, the girl. There was a city map posted on the Metro entrance across the street. I took out my phone and headed over to the map. I called the US embassy.

"Thank you for calling the American embassy in France," said the automated machine. "*Bonjour, vous avez appelé le numéro . . .*" After pressing a ton of buttons, I got a human being named Charles.

"This is Charles."

"Hi. My name is Adam Macias. I'm an American here in Paris and I've just been wrongfully terminated by my employer while being wrongfully listed as a suspect by the Paris police for a crime."

"Oh, uh, there's no—"

"I know you can't officially advise me but I need to ask you about something." I started to trace a route on the big map in front of me, the fastest route to his embassy. "My company somehow saw whatever list of persons of interest the police have and took premature action against me. Can we urge the police to downgrade me? Downgrade? Does that make sense?"

"Uh, does—?"

"Whatever it is they're investigating has my name on it and my company made its decision about me *based* on this naming."

"As a representative of the embassy, I can't really—"

"Yes, I fully understand, but when I get thrown into a dark cell and can't talk to a lawyer, I want at least one American to have heard me out. That's you. That's wise, right?"

"Adam, is it? That's not how France works, Adam. They use a structured legal syst—"

"Just hear me out. This is a recorded line? There was a girl, likely from Latvia or Russia, approximately twenty-five years of age, five-ten, fair skin, possibly a sex worker. That's the entire reason I'm calling you. If we can find this girl, we can track her history, because I'm sure she's a pro. She had a bottle of sex oil, this girl, in a fancy bag, from, uh . . . from, uh . . ."

I couldn't remember the name.

"What the embassy can provide is a list of attorneys who speak English," said Charles. "We can also contact various fam—"

"I'm telling you—she can speak on my behalf." If I'd actually seen our CEO with her, it'd be one thing but I had no idea what kind of connection they had. What I *did* know was there was sex oil in the bag, which I barely noticed at the time but, flashing back, I was now sure of what I saw. "And if you don't believe me, I have someone who can vouch for where I was each minute of the night last night. That person's name is Jennifer Graham—"

"Adam—"

"I'm meeting Ms. Graham for lunch in about one hour—"

"We can't interfere."

"I know you can't interfere. Radiance! The name of the store is Radiance."

"Adam—"

"I *know* this sounds like fourteen wrong things coming at you at once but a girl I never met before is at odds with people high above me, people involved in what could be a cover-up." I was building the airplane in midair, not even knowing where it should fly, praying the authorities would find relevant info if I could tell them where to look. "I don't know the extent of it but our top brass has a history of illicit behavior and now they're using me as a scapegoat because last night their behavior got messy."

"Adam—"

That call would be over within the next minute. He was a nice enough guy who insisted he couldn't help and I had no rebuttal to his rebuttal. The conversation was sloppy on my part. A knee-jerk reaction. I looked on the map at how far away his embassy was from me—fifteen minutes' walk. Should I just show up at his gate? At least I'd be inside some kind of green zone, right? I had a lunch scheduled with Jenn, that wasn't a lie, but would that be doing enough? I looked around for the nearest knowledgeable individual. Somebody who knew . . .

"Excuse me." I went up to a clerk at a magazine stand.

"*Oui, Monsieur?*"

"Have you heard of a store called . . . uh . . . uh . . . Radiance?"

"Radiance . . . ?" The guy shrugged.

"Maybe *La* Radiance? With a *La* in front?"

"It is a bar?"

"It's probably a sex shop."

"Sex shop?"

"Yeah." The time had come for me to chase down the girl.

# CHAPTER 11

The responsible move on my part was to find the one person whose identity alone could settle all this. If you find her, you confirm that maybe, just maybe, she was at the hotel as an escort. La Radiance is a sex shop—I was betting on it. I saw a bottle of what had to be sex lubricant in the small, fancy bag she was carrying, which meant somebody behind a store counter had to have seen her, right? An hour later I was standing in the middle of the red-light district across the street from the Moulin Rouge, surrounded by hordes of tourists trying to get the best photo angle to mask out the disappointing neighborhood, which was a stretch of homeless people, drunks, damp trash, and, no kidding, the most sex shops I'd ever seen in one place. La Radiance wasn't hard to find. Within minutes I was walking through the front door to find a rather decadent lady sitting behind the cash register. Late fifties. Huge pendant earrings. Weathered yet seductive.

"*Bonjour*," she said to me from across the store.

"*Bonjour.*"

"You are . . . looking for some nice toy?"

"Uh . . . well . . . that's a nice question."

"You are American?" She smiled through a set of yellowish teeth.

"Yeah . . . um . . ." I smiled back.

"My name is Mathilde. What excites you?"

"Well . . . actually I was wondering if you . . . saw someone. If you saw someone who came in here. She would look like . . . like . . . like . . ." I had my phone out. On my way there I'd dug up random photos of celebrities from the Internet, whatever I could find, piece by piece, cropping and reassembling them in a bizarre array of womanhood. The eyes of Kate Moss, the body of Gal Gadot, hair like Milla Jovovich. "Like . . . her . . . or . . . or . . . her."

"No," said Mathilde.

"She'd be a . . . Wait . . . a combination of her . . . and sort of . . . maybe her and . . ."

"No."

"Or her. And a scar on her neck. No scar? Has anyone age twenty to thirty come in this week? For oil? Lubricant?"

"If you are not buying something, you go."

"Nobody came in for maybe massage oil?"

"You go."

"Can I just leave my info? I'm on a plane at four p.m., but I'm willing to pay you three hundred euros if you connect me to her." I laid my business card on the counter, which she didn't reach for. She just defiantly let it sit there. But I caught something—a little pause in her eyes when I'd mentioned the scar. I saw it because it's my job to see it. "Cash. Three hundred. If you can let me know before my flight if she happens to come back." It's the instances of vulnerability that tell you everything.

"No," she said. "I am happy to have you leave now. *Merci.*" And she brushed the idea of me out the door with a high flick of her fingers.

I walked outside her store and stood there while getting on my cell to check in with Jenn. No answer. My tenth attempt. "Hey. It's Adam. Not sure if you're getting these but . . . Not sure if you're, like, infuriated about . . . I mean, well, anyway . . . I should be on time for the lunch, so, yeah, let's, uh, let's just talk at lunch." I hung up. I'd been trying to avoid saying anything serious over the phone but at this point why play it safe? I dialed her again. "Heya. Me again. Just in case you didn't hear, they fired me. Fired. Yeah. So I'm . . . uh . . . Yeah . . . I'm freaked out. Probably banned from the conference. Not sure why you're not replying. I know you're checking these because otherwise your inbox would be full. Some detective called me and was only—"

I was staring right at it.

In the window, in the display case. It was right there. A rack of lubricant bottles. They all had purple caps. The same purple caps on the girl's bottle. I hung up the phone and pushed my way back in through the door of the shop, going up to the counter and pointing back at the display.

"Sorry, I just have to ask," I said to her.

"Get out!"

"The bottles in the window . . ."

She'd already lost her patience with me. "You please leave!"

"Do you know if that stuff is flammable?"

I made sure to look at her and not the bottle when I said the word.

"Like . . . as in . . . on fire?" I continued. "Like . . . it would catch on fire?"

Mathilde didn't budge. There was no way she was about to give me a straight answer but I wasn't looking for one. I was looking for that hesitation. In the eyes. The hint I'd seen earlier, the slight lingering wherein you confirm that your sentence had penetrated some region of someone's brain that held some particular thought that shouldn't be there.

"*Connard!*" she said to me.

"I'll take that as a no."

"*Putain de sac à merde!*"

"Okay."

"*J'en ai rien à foutre! Va te faire enculer! Putain de mauviette! Putain de pauvre type!*"

She continued listing what I could only assume were helpful words of encouragement as I turned and headed out. Clock ticking, I hurried to the Metro. I'd have a chance to shower and change out of my smoky clothes to meet Jenn at the group lunch, to convince her to go to the US embassy with me to convince them to help me out. One hour, round trip. Sex lubricant is flammable. I read that once. Oil is a nightmare to remove from a burning person. And gel? It was a long shot, a thousand to one, but even if I were wrong, even if that girl had nothing to do with this, I still had enough notable factors to get the detective started. It'd at least *seem* compelling to an embassy, which was the long shot I needed, plus if Jenn got involved, she'd make it all convincing because she had that kind of sway. So, I needed to groom myself because at the moment I looked soiled enough that people on the street were staring. France has less eye contact than LA but I had that slept-in-a-puddle-of-pee look. The trip from Metro Blanche to Metro Odéon took only thirty-five minutes. I knew if I could rush up to my room and take a fast shower, I'd have a chance to shave, comb, look trustworthy, smell like the type of guy a bank would only *mistakenly* terminate, then go convince Jenn to help me out. At Odéon I hurried off the train, then hurried through the turnstile, through the crowded streets, past the pedestrians along the busy block that led to my small, antiquated hotel—where the clerk at the front desk barely nodded as I passed him—taking the stairs two at a time, so that when I arrived at the third floor I was completely out of breath, nearly hunched over, rounding the corner on autopilot with no thought other than to get in that shower, fishing in my pocket for the room key, noticing that down within the horizontal strip of light at the bottom of the door a shadow had just moved.

Just now. A shadow from inside my room. Moved.

I'm standing there, staring at it, wondering if I saw what I just saw, wondering whether or not it *was* a movement, while also becoming aware of another detail I'd inhaled a moment ago. I'd inhaled it. I'd smelled it. A waft of someone's cigarette breath hovering in front of my door, the exhalations of someone who took a drag somewhere else and transferred the airborne remnants to the cloud that was now around my face, all while I was gazing down at the light below my door, squinting to confirm whether that movement was a movement, already having involuntarily inserted my key into the lock—caught up in the momentum of it all—opening the door, pushing it inward, and seeing the thing you just don't want to see.

There was a guy in my room.

There was a guy standing next to my dresser. He had on a leather jacket and leather gloves and was in the midst of rifling through my luggage when he looked over at me and, without hesitation, without anything but a horrifying intensity, started walking toward me.

"You," he said.

I immediately started backing up.

"Stop," he said.

I turned back toward the stairwell, surging with adrenaline.

"STOP!"

"HELP!" I yelled out as loud as I could. "HELP! THERE'S SOMEONE IN MY FUCKING ROOM!"

# CHAPTER 12

My grandma, bless her soul, thoroughly hated the smell of cigarettes. She hated the sight of them, hated the packaging, hated the ads, the billboards, the butts, the ashtrays, the ashes, the word itself, and definitely hated the fact that her only daughter, my mom, *chose to have a child* with a man who smoked hourly. That would be my dad. That would be the barely sober individual I barely saw, barely knew, who had spent most of the years of my life sleeping in an auto-repair shop on the other side town—at my grandma's request—who convinced my mom this was the only way not to end up in the ICU. So I didn't get a real dose of fatherhood until the day of my junior high school graduation when my father had arranged for me to begin working at his garage. The grand plan was scheduled to commence with him driving me to my graduation, an image that sickened me to the core because I'd be arriving in a parking lot full of wealthy classmates in a rusty half-ton pickup that said "Pepito's Garage." This seems like a petty concern in retrospect but let's note that I'd spent my years in the smart classes with all the smart rich kids, slogging from room to room, period to period, desperately pretending they were my socioeconomic peers, hoping they might one day see me as I saw them—admirable, white, promising. Summer vacation was now starting and my dad considered his plan the long-overdue obligation of a son to help his father's business: answering the phones, using good English, managing the books, cooking the books, schmoozing clients, mopping the floors, checking emails, and, of course, setting up tax evasion—all at the ripe old age of fourteen.

You're the only one I can trust, he said to me.

He needs to be in summer school, said my mom.

This *is* summer school. This is life school.

He needs to study. He's competing with kids who have tutors and computers.

It's my decision.

The—

I'm his father.

What he needs is to marry a good Catholic girl, said my grandmother well after he'd left, well after the argument had been won. Irish Catholic, she said, believing we needed to lighten the bloodline. She opposed my mom on most issues, generally leaning too old-world for us, disagreeing on small things like how could Frida Kahlo be a real Mexican if she abandoned God? My grandmother led a challenging life, staying healthy just long enough to see me get my first promotion within the financial world, with a title that left her confused on every level, never understanding how the word "bank" could apply to someone whose job looked nothing like a bank.

Then why I can't be one of your customers, she'd say to me.

I told you, Grandma.

Because I don't have enough money?

No, because I don't have customers. I handle accounts. It's banking for institutions. There's no, like, ATM.

But you handle accounts.

The *people* are the accounts.

People are not accounts.

*Si*, grandma.

That's not nice, *hijito*.

I *manage* accounts. That means I interact with representatives from each institution, with people who are my contacts at different firms.

So you're a manager?

No, I manage their *satisfaction* in terms of how they've done business with us. I buy them drinks. I buy them golf. I get them schwag. Ninety percent of my day is mailing out logo'd schwag to reps who choose our company for an interinstitutional transaction.

I don't know that means.

Grandma . . . neither do I.

It was an odd thank-you to the one person who sacrificed everything for me, having shielded my youth from the brutality of my own DNA. She had to support both me and my mom in the face of how badly my father tried to undermine us. You need to stand up to him, she'd tell my mom, over and over, and my mom would speak up, occasionally—and got hit for it—occasionally—and did finally ban my father from our home, which led to a month of hope—my hope—that maybe this ban would last, which, of course, it didn't because he *did* come back. I'd see him in the kitchen the next morning and he'd put his hand under my chin and say, *Mijo*, if there's one thing I gave you in this world, it's this nice face. He meant how likable I looked, using some word I refused to remember—*poso* or something. He meant slick and charming, and he took any opportunity in line at a store with me to ask the people near us if they'd ever seen such a likable face. Watch him charm you out of your last dollar, he'd say. And within several months came his suggestion that I stay with him long term, which my mom fought against hard enough to bring to a stalemate. Several months went by with no word from my father and I was praying *daily* that he'd somehow lost interest in me, or forgotten me, or a meteor smashed his head, or he was recruited by a distant military. I was praying and praying—praying right up until the day before my graduation, walking home from school, walking through my front door, crossing the middle of my living room to pass through a startling wall of cigarette breath, several million singed molecules of nicotine informing me that he was back in our home that day and that my summer with him was now inevitable. No, I would *not* be embarrassed at that graduation ceremony arriving in a rusty pickup truck because my father never took me to it. He drove us straight to the auto shop instead, and within a week beat the shit out of me for having miscounted the cash and beat the shit out of me all summer, actually, so that there I would be, twenty-three years later, older, wiser, in Paris, at the top of the stairs of a small hotel with my head immersed in a cloud of someone else's fumes, reliving a pent-up dread I didn't know I still carried, replaying all the irrational conclusions that came along with it. I was about to run from something totally unknown with no capacity to see the mechanics of why—no capacity to see that it wasn't the *fear* that was forcing me to relive that childhood memory. It was a childhood memory that was forcing a grown man to run.

# CHAPTER 13

I stepped back as he yanked the door open wide enough to have us facing each other—me and the stranger who broke into my hotel room—frozen there, exchanging a hostile look for what lasted merely a fraction of a second.

"*Ne bouge pas*," he said.

I didn't reply. It wasn't friendly, whatever it was.

"*Tu comprends? Ne bouge pas!*"

He was slowly inching backward while staying focused on me. There was something behind him in the room he needed to get but he also needed to keep me with him, and those two opposing forces were trapping him in place. He was taking off his gloves, slowly, while reaching into his jacket, slowly, while inching backward, while watching me the whole time.

None of this looked okay.

I ran for it, hurrying down the stairs, banking on the fact that he might have a delayed start, picking up speed, stumbling but recovering, somehow knowing I had to get away as quickly as possible, down the stairwell—descending—first flight—second flight—descending. My body didn't give me time to contemplate what could be going on with him. Seeing his eyes, his posture, his active hands, my legs began moving me on their own, faster and faster, and, with one last set of stairs to go, I stopped.

I had to hide.

I don't know why my instincts dictated it but somewhere in the recesses of a childhood fear of the unpredictability of adult males came a fixation on the idea that this would be the only safe option. I hid, ducking out from the central staircase and into a hallway. I could've continued down the stairs full speed or I could do what I was doing. Cowering. Here. Pressed up against the hallway wall.

I listened. I tried to hear every step he might make.

"*Attends!*" he yelled to the empty stairwell from way above.

He was on his way.

High up there I heard him lean over the railing and yell downward toward wherever he thought I currently was. "*Attends!*" he yelled, waiting only a moment before thundering down the steps, descending just as fast as I did, if not slightly faster, and definitely harder. I honestly thought the structure would break beneath him. He came crashing onto each level, full weight. Two flights above me. One flight above me. Half a flight above me.

Then stopped.

He fucking stopped. Right beside the door I'd just come through.

I couldn't see him. I could only hear him—my mind blitzing through all the scenarios that could be unfolding there. Did he notice something of mine on the floor? Did I drop something? Did I leave a sweaty handprint on the door?

"*C'est toi?*" he whispered.

I absolutely froze. I swear he could hear my heart raging against my chest. I'd tried to stifle my breath, having slowly sucked in air through my nose before holding it in attempt to stay quiet, already bereft of oxygen, trying to subdue the physiology of panic, while my heart slammed against my rib cage at a hundred-and-forty slams a minute. Why in God's name did he stop next to me?

I slowly, quietly, began to raise my hand, going inch by inch, to get my fingers to line up with the rim of my pants pocket. I waited, I waited patiently, then slid those fingers downward as quietly as I could. To take inventory. I had coins—I knew about those—three euros in coins. I had two credit cards. I had a pen in my other pocket. I thought I had a packet of plastic utensils—a fork or a knife, from breakfast—but, no, that was yesterday. You didn't eat today, man. I needed a weapon. Anything. The guy chasing me looked so hideously determined. I had no sense of how to confront him. He had to be a pimp, right? For the girl? He somehow thought I messed with her? Because he looked the like type—not a TV-show pimp, not all ornate. More like the guy who solved things with brass knuckles.

The interior metal coils of the knob started to crackle. Slowly. On the verge of its being turned. My heart rate doubled. I had to cease breathing altogether. I still wasn't sure whether he knew I was *by* the door or well beyond it. Maybe he thought I'd disappeared down the corridor behind me. I glanced back at it. I could see a window at the far end leading to a narrow courtyard. He was going to open this door but he was doing it so slowly, almost rhythmically, like softly prodding it with his index finger to test the inertia of what might exist behind it. *Christ, he's gonna kick it open. He's gonna stomp the thing into my skull.* I heard his fingers grasp the knob tighter. I heard the floor creak slightly, his feet apparently finding a wider stance. The wood was old and hollow, loudly announcing any movement anyone might make. This was it—he was rearing back, ready to ram my door. My hand gripped my pen as I checked the corridor one last time, then closed my eyes, waiting until I felt ready. His face and limbs could be in virtually any orientation on the other side of that door—crouched, reared, pressed up close, far away, low, high, anything—but the one thing I knew with certainty was that his fingers, his *fingers*, were on that knob. So I did it. I yanked the door open and stabbed directly down into the other side of that area, my pen gripped like a dagger, plunging it directly through the back of that hand.

# CHAPTER 14

T he guy let out a cry of agony as my lance came straight down into the valley between the first and second knuckles on his clenched fist—all the way through the tissue, all the way through the other side of his hand. I mean, Jesus, I penetrated *ligaments*—stabbing as hard as I could at the only occupation of space I knew of.

His voice registered every decibel of the start of our war. "Ggaaaaaaaaaaaghhhh!"

I sprinted—the opposite direction—heading straight for the court-yard window. If I had any common sense, I would've jumped through the glass, shattering it into a thousand shards of emancipation, but I was still operating on a stunted IQ and concluded, decisively, woefully, that the best course of action was to come to a stop, take a moment to search for a window handle, find no handle, check for a way to break the window with maybe my elbow, realize that the window was too thick, then turn around to return to the stairwell, which was a decision that took far too long, because the guy plowed right into me.

He tackled me with everything he had—undeterred by his mangled hand—his momentum taking us both directly into the back wall so that we tumbled into a fistfight on the floor. Despite punching me with his free hand and kneeing me in the ribs, the pen stayed lodged. All I could do was hold my arms over my face in pure terror as I got hit and hit and hit—a doomed boxer on his way to a loss. I must've been struck six times before I caught him in the chest with my foot, shoving him backward, which gave me the chance I needed to grab that free hand of his, the one he was hitting me with. *This is not your life.* You flash on the profoundly useless, metaphysical thought. *This is not really happening.* You can't imagine how detrimental your mindset can be in a fight, violating every rule of tactical engagement, rendering you the laughable victim you see in the evening news—the panicked pedestrian who runs *toward* the shooting. In the midst of this struggle, I looked over at his other hand, bent backward against the carpet, functioning as his primary support, and realized I had only one chance to survive and this was it. I held him and held him and held him, then as fast as possible rolled sideways, giving up all control of his free hand to grab his impaled hand—grab the *pen* in it—and push that pen as hard as I could in the ugliest, nastiest direction possible.

He convulsed instantly. "Ghhhaauuuuuugh!"

I scrambled to my feet, sprinted toward the window, and stomped the frame outward so that I and the whole glass assembly fell forward onto the pavement of the atrium. Everything about it hurt—I must've twisted both ankles and bloodied up both hands, but my adrenaline was flowing full bore and I was up and running before I even decided where I'd go, bursting through the nearest door, through the short hallway beyond it, and out onto the street, spattered with his blood, drenched in my sweat, smelling like a concoction of the worst odors a city has to give, as I ran left then right, then immediately started walking. Normally.

"Walk . . . *Walk*," I murmured to myself. "Normally." Don't attract attention, just walk. "*Excusez-moi*," I mumbled to the lady I bumped into. "Walk," I whispered to myself again, scolding my legs for hesitating to do so. I didn't want to look behind me. I couldn't. There was a chance that the back of my head was blending in with the rest of the people around me—with the foot traffic in Paris being so constant—but the sidewalks are so narrow, so deathly narrow, that you can't pass by anyone without first dipping into the street, into plain sight, and you might not easily be able to stay out of a psychopath's view.

I took the first left turn I could. I needed my path to wrap around the block, away from the front of the hotel. This would give me a chance to get a quick glance backward through the window of the corner boulangerie and, Christ, there he was. The guy. The moment I saw him, I veered right, not letting even a fraction of a second elapse, turning street-ward without checking for cars or vans or scooters, and thereby was broadsided by a bicycle—wham—instantly slammed sideways along the street.

I was no longer on my feet. I didn't contact any vehicles and I ended up crouched on my knees, stunned. After an unknown duration of seconds—Three? Five?—I stood up just as the bystanders were starting to converge to help me. *"Est-ce je peux vous aider?"* *"Ça va, mec?"* Glancing to the right, I could see the cyclist who hit me tangled up in his own mess. The crowd hadn't yet cinched up around us but they were approaching fast.

Barely processing the full parade of visuals in front of me, I tried to get a look past all the legs and tires and caught sight of my nemesis. The guy. Now running toward me. I got up, staggering, but got to my feet and pushed forward, soon getting to full speed, full stride, pummeling some poor high school kid who was trying to lift me up, then charging toward an alley. I ran as hard as I could. I had no other thought in my brain. Run. Hard. Alley. Run. Raw fear finally reducing me to only one function. Fleeing. I skidded through a tight turn leading to a second alley before turning again—an act that ultimately had me rounding a corner into a dead end. God no! It was a small construction site, probably abandoned for the week, tucked in the alley, one of a hundred you'd find on any given day in a city constantly undergoing surgery. Nobody was around. The fence was too high to climb but it wasn't too low to crawl under, so I ducked down to scoot below the jaws of the very tight gap—below the sharp tips of the chain-link fence—and, contorting, had a chance to look behind me to check the entrance of the alley from where I'd just come from, from where this lunatic might emerge. I pushed harder with my legs in an effort that got my front shoulder through, having dragged my chest across the ground to do so, clawing at the loose dirt with my hand to dig myself another half inch forward, pulling with my free hand, pulling as hard as I could, finally starting to slide myself through, finally getting a good look at the inside of the construction area, just in time to see this same fucking guy coming at me from *inside* the site.

Christ, he'd gotten ahead of me!

Carrying a large rock now, arriving just in time to slam that rock toward my face.

I recoiled just quickly enough that the rock cratered itself in the dirt, missing me, then I lurched in retreat—never pulling so hard in my life—still stuck under the fence, feeling my chest bone flex inward as I tugged with all my might.

"You understand?!" he growled threateningly.

He'd grabbed my elbow. He'd circled around the block to intercept my escape. I could see that his bloody hand no longer had a pen piercing through it. *Did I understand?* He'd knelt on my arm and the leverage was crippling. His venomous face was now visible through a crack in the partition. He obviously wanted to ruin my world, pulling at me ferociously—you could see it in his eyes. *Understand what?* He'd been saying something to me the whole time, but, deafened by my own adrenaline, I was only now finally hearing it.

"You understand?" he said. "I'm a cop. I'm a *cop*."

# CHAPTER 15

Y ou play out a hundred scenarios in your head. Your intellect having been in limbo the prior nine minutes, unable to process anything other than the raw escape—your mind now roars to life, reactivating so that every permutation of the three-letter word was laid out in front of you: C-o-p. Cop. Cop. Cop. All my synapses went to work, flashing a giant decision tree with a thousand different realities growing from one lone, gnarled trunk. *I stabbed a cop?* Whether he was lying or not, if making me hesitate was his goal, he'd done well. That single word might as well have been a guillotine. He'd said it to someone who grew up on the wrong sides of the tracks with a wrong shade of skin. Cops were never a simple noun in my vocabulary. I stopped struggling, stopped pulling, stopped resisting, stopped everything—*salvage what you can because life as you know it is over, Adam*—my brain switching to the urgency of what to do with a bombshell like this.

"Don't move!" he said.

*You can still mitigate the damage, man. Just do what he says.*

"Don't move!"

*Do whatever he says.*

"Y-yeah," I said.

But my central nervous system refused to concede right now: my muscles twitched, my body surged, my legs flexed to shove downward as hard as they could, twice as hard as before, and rip me from the grip of both the guy and the fence—my jacket coming clean off in the process—scooting me back until I was clear of him. For a fraction of a second, I stayed there on the ground, transfixed by the spectacle of it all—a guy gazing at me, a guy who was a cop—and then I got up and ran. How could this end in anything but jail? I was already sprinting toward the intersection where I'd come from on a route that'd take me through the heart of the third arrondissement. I didn't know the city well but I knew I had to head away from the river, away from what would be a wide swath of open space that offered zero cover, so I ran north, several blocks north without blinking—dodging traffic, dodging people, carts, bikes, dogs, running north, along a path that emerged onto a quaint street corner at the base of a giant cathedral called Saint-Eustache. North. Which led me to—to—to—I had to search for a street sign. Where the hell's this? Rue Coquillière. A smaller street, sparsely populated. Which meant I could hurry. All out. Wishing I were in any kind of decent shape. Pushing myself beyond exhaustion. I honestly thought I'd end up falling to the pavement, knees buckling, desperately in need of a next move. Somewhere in front of me was the optimum choice for getting out of this. Would it be a *fromagerie* with a storage room? A dry cleaner? A park? Some timid kid in a bookstore guiding me to the bookshelves in the back? No, you couldn't afford to stop. The guy had already out-mapped you once. What if the problem was that I was easy to follow? "He fucking has my wallet," I said out loud. My wallet was in my jacket pocket, ripped clean from my upper body. Now he had my credit cards and ID. "No, no, no, he already knows who you are, idiot. He was in your room." I stopped running. One way or another, I now had to operate under the assumption that this man had my home address, my credit cards, my personal info, and my itinerary. I told the sex-shop lady I had a flight at four o'clock but, realistically, there was no way my company was letting me travel with them. I stopped altogether. I did a three-sixty in place, gradually recognizing the inevitable. I only had one place to go. One port in this storm. Cash, info, embassy access, corroboration, credit. *Jenn.* I had to risk everything and meet Jenn at the restaurant as originally planned.

# CHAPTER 16

L unch with my best friend and three colleagues was slated for
1:15 p.m. in the eighth arrondissement at a restaurant called L'Isle
de Soleil. We booked the reservation over a week ago. I hadn't heard
from her in twelve hours but this is a woman who never misses a single
commitment. On time. On point. Detailed to a T. That meant the two
of us would finally be in the same place and she could give me some
cash, after which, without implicating her in the nightmare, I could
buy myself a train ticket to maybe Marseilles or Lyon or Cannes or
Bordeaux, lay low for a day, sign a waiver, find a flight back to LA, or
drive to Italy, fly home from Italy, or first rent a car and go wherever,
and then lawyer up and get this all straightened out *after* I left the
country. I could basically do anything other than stay out on the streets
waiting for my demise.

I walked all the way to the eighth. I had nothing left in the tank but
I walked and walked and walked, opting for the smaller roads with
less visibility—keeping my head low at every intersection. Near a street
called rue de la Bienfaisance, I looked up and briefly saw the guy's face
in the crowd. It wasn't *actually* him but I saw his eyes—those lifeless
eyes—stinging me with that spike of fear where you flash on the image
of someone you never want to see. Finally getting near the restaurant,
L'Isle de Soleil, I switched to the opposite side of the street and stayed

along the far wall to scout the location. I wanted to be outside when meeting her—Jenn. She'd be arriving with other colleagues any minute. But being outside would mean being exposed.

I had to go in.

*"Bonjour,"* I said to the well-dressed host. *"Nous avons une réservation pour cinq. Est-ce que . . . ? Est-ce qu'elles ont . . . ? Elles ont . . . ?"* Reaching my mental limit in French, I switched to English. "Have my colleagues arrived? Jennifer Graham? We have a reservation under her name. Graham." Someone was on a grand piano, playing in the corner—Flaubert. There was a sommelier. There was tapestry. It was that kind of place. I didn't have a way to excuse my appearance. I looked like a guy who lived in their alley.

The young host did his best to hide his reaction. *"Bonjour. Votre nom s'il vous plaît?"*

Jenn had booked us a table by the window. I knew that much. She hadn't arrived yet but, again, I was early. The host was nice but he kept eyeing my general look and noting a general odor. After a few more awkward sentences, he told me he needed to go check on something with his manager.

*"Alors . . ."* You could see right through him. He wanted to get a directive from his boss on getting me the hell out of here.

"Wait." I grabbed him before he could go, pulling him close to me—desperation kicking in. "Wait. Listen, man. Listen. I'm really sorry but I'm in a serious jam. *Je sais que j'ai l'air de merdre froid.* I know your restaurant is high class but my colleagues and I are about to drop six hundred bucks on lunch and you can just seat us in the very back where no one has to see me or deal with me. No one." I reached in my pocket. "Here." I took out my sunglasses. "Here. Here. Sunglasses. Take them. For you. Personally. Here." I'd still had them in my pants.

A $449 pair of Bulgari shades. They should've been bent by now, given what they went through, but luckily they only looked ever-so-slightly dirty. "If we could just, y'know, avoid your manager."

He passively watched them arrive in his hand. "*Monsieur*, I cannot—"

"Just don't talk to your manager. That's all. Take them. Please. Just . . ." I'd placed them in his palm and was folding his fingers closed. "Let me sit in the back. I'm waiting for a woman. Jennifer. Half Asian. Attractive. Take the glasses."

He was young and had a pricey haircut—the type of kid who might actually wear stuff like this. He stood there a moment, then looked around, then led me to the back where he rapidly rearranged a table for me. "Your companion . . . she is, uh . . . to come soon?"

"By one p.m., yes. Probably sooner. Just give me until one p.m."

Even from all the way in the back, I could see the face of each pedestrian passing out front. The place had large windows overlooking a constant supply of foot traffic. I looked for Jenn—no sign of her. I carefully put my hand on top of my dinner knife, carefully, slowly moving that knife toward the edge of the table, taking a couple of *minutes* to do so, looking around, then sliding that knife into my lap. I held it tight there. It wouldn't be impossible for me to surprise attack someone who approached me at this table. If that guy didn't know what was in my hand, he'd lean over and expose his chest to me. Once you have a sharp object like this, you can change the game. The only question would be finding the willpower to do so, to cross a line that can't be uncrossed. As of now the vision I had of myself as the successful, cooperative, well-liked, well-received, reputable, nonviolent man named Adam Macias was dissolving. Actually, I'm not even sure that person was ever me.

# CHAPTER 17

The restaurant host returned for a brief, wordless visit wherein he brought me four drinking glasses, a basket of bread, a tiny spoon, a tiny jar of mustard, gave me a menu, asked if I wanted a drink, said he'd bring a house red, then left.

"Talk it through," I said to myself once he'd gone.

You need to simplify things, man.

"Talk through the day."

Who broke into my room? This man had to come from one of five possible realities: a pimp, a boyfriend, a guy who set fire to the hotel, a guy who sabotaged my employment, or an actual cop. Let's start with how he found you. How would he know your hotel room? Occam's razor—the explanation had to be simple. He had to have internal info. I looked toward the front window—a mom passed by, along with two college kids, followed by an old lady. I noticed my heart was racing. The calmer the restaurant became, the more frayed my nerves got—shredding my ability to focus. I picked up the salt and pepper jars. I placed them on opposite sides of my butter knife. "Picture it." I began to map this guy's physical path. The hotel. The river. The office. If he were a cop, would he have searched my room like that? What did you see him *do* exactly? "You saw him with your suitcase open." What else? "Nothing." What else was there, man? Think! I closed my eyes. I tried to envision the room. The moment. The geometry. The problem was that the more I concentrated on remembering details, the more I started to *invent* them. I saw hints he had a gun. "No, you didn't." A handgun. "There was no gun." Simplify! I moved the saltshaker over, losing patience with myself. "*That's* the hotel terrace." I scooted the butter knife. "*That's* the river." Spoon. "*That's* me." Tray. "The girl, the guy, *me*." I stared at it, frustration mounting. I had no idea what this would lead to, not just here but in general. I should've seen it coming long ago—I'd agreed to go on this trip, this European business trip, sort of lost, wanting to define who I was, not just in terms of a career but, as cliché as it sounds, a man. Stupid—but the sentimental avalanche was coming. Now I was facing a total loss of control. I'd never expected anything insane would occur, good or bad. Get a job. Meet a wife. Fatten. Mow a lawn. Nothing crazy. I could hardly believe the past twenty-four hours. Jenn will be here any moment. She'll be fearful of you, right? No, whatever slanderous info your company disseminated to the rest of the team about you, it wouldn't drive a wedge between you and her, right? "What does this guy *want*?" I promised myself I'd convince her to get the embassy involved. Period. I was already rehearsing the first things we'd say to each other. I was picturing her apologizing, me being passive aggressive about it, her criticizing my choices, then me criticizing hers, then us making a plan. I couldn't see the clock. I knew time was passing. Why was she late? I was honestly ready to strike back. I didn't care how trivial my proof of the corruption was. I could start a war if I had to. Would Jenn help? Would I even see her? What if this guy followed her and was waiting to attack both of us once he had us *together*? Damn, dude, I hadn't thought of *that*. A random male pedestrian stopped right in front of our window with his back kept toward me. He had the same jacket as my enemy.

Beige leather. He got on a phone call. Under the table, I changed the position of the knife to a downward-stabbing grip. I felt my pulse rise. *I'm not violent. I'm not that guy.* I moved my arm closer to the edge of the table so I could stab faster. *This is not my life.* I'd need to puncture his torso. A quick jab. Something secretive. One of those crippling, prison-yard stabs.

The waiter returned. *"Alors . . . Voulez-vous commander?"* He'd brought a glass of red wine, which looked quite thirst-quenching right now and was asking if I was ready to order appetizers. I tried to look calm but was teary eyed. It wasn't from self-pity. It was sheer exhaustion. I immediately faked a yawn to justify the wet eyes.

"Sir?"

*"Non, ça va,"* I said to him, playing it off. *"Ça va. Ça va."*

He knew it wasn't from the yawn. He'd brought my sunglasses back, having cleaned them, and placed them on my table.

I didn't know what to say.

I glanced at his wristwatch—over an hour had gone by. "She . . . uh . . . She didn't call? Ms. Jennifer?"

"No, sir."

She wasn't late; she wasn't *coming.*

Jesus, was there any bottom to this abyss? I'd never once entertained the possibility that she might not come. I didn't want to consider the implications. Jenn. In all our years as friends, I'd never expect something like this from her. She's yelled at me, criticized me, thrown a drink in my lap, lashed out at me—she's never *not* shown up.

"Okay," I said to him. *Can you tell me how much jail time you get for stabbing a cop?*

He'd been a good sport. I didn't ask any more questions. I didn't want to freak him out while I was holding sharp cutlery.

"*Monsieur?*" came a female voice. My civility wouldn't matter. Behind him his manager was briskly approaching. A young woman with a no-nonsense hair bun, whose subordinate had let me stay well past her own deadline of 1:45 p.m. "Sir," she said, in no mood to be accommodating. "We will need you to exit."

"Oh," I said. "Okay, uh, can I just use your phone?"

"No."

"It's a fast call. It's an emergency."

"Sir." She was about to raise her voice to the everybody-around-you-shall-notice-you-getting-scolded level, a level I absolutely couldn't afford to tempt. The pedestrian in the beige jacket outside had disappeared from view. "*Sir . . .*"

She didn't realize I'd reached my own boiling point. "No problem," I said, getting up, cordially, humbly. I did this before she could say another word—"All good, no problem"—motioning for her to step aside to give me a clear route to the front door.

And she did.

And I wasn't walking toward the door. I walked the other way, toward the tight spiraling stairs that led to the basement, toward the counter *next* to those stairs, toward the phone on that counter.

"*Monsieur!*" she said, calling after me when she saw all this.

It was time for me to call the detective. It was time to throw myself at the mercy of a foreign country with their foreign laws and face a foreign jail.

# CHAPTER 18

I grabbed the cordless phone off the back counter, a landline, picked it up, and kept walking with the receiver, never breaking stride, heading down the steps into the labyrinth of the busy kitchen.

"*Monsieur!*" the manager called after me.

I dialed 17—the French version of 911—knowing it'd be foolish to pass up the only phone I might be accessing for quite a while, with the line connecting immediately.

"*Dix-sept Urgence.*"

I struggled to hear the operator. French is a rough language in person, let alone on a call, let alone against the backdrop of a one-star kitchen. "*Salut, je suis Américain,*" I said. "I'm calling because I know where a key witness is in the arson incident last night at the Astoria sur Seine."

"*Pardon, Monsieur?*"

"Arson. Last night. Fire."

"*C'est dix-sept. Quel est votre urgence?*"

"Yeah, I need to talk to Detective Élodie Michel. *Je m'appelle* Adam Macias. Arson. Urgent."

"Uh, it's . . . Do you have . . . some emergency, sir?"

"Yes. I'm her arson suspect but I have proof that I'm not her suspect."

The operator didn't understand most of this but he seemed bewildered enough to break protocol and connect me to her. "One moment, sir, I will try to tran—"

*Wham!* I was shoved from behind.

Sent stumbling into the wall directly in front of me.

The head chef had arrived, delivering a heavy blow to my back. I'd held on to the phone and stayed ready to square off, but when I looked back, I was facing a massive, two-hundred-fifty-pound boulder of a guy, along with that tight-bun manager flanking him. There wasn't enough room in the hallway for me to avoid confronting this rhinoceros, yet as soon as I finally turned to fully face them, they both froze. Both of them.

I forgot I still had the dinner knife in my hand.

I absolutely didn't threaten him with the blade, I swear. But he saw it and saw the crazed look in my face and kept himself still.

Just as a female voice came on the phone in my hand. "Hello, this is Detective Michel."

No one was sure how to react to the weapon, seeing it wielded by someone like me who'd lost all sense. I stayed there a moment before deciding fuck-everything and waltzed into the narrow bathroom, entering one of the toilet rooms and locking the door while I listened as hard as I could to the handset.

"Hello?" said the detective.

"Am I wanted by the police, *Madame?*" I said to her. "Are you sending police after me? A man is chasing me in the eighth arrondissement, but I have no way to be sure who he is."

"Mr. Macias, I instructed you to come into the local station. Why are you telephoning me?"

"Because I can help you get what you want! But first I need your assurance that I'm okay. I acted in self-defense." I had to stop being passive. "I know where she is. The girl. And I know where this girl can be found."

"What girl?"

"She can clear me of suspicion. The girl I told you about. I'm not part of any arson. You can take me off the list. Somebody broke into my hotel room. This man, he broke in and he chased me. I had to jab him with a pen."

"You assaulted someone?"

"No. He tried to hit me with a rock. He said he was a cop. He's lying."

"What do you mean you—?"

Bwoosh! The chef slammed himself against the bathroom door. Loud. Jarring as hell. Must've been using his shoulder. I didn't fall over this time because I was braced for it. Staying on this call was all I had left.

"What was that noise?" said the detective. "You need to listen very clo—"

"NO, YOU NEED TO LISTEN! You need to listen. I am being pursued because he's angry at his prostitute. This girl is a prostitute—you can interrogate her, and you can confirm she was at the hotel and that she accessed the elevator and *never* met me prior to last night, and I know where you can find her."

"Mr. Ma—"

"I'm prepared to give you key information about the criminal behavior of the heads of Euro Mutual Bank, which I know sounds insane but I'm talking about: girls rented, girls abused, financial embezzlement, fraud, all connected. I can expose it, a lot of it, but the first step is clearing my name, which is you and me working together to find this girl."

"The girl isn't my concern. You're going—"

"No!" I pressed myself against the door to prevent the chef from edging in. "What do you mean the girl isn't your concern? She's a sex worker. That's what I can prove about our company. That we have a history of engaging—"

"Mr. Macias, if you try to leave the city, you'll be charg—!"

"How do I know I can count on you?! You want me to come in but you got a guy out here pretending to be a cop! Faking it! He assaulted me!" Every video of every police beating I'd ever seen had come screaming to mind, showcasing the potential of what could go wrong here. "And I'm getting no assurance from you that you see the complications. That's why this girl's relevant. Listen! I'm up against a former employer who's using leverage against me. People high on the food chain are clearly—and I don't have proof—but I will—I will—*clearly* trying to paint me into a corner and cover up illicit activity and this girl is a disgruntled part of it, or a victim of it, or a catalyst, I don't know, but she can confirm I've never met her before!"

"I repeat: if you try to leave the city, you'll—!"

"ARE YOU LISTENING?!" I hung up the phone on her and shoved the door open to find the big guy standing in front of me, now staring at my knife. I didn't advance on him. My pulse was racing in three different directions but handling this guy was the most straightforward of all the things I had to deal with.

I didn't move.

"Ça va," I said calmly. "Ça va . . ." Assuring him it's all good. We're good. Making a truce gesture, I gently crouched down, never breaking eye contact with him, bending gently, like facing off with a wild dog, gently placing the knife on the ground in front of me along with the phone, which these people seemed to regard as only half the disarmament necessary to feel safe, still suspecting I had yet another weapon hidden on me.

"You win," I said slowly. "I'm leaving . . . quietly . . . quietly, okay? *Nous pouvons le fair avec la . . . la . . . paix.*"

There was a moment where they could've bull-rushed me. They could've. They had that edge.

They didn't.

Everyone remained in position. "Go," said the manager, infuriated. "Yes. Okay? You just go." She took a step back to let me complete the act of abandoning the knife on the ground, with all three of us nervous that one of the three of us might actually lunge for it—both of them letting me then proceed backward to the steps that led to the rear exit—going slowly at first, then faster, then running.

Running.

The chef didn't follow. He watched from the hallway, just wanting me to get the hell out of his world. I ran out through the alley as hard as I could, crisscrossing two busy streets full speed. I couldn't take a chance on anyone in a beige jacket seeing my route. I couldn't trust anything to go as planned. That was the lesson here—the distrust—the fact that the big players involved didn't give a shit about you. Not even the cops were quick to help. I mean, Jesus, what the hell did I just say to that lady on the phone? What kind of puffy bullshit did I just spout out? Even if I *could* prove any of it, how exactly would it help me survive even the next *hour*?

# CHAPTER 19

The fastest route to Paris Charles de Gaulle Airport is to take a metro train called RER B. Tickets cost ten euros—ten euros I didn't have. I'd seen enough people hop turnstiles to know it's a risky but feasible endeavor. You prop your hands on the turnstile dividers, tuck your legs, rise up, then hurdle the trio of bars. I've seen girls do it, guys do it, teens do it, kids do it, businesspeople . . . If you execute the maneuver smoothly enough, your head maintains the same height as everyone else so that even the person directly behind you, caught up in the general stampede of his or her business day, doesn't notice. That's what I theorized. That's what I'd envisioned. What I was failing to account for was that I'd also need to hop a turnstile to *exit* a station—a very particular station located *inside* the airport—which meant I'd be hopping a turnstile in front of airport-level security.

I was done giving a shit. I had no scruples. Jenn had something I needed and I'd be damned if I didn't get what I came for.

Proof.

She'd be on the next flight to the next conference. Paris to Amsterdam. That meant right now I had her thumbtacked at a known location at a known time. Charles de Gaulle, Terminal One. Yes, it'd be risky to walk into a highly surveyed airport with all that was dangling over my head, but it'd be riskier not to try. You can't be negligent, man. You're gonna turn yourself in to the cops but before you do, you're gonna cover your ass. I slipped through the second exit, vaulting the glass, and emerged into Terminal One just in time to come within machine-gun distance of a roving quartet of Paris cops—each armed with an MP5 automatic weapon—strolling through the airport lobby, not really noticing my arrival.

Not fully.

I didn't retreat. The upcoming transaction was all that mattered. If you want to survive, you gotta take a stand. If you want to take a stand, you need leverage. That leverage would be the emails I could access, access which was blocked by firewalls, firewalls which were to be penetrated by me if I got my hands on something rather precious inside of Jenn's purse. Her employee card.

I stopped in front of the row of departure-info screens to check how many gates had flights to Amsterdam in the upcoming hours. Mentally, I started to organize what I could say to counter her inevitable rebuttals: (a) You won't need your card in the Netherlands, Jenn; (b) I'm just checking my own email account, Jenn; (c) They could be deleting me soon, Jenn; (d) I'm not retaliating, Jenn; (e) I'm exonerating, Jenn.

I had to hurry to be on time—she always arrived at exactly the designated airline time, down to the minute, and if I missed her before she passed through security, I wouldn't be able to get to her at all. I had to hurry, sidestepping the various travelers along the way, staying focused, staying alert, which meant I hardly noticed that someone was tapping my left shoulder. It happened on the main escalator when I'd arrived at a clump of stagnant people. And it was without me noticing at first. I'd stopped to wait for the clump. That person then tapped my shoulder again, at which point I moved over to the right to let him or her pass.

"Adam?" said a voice. A female.

I turned around.

"Adam." It was the girl.

"You . . . You're . . ."

It was *the* girl. "Hi. Can we talk?"

# CHAPTER 20

I stepped off the escalator, completely at loss for words, having had no expectation I'd see this person now. Certainly not here. Certainly not this soon. Probably not ever. Impulsively, I yanked her by her hand to pull her away from the streams of people coming at us from all directions, looking around to see who might be studying the conversation we were about to have. I brought her to a corner. "This is not the time."

"I need your help."

"I'm sure you do."

"You need my help."

"Like I said . . ." I turned. I left. "This is not the time." With ten different objectives clashing in my head, I couldn't be sure which ones logically outranked the others, but despite how important this girl was to me, the imminent fear of losing Jenn dominated them all. I started walking toward Jenn's terminal.

"Will you please stop walking?" she said, following me for a few steps. "So we can talk?"

I stopped.

"You don't know what you're dealing with," she said.

It was exhilarating to be inches from her. I had to be honest. I'd never gazed at someone so beautiful while telling her to go away. It was a rush of fear, nerves, anger, hope, adrenaline, sleep deprivation, and confusion. "How did you know I'd be here?"

"I'll explain everything to you but right now you don't know what you're dealing with, so you need my help."

"You're drawing a lot of attention to me and that does *not* help, and I absolutely can't talk right now, so . . ." I couldn't think fast enough, logically enough, to wrangle all the conflicts involved. I *did* need her, but I also needed her to get the hell away from me if I were to have any chance of convincing Jenn of anything. If Jenn were even here. "Please let me do what I have to do."

I started to walk off again.

"I have no one else," she said.

"For what?"

She caught up to me and accompanied me this time. I saw it in her face. The pleading.

"For what?" I repeated, knowing I wasn't going to give in. I told myself I wouldn't give in. "Fine. I'll let you explain to me whatever you need to explain to me, but you'll do it after this thing I gotta do, okay? Not now. After. I need to meet someone now and you need to disappear."

"Where will I find you?"

"I don't know."

"Where will I find you?"

"Not here. Inside . . . Inside . . . Sacré-Coeur."

"No."

"Then?"

"It has too many people."

"Then . . . the Pyramid."

"At what time?"

"I don't know. I have to go." I looked around. There was this sinking feeling that police were slowly assembling around us in an arc, whispering into their headsets. Male. Five-ten. Light-skinned Hispanic. "In several hours?"

"The Pyramid closes in several hours—"

"God!" Is nothing simple? "Then *you* pick a spot, okay? Pick one. Hurry."

"Pont des Arts. It's a bridge—"

"Fine."

"City center—"

"Yes. Fine. That."

She was now looking at me almost condescendingly, almost like she was about to say more but decided I wasn't worth it. I started to respond but she turned and walked away.

I didn't have time to figure out just what that look meant. I hustled up to the third concourse where the main security gates were located. They had a ramp crossing diagonally through the courtyard within a multilevel stack of floors. Fortunately, the whole thing was weirdly transparent, and I could see people crossing to any floor and, like clockwork, right on time, within her patented two-hour cushion, I saw Jenn rolling her luggage ten yards ahead of me. I felt like I was dreaming. The sight of her. Nothing else had gone right in the past twenty-four hours, yet there she was, and when she saw me, when I saw that she wasn't going to run in the opposite direction, or slap me, or whatever the hell any of this warranted in her unpredictable Jenn mind, I forgot all my counterarguments.

"Hey," I said.

Her presence did that to me. A slight rush. A slight escalation of breath.

"Hey," she said back.

I tried to pull her aside so we could talk discreetly but she flinched as soon as I touched her, so I moved back a step, not wanting to create a spectacle. "Okay," I said. "Okay, okay. What's going on?"

"I don't know. You tell me." She seemed furious, which was something I hadn't really prepared for.

"Uh . . . okay . . . okay . . . Here's the deal . . . Here we go . . ." I turned my back to the nearest video camera, knowing the effort was futile but doing it anyway. "I need something from you. I don't have a lot of time to convince you I need it, but I need it. I'm getting a sense you're upset with me, though I'm not sure why, though I'm also sort of entitled to be upset in return, based on you missing lunch. *Upset* is a strong word. I'm not upset. I'm just trying to say I'm in a serious situation. You don't need to be part of it. I just need you to let me have something of yours without fully authorizing me to have it. Just . . . Well . . . I thought this through and here's how it could work. You'll tell them you lost what I'm about to ask you for. And I'll tell them that I *stole* it from you when—"

She pulled her employee ID from her purse and held it out toward me.

She did it so effortlessly I couldn't even process it at first. "The—?" I didn't know what to say.

"They locked you out of the network, right? And now you need to access your account?"

How could she know that this is exactly what I'd be asking?

"Is that right?" she said. She was fatigued. "Look, I don't really want to hear all the details of what you're about to do. You stole this from me, fine. I'll say it's lost, fine. The fact that the only reason you hunted me down is to grovel for some bullshit scheme that probably won't even come—"

"Whoa."

"—close to—"

"Whoa. The only reason I hunted you down? I fucking texted you up the ass."

"I'm not doing this."

"I called you and left messages all morning to make sure you—"

"All morning? All morning?! Let's process that for a second. All morning. First of all, I was *exhausted*. I inhaled approximately nine thousands pounds of smoke last night, I had to take all these heavy meds, so I'm sleeping in just to *survive*, then I wake up and literally half the planet has texted me asking for ridiculous shit, like, everything that ever existed, and so here I am just doing *our* job, just piecing together a halfway usable battle plan for damage control for the *Paris* leg before they confirm *Amsterdam*, and when I finally *do* get a chance to read your passive-aggressive text-vomit, during which you go from Zero to Guilting-Me-Out-for-Not-Being-at-Your-Disposal, maybe I didn't have the time to apologize for things I didn't do in order to protect our friendship, which in your eyes is utterly delicate because I was too busy doing *both* our jobs to keep a last-minute lunch when you couldn't even keep yourself out of trouble for our most important night ever, even after I told you seventy-five million times how important last night was to me, yet here I am still willing to do you this favor that could get me fired."

She put her employee card in my hand.

I couldn't think at first.

"Okay, first of all, uh, thank you . . . for this . . ." I said, holding up the card. "Second of all, I mean, no, wait, *wait*, how in the world is this my fault? I didn't drop the ball. I got terminated. They—"

"You were flirting with some girl."

"Me?"

"I'll never forgive you for that. The whole reason we were late was because you let your dick take over your spinal—"

"Whoa, slow your—You cannot say Evan Goldman happened because of me."

"I'm saying you knew how important last night was to my *career* and you couldn't even be reliable for half a *day*."

"I got suspended. I did *not* chase down a girl."

"Trevor said you went to find her."

"I nev—What? No. Trevor's—No. I'm not gonna go into the details of my day but just know that my day was by your own medieval standards of hard, hard." I couldn't tell her exactly what happened because I couldn't make her liable. The more she knew, the more she could get fired. "But what you went through on the roof last night . . . is . . . yeah . . . Okay, you're right."

She seemed to sense that I'd experienced something dire. Her posture relaxed ever so slightly.

"Okay?" I said.

Best friends are like that.

She took a new tone.

"Okay," she said.

"Okay." I took a new tone too.

"I'm sorry I accused you of anything with that girl."

"It's fine."

"You're stressful sometimes . . . but . . ." She felt bad. I could see it. She'd said whatever nastiness she needed to say to me, probably directed at the universe in general, and not my head, but I happened to be in front of her nozzle. "I'm sorry to accuse you of anything. I understand you're up against a corporate wall. I'm sure it's ugly. I might be able to talk to our legal team and see if there's—Oh my God."

"What?"

"Oh my God."

"What is it?"

She saw something behind me.

And once I saw her see it, I didn't even need to turn around to see what it was. I could read the entire situation on her face.

The girl.

The girl had approached us, coming up from behind me to stand directly by my side, facing Jenn.

# CHAPTER 21

The three of us were now standing together with Jenn so livid she wouldn't even *look* at the girl. She just glared at me—only me—flooded with exasperation and anger and a sense of betrayal and disappointment. "Are you kidding?"

"I—I—I have nothing to do with her. I'm—I'm—"

"What the fuck?"

I pointed to the girl. "She followed me."

"I hope you get an STD, Adam."

"No, no, no, we never—"

"I hope you get an STD that's *visible*—that kids on the street point to and laugh at."

"Just if—"

"Do you even know how dangerous and irresponsible you are?!"

That's when the girl spoke. "Your name is Jennifer?"

"You know how *reckless*?" said Jenn.

"My name's Katarina Haimovna." She spoke in earnest despite the fact that Jenn wouldn't even blink in her direction.

"At what point do you grow up?" said Jenn.

"I need to ask you for your help," said the girl.

"At what point do you look around, Adam? Huh? Because I wanna tell you something about your little virtue crusade—whilst you moan how unfair things've gotten, how the process is so unjust. Did you stop for one second to notice that *you're part* of that system?"

"I'm—"

"You're in it! You're working it! Every day. We both are. And you're doing exac—" She recoiled as the girl reached over to put her hand on her shoulder. "Wow, please do not touch me. Ever!"

She picked up her bag.

"Like, ever!"

I tried to get in front of her but she was leaving. "We're not together," I said. "I don't—"

Gone.

That was it.

She walked away and I was left standing there with the girl named Katarina Haimovna.

"I'm sorry for this," said the girl, waiting almost a minute before saying anything, the situation now growing borderline absurd. "But let's not worry about it."

"Excuse me?"

"Let's not worry about what just happened. Let's help each other."

"Incorrect."

"You're in danger. I can find safety for you."

"Incorrect."

"I'm sorry about coming over just now. She was the last chance I had."

"*I* was the last chance you had—is what you said. She was *my* last chance!"

"We've—"

"Either way, I don't care. *I don't care.* You've done enough. And now you're going to them. *We're* going to them. I'm obtaining records of specific conversations, which will be the last step before coming clean, and you're coming with me." I took her hand and started leading her toward the front check-in area.

"What're you doing?"

"You go to the police. You present the whole story."

"That's not going to help us." She stopped walking, which caused a hard tug on my arm, so I had to stop too. "You can't do that. That's not going to work."

I got up close to her face. "I don't know what you know about this particular game you're playing but it's a game won on paper . . . on *paper* . . . long before people like you even know what the hell hit you. I'm sorry that's the reality for your demographic but that's actually the reality for *everyone*. We live and die by what's written. You and I are going to a detective and you're going to *tell* her that the two of us never met before and what exactly happened at that hotel."

"You can't risk exposing yourself."

I started to pull her arm to bring her even closer to me but this time she snapped away from it.

"I'm not surrendering to the police!" She literally took several step backs from me so that we were now standing ten feet apart, awkwardly, visibly having an issue now. In the middle of a Goddamn airport. There could be cameras anywhere. There *were* cameras everywhere. There could be *anyone* watching any monitor. What would that look like—me barking at a nervous Eastern-bloc girl? How fast it would it take INTERPOL to spot her level of discomfort? "You can't go to the police."

"Stop backing away," I quietly growled at her through gritted teeth. "Act normal."

"You can't go back. You can't go anywhere they can know."

"What are you talking about? Yes, I can and am going back. *We're* going back. I'm taking a stand and you're—"

She walked away.

Literally turned and walked away—so decisively, so abruptly, that any pursuit of her might look exactly like me chasing an attractive Slavic female through an airport, which even on the best of days would look catastrophic, which meant that right there, inches away from a very crucial acquisition in this hunt, I had to let her go.

God help me.

I'd managed to lose two allies in two minutes. I looked at the escalator, I looked at the sliding door that led to the curbside area—the only two options for me getting back into the city. The RER train wasn't viable anymore. I'd already shown my face to over a dozen airport security cameras, meaning, I had to assume, I was being tracked by the detective, meaning any train would be an extension of her ability to see me, so to return to the bank office safely, which was all I had left in terms of a way out of this toilet swirl, I'd have to walk there. Directly out the sliding doors. Directly onto the streets. Walk.

"Fine."

Walk. Armed with the only weapon in the whole equation that mattered thanks to Jennifer Graham, who, let's note, despite her display of defiance, animosity, disappointment, and bile, never did actually take her employee ID card back from me. So here it was, in my hand, thin and powerful. So here it was—the thing I needed to start my small world war.

# CHAPTER 22

Throwing stones at an institutional empire takes more than just courage. It takes savage quantities of acceptance. You have to accept the fact that you're eventually going to jail, that you yourself will also be included in the drainage of the swamp. Because if you deny this possibility, if you fixate on the hope that you'll somehow escape unscathed, you'll hesitate at a crucial moment. You won't jump into the fray. You'll fail to do what's needed exactly when it's needed most. And you'll lose.

Case in point, right now what I was facing was the potential repercussions of illegally entering a bank office to illegally access material I shouldn't access. The plan was basic: if I could expose them before they publicly attacked me, then anything they'd do to me would be recognized for exactly what it was, an attempt to scapegoat an innocent employee. Hurrying through the neighborhood of Saint-Denis, one of the more dangerous places in Europe, an hour north of Paris, taking advantage of the fact that in a giant ghetto like this, I had a decent chance of eluding whoever had been chasing me earlier. There were sordid individuals on every corner, along with broken windows and graffiti. It was ideal cover from the fake cop—the one who searched my room—but even the remote odds of this guy lurking behind one of these tight corners, even all the way out here, scared me just as bad as the prospect of jail. What was he capable of? What kind of retaliation had he been contriving these past few hours? What did he even *want* from me?

I deliberately chose the most illogical streets possible. Each time I arrived at an intersection, I asked myself, What route would this guy guess I'd take? Metro Fort d'Aubervilliers or avenue du Général Leclerc? Turning left looked safer and faster, so I turned right, not stopping, still hurrying, going against my default logic, choice after choice, turn after turn, contradiction after contradiction, even sneaking on and off a crowded bus for a minute, so by the time I'd hit the final half mile inside the posh eighth, my zigzags had tripled my fatigue. I was approaching the Euro Bank headquarters just before the end of the lengthy Parisian workday, which would become, ironically, ideal timing. At 6:45 p.m. the majority of the local staff would be out, yet it wouldn't be so late in the day that the security team would wonder why someone would be entering instead of exiting. When I rounded the final corner and was within direct view of the office, ready to get right to the task at hand, I felt good about what was to come, and that's when I saw him—the guy—the fake cop—sitting at a café across the street, patiently waiting at a small table in the corner, having perfectly anticipated my choice of destination.

# CHAPTER 23

The worst of luck? Or the best of luck? That I spotted him before he spotted me—a miracle. That he'd be fucking sitting across the street from the front of this office—a nightmare. I stayed standing on the corner out in the open for way too long, gaping at him before snapping awake to the reality that I had to duck out of his line of sight immediately. As quickly and discreetly as I could, I moved behind the tall racks of a nearby magazine stand, doing anything I could not to be noticeable in the process.

Of the two possible explanations for how this happened, it had to be either Jenn or the girl who'd warned him, right? They were the only two people with knowledge of where I was going. I mean, this wasn't me being paranoid. This wasn't an exaggeration of a threat. After what had just happened, it'd be negligent to believe that everyone around me was who I assumed they were.

The sun had just fallen behind the buildings. The guy was smoking cigarettes as he staked out the front door of the building, wearing the same beige jacket, same pants, same everything. His hand was bandaged. He was seated in the back row of the terrace seats, so it was pure luck that I'd seen him at all. I was taking slow, strategic, ambitious glances at the front of the building, calculating whether or not I could actually sprint across the street, swipe my card on the scanner, open the door, close it, get to the elevator, get to the desk, get to the computer, retrieve the files, then call the police. I'd have to pray this guy wouldn't plow through whoever else might open that door behind me after I'd gone through. I'd also have to consider that maybe David versus the corporate Goliath wasn't a promising enough tale to risk my life in a street fight for, that maybe I should just go to the cops *without* trying to topple a kingdom.

"You know where is Arc?" An old man was talking to someone near me.

The only problem with going to the cops empty handed was that this was a game of leverage and I'd have none. So when it came to the mission at hand, there was no turning back. I didn't truly hear him—the old man. I was still dwelling on maximizing the odds of getting across the street before my enemy might cut me off. He had fresh legs, the fake cop. He could easily outrun me. He'd already kept pace with me earlier today when I was at my physical best. In my current state, he'd tackle me before I even got halfway to the building.

"Arc . . ." said the old man again. He had a thick accent. "Excuse me, my friend, but . . . are you . . . are you knowing where is . . . Arc . . . Arc of Triumph?"

I'd heard him but I hadn't understood that he was talking to me until now. He held up a small tourist map for me to reference. Apparently, I seemed knowledgeable. I couldn't imagine how awkward I must've looked, spying on someone across the street while loitering in front of a book rack.

"You want to go to the Arc?" I said to him.

He held the map up higher, one of those ad-ridden sightseeing things, the kind of garbage you get handed on the street for free then toss ten feet later. "I and my son . . . I and my son . . . we are looking for this . . . to make visit."

There was a van pulling up to the curb, a blue delivery van that the old man pointed toward, inside of which I could see the driver, who was, apparently, his son.

"Uh, I think it's just down the big street," I said. "It's big."

"Big? Yes, but is which?"

"What?" I glanced back at the café—to make sure my enemy was still there, which wasn't easy to do with all the crisscrossing cars and buses between us.

"Which?" said the old man. "Which street?"

"The big street."

"Is which?"

"The big street. This. This."

"Where?"

"*This* street. This."

He wasn't there. My enemy.

"Is where?" said the old man.

He was gone. I'd let my guard down for a matter of seconds and the guy across the street had vanished.

"Can you show my son?" said the old man. "My son is needing direction." He pointed to his son in the van as my stomach sank. "Show, please. To him."

I scanned around the large sidewalk area—there were a couple other tourists around, but it was mostly empty. I took a few steps sideways, literally turning in place, scanning three-hundred-and-sixty degrees, trying to process the ensuing whir of visuals. Two girls on the far corner. A guy walking his dog. A group of Korean tourists. The van now with its side door open. The kids on a scooter. A lady. A bicycle.

"Please!" yelled the driver. "We pay five euro you to help. Please!"

The old man was already over at the passenger side, having opened the door of the van for me. I turned back to check if anyone else was seeing all this, which was when I saw him, my enemy, charging right at me full speed, tackling me into the back of that blue van. I'd been too slow to brace myself or lower my center of gravity, so my body flopped like a rag doll, freely traveling midair until my head hit the metal interior, hard as all hell, not quite knocking me unconscious but rendering me virtually inert, as the old man got in and quickly began punching my torso.

"*Vite!*" he yelled to the driver.

The driver floored it. I heard the tires peel out as our engine revved to get us into the main traffic of the main road while the blows kept coming—my body tucked into a fetal position, my forearms over my face. The original enemy, the supposed cop, began punching me as well, everywhere—head, ribs, head, gut—everywhere. Their van sped to about fifty miles an hour before rapidly slowing down to thirty, the driver likely wanting to blend in. They had to evade the scene and vanish. I could hear him up front shouting in a language that wasn't French. He must've needed me alive for something because I couldn't hold my arms up and they could've easily kicked my head in but they hadn't done anything—the old man was sitting on my legs to negate my leverage while the other guy, the fake cop, was clamping me down in an arm lock.

"You stay fucking quiet," he said, shoving me up against the interior side of the van, mashing my face against the metal. "You stay down, quiet, you understand?"

An endless minute went by, then the van stopped and a door opened—the driver's door. I couldn't see much. It was slammed shut and we accelerated again, our whole world dipping forward as we drove down what felt like a ramp, which meant we had to be in a parking garage, swerving a few times while these guys continued shouting at each other in that other language. *"Kaaaffkkka noll."* Then *"Jeee brooozh. Jeee brooozzzhh."* *"Kaaaffkkka noll."* Back and forth they went, one of them barking orders, the other reporting how problematic those orders were to execute. The van came to a hard stop and the traffic noise became completely muffled. I no longer heard city sounds. All I heard was their new argument. The old man slid the door open so I now saw the concrete wall of what should've been a parking structure, but it wasn't a parking structure. The men were shouting at someone new and we were on a small road along the bank of the Seine river, having parked in the ideal position to dump a person in the water.

# CHAPTER 24

All three of these guys were yelling at someone just out of my view. I could barely discern the weak voice of what sounded like a seventy-five-year-old woman. A predicament had arisen. She was talking back at them, and things were getting extremely hostile. The old man shouted some foul words at her, then shouted something conclusive to his partners, then slapped the side of the van twice before scooting back over to kneel on my chest, holding a gun now, which he pushed against my temple.

"Keep your mouth shut," he told me.

This was the first time in my life I've had a gun pointed at me. I became useless. Physically, mentally done. I knew—knew—I was going to die and it'd happen within a matter of seconds. I knew it. I could feel it. The back door opened up again and I could see the guy with the injured hand standing there—the fake cop—who the old man called Oleg. I couldn't tell if he, Oleg, was getting cursed out by the old man or if he was just getting instructions but I soon understood that the three of them were yelling at a homeless lady. I could see her unwashed feet. She was sitting on the ground just outside the van, maybe directly in the way of their tires, and the guys were telling her to stop speaking. Oleg wanted to throw her into the water but the old man suggested something else and, whatever it was, the driver agreed to it, then Oleg agreed to it, then Oleg slapped the side of the van again twice, and I heard the old lady switch from arguing to pleading, to agonized begging, to outright screaming.

Horrific—you never forget the sound of desperation like that.

The van lurched forward several feet before Oleg slapped the side of the van again to have the driver shift to reverse and back up *over* the lady. They crushed her, the whole vehicle bumping up then bumping down, one, two, just like that. Then the back doors opened and they dragged me out and shoved me onto the pavement where I could see that the van had stopped on a narrow road underneath the main road, low down along the bank of the river.

"Take it," the old man said to Oleg. "The photograph. Go."

They were trying position me for a picture, wanting me to look like I was, what, maybe a hostage? I don't know. They continued bickering about how to do whatever would come next, then abruptly stopped. I wasn't sure why until we were all hearing it—a distant scooter was approaching us. I held my breath—Please, God, be a cop—Please be one—I'll never think of them badly again—all of us going silent in anticipation, with me also starting to wonder if they were the type of people to *kill* cops. The scooter was just a regular scooter and sped by without slowing down, passing our van before disappearing around the bend. All that'd happened was they were delayed a half minute and I'd gotten a longer look at what part of the river this was. We were across from the backside of the Notre Dame—lit up from below, Gothic and imposing. These guys must've busted a padlock at a gate to get down here because no one else was around. With the scooter gone, they turned back to me. The old man then pressed the record button on his phone.

"Tell me what you saw."

What? I stared up at him blankly.

He held it closer to me. "Talk for microphone. You say. Say!"

"...S-say?"

"Say what you are knowing."

"I have...I have..." I was shaking. Hard. My eyes watering. These guys didn't want anything from me. They just wanted me dead and this was the exit speech. "I have...I'm...I..."

"Finish him," said Oleg. "He doesn't know."

The old man clicked the recorder off.

"Noooo!" I yelled.

The old man picked up a dirty piece of cloth from the ground and wrapped it around the muzzle of his revolver.

"Nooo!" I yelled out. "NOOOOO! NOOO! NOOOOO!"

He put the muzzle in my mouth.

"NNN—mmmmppppphhhh." I tried to fight it but the barrel's invasion was merciless. All I could do was grab at it, grab at anything, and flail with Oleg quickly descending on me to lock up my arms in a bear hug from the side.

"Stay still," said the old man.

"Now!" yelled Oleg.

My vision was flooded with tears so I couldn't see well. Holding that gun away from me was all I knew in this world. *Just keep that muzzle away from you no matter what.* Oleg stood up and started kicking me in the ribs, once, twice, a third time, a fourth, while the old man tried to torque the gun back into the center of my mouth for a direct trajectory. I convulsed, trying to move away from them, turning myself down toward the concrete, pulling away as hard as I could.

Which was exactly what she needed.

Katarina.

Out of nowhere she marched up and decked the shit out of the driver. She'd come from the guy's blindside and swung her motorcycle helmet at his head, swinging at the soft side of his skull so that upon contact, his legs buckled and dropped him straight to the ground. And she didn't stop. Before his body even finished tumbling down, she straddled him, raised her helmet up high, then with both hands swung down on him full force *into* the center of his face. Shattering him. The guy didn't even whimper—he went from squirming to zero. Inert. Gone. Instantly. And she was already coming for Oleg, who was now getting up. It was all that fast. Two and a half seconds had elapsed—maybe—since her arrival—it couldn't have been more. She was dealing with Oleg while I still had the old man tangled up in a wrestling match for his revolver, soon believing that my fight-or-flight strength would overcome his aging musculature, yet this guy had fingers like granite, and instead of trying to pry *me* away, he began crushing my hands *tighter* inside his fiendish grip, mashing them against the metal of the muzzle, while, from my sideways view, I saw Oleg pick up a rock to square off with Katarina right before she swung her helmet at him. He dodged, then lunged for her, which led to their entanglement as they both fell to the pavement. Now the four of us were all on the ground going at it and I'd gained nothing on the old man.

At best, I was delaying him. His face eventually came to hover over mine menacingly. You could see that this guy didn't care what would happen to him. He wanted me dead and had no concern for any damage he might incur. Marks, scars, fractures, torn flesh—he didn't care. You couldn't tell if he was wincing in pain or smiling. Both rows of his crooked, wet, gray teeth gleamed in the dark. I wouldn't have been surprised if he'd leaned down and bitten me.

"POLICE!" I couldn't think of the French word for help so I shouted for the cops. It took me all this time to think of doing it, which didn't amount to much volume with the old man's weight directly against my chest. Plus, nobody was around. The sun had set and the big van eclipsed us from anyone's view. The random people on the far bank a quarter mile away could neither see us nor hear us. "POLICE!" I yelled again.

Oleg was strangling Katarina with his one good hand—his legs around hers in a scissor lock. It was ghastly what a real street fight looked like—hardly the dance of two Hollywood heroes taking turns punching. This was ugly, clumsy, sloppy, dirty, barbaric. Our sounds were inhuman.

Katarina's body was losing vigor, losing leverage, until, abruptly, with no buildup, Oleg lost the battle.

Done.

His mouth slurped its last breath.

Just like that.

I couldn't see how it happened. I'd seen no indication she'd even been gaining the upper hand on him, yet, bottom line, she choked him out before he choked her out, apparently outlasting him through sheer will. She quickly got up, grabbed her helmet, and walked over to us, to me, to the old man—who was totally unaware of her presence—and stoved the side of his head in, instantly rendering him unconsciousness as he slumped down directly on top of me.

Also done.

She took a moment to catch her breath, then knelt down near me. I could barely recognize her—every part of her skin had reddened—her veins pulsed—her hair was a wreck—knuckles scuffed—blood dripping, hands shaking, sweat and saliva gleaming everywhere. "Can you stand up?" she said.

I wasn't able to speak. I was just . . . gawking at her.

"Can you stand up?" she said again. She reached down.

I wanted to tell her that if she was going to get me out of here with a torn-up back, the maximum effort I could make would be to take several steps and lie across the back of her scooter—wherever it was—assuming it was her that'd ridden by. But she wasn't reaching for me. She was reaching for the old man.

"Can you?" she said.

She'd waited for him long enough in her opinion and grabbed him by the scruff and dragged his wobbly body toward the back of the van, where she started to load him in. I got up onto my hands and knees, semi-crawling to make my way over to her to help her shove the rest of him upward. It was a serious effort, but we finally got the guy in there, then she picked up her helmet and tossed it into the back, looking over at the other two guys, then looking over at me. "We won't kill them here."

## CHAPTER 25

"I'm not killing anybody," I told her. "We're going to the police."

"We can't."

"I'm not part of this." I pointed to the stagnant mayhem all around us. "I'm not part of any of whatever this is. I'm gonna turn myself in and I'm gonna be safe."

"You're not safe."

"Exactly. I'm not!"

She walked over to the other guy. Oleg. She was barely engaged with me, staying focused only on what she was about to do with him.

"I mean . . . thank you . . . by the way," I said to her, finally realizing it needed to be said. "For, uh, rescuing me. Thank you. I owe you more than . . . more than I can, uh . . ." She had blood on her neck. I couldn't tell if it was hers. "I want to help you do whatever you need to do to confirm your story with the police. I'll vouch for your side. I'll help you prove whatever you need to prove to them."

"The police can't help." She grabbed Oleg by the calves. "They can't help me, they can't help you. It's bad if we stay out here. We need to take these men into the van." She nudged the door open wider with her back foot. "And it must be quick."

She started dragging Oleg to the back door. I had no idea how any of this worked—not just the basics of moving a one-hundred-and-sixty-pound male up to the cargo bay of a van but the broader concept of administering justice within the gaping absence of it. What exactly was a "right" thing to do here? My hands were jittery. My stomach felt like it puked inside itself. I was both debilitated and hypersensitive, discerning every individual noise around me yet having no capacity to make a moral decision. Oleg stirred. A burbling sound came from his mouth as he started to slightly struggle. Katarina let his legs fall and moved behind him, quickly, quietly, efficiently sliding herself into a combative hug. He'd found a new lease on life and she was right there to quell the uprising, holding him in a headlock, trapping half his arm across the top of her own. I wasn't alert enough to realize I should probably rush over and help her but she didn't need me anyway. She sat there blankly gazing at nothing for six seconds while neutralizing him. You got the distinct feeling that today wasn't the first time she'd fought with a grown man.

"Take the helmet," she said to me.

I looked around. I saw the helmet. I picked it up.

"Get the driver," she said.

Oleg started grunting in protest.

"How?" I said.

"Get him."

Get him? Jesus, did she mean for me to beat him unconscious? *Get* the driver? I didn't argue. In the throes of dealing with the potential revival of three of the nastiest humans I'd ever known, I saw no convenient morality. I saw only panic and pragmatism. I hurried around to the front of the van. I looked. I crouched. I turned. I looked. I shifted. I crouched. I looked more. I turned more. I looked again. I turned again. That driver was gone.

## CHAPTER 26

We hurried—Katarina and I. We quickly shoved both of the remaining guys into the rear of the van, then she ordered me to drive while she crouched down in the back.

"Me?" I said to her. "I'm driving?" We were leaving. We'd given up on the driver just as quickly as we discovered his disappearance. "Why me?" Why would I be the one at the wheel? I'd driven a car every day of my life in LA, but Paris roads are another world. Even the first turn in front of us, pulling forward along the edge of the river, would be mortifying. I got in. I got started. I had to go slow yet fast, then accelerate, then decelerate, controlling it but hurrying, getting us squared up with the narrow ramp leading back up to ground level, then quickly merging to get us wherever the hell we were going. Maybe she had me at the wheel because she didn't trust me to stay in the back area with two full-grown thugs? Maybe.

"Turn left. Tight," she said. "On rue du Fouarre."

Paris street signs aren't posted where you can see them. They're sunken onto small, illegible blue plates on the *far* side of whatever wall you're passing, completely out of anyone's view.

"Here, here, here," she said, trying to get me to see the street I was missing. "Turn!"

I turned. I thought driving in New York was hard with its swarms of chaotic yellow traffic. I thought Tokyo was hard—on the opposite side of the road. Paris was a new standard of pain.

"Don't look back!" she said. "Look at the road."

I glanced back at her, just for a moment—both men were on the floor, inert. I quickly looked forward again. I honestly didn't want to see what she was doing. I'd been going sixty kilometers an hour, which felt obscenely fast—partly because I couldn't convert the metric system in my head but also because the streets here were insanely narrow. Parked-car doors left open, pedestrians crossing, scooters moving diagonally. You had potholes, bikes, electric bikes, dogs, carts, buses—absolutely none of which was predictable. Then you factor in that the blocks aren't square. They're all a triangle. Every street hits every other street crookedly and very few have two-way traffic, so whichever turn you choose is a wrong direction. And now one of the men who'd tried to kill me was kicking the inner wall of the van.

"Stop moving," yelled Katarina.

He didn't listen. He'd woken back up with enough strength and determination to keep banging despite the fact that she had a gun aimed at him.

"*Bouge pas,*" she said.

"You won't," he said.

"*Bouge pas!*"

He started flailing even harder, so she tried to shove him against the wall, to pin him down. I could barely concentrate on the road. "YOU WON'T SHOOT!" he roared at her.

"Go left," she said to me. "At the store."

I yanked the wheel left and we peeled onto a dark, unlit street that took us away from the bigger roads. Every part of this town was walled in by jam-packed rows of buildings, exactly the same height, seven floors tall, in every direction, rendering it all one big maze. The smaller streets crisscrossed even smaller streets until we found ourselves turning into a particularly tight stretch of nondescript buildings.

"Up here," she said.

She had me pull to a stop in front of a padlocked apartment entrance where no one was around. She yanked open the side door of the van, got out, then dragged the old man onto the pavement, mercilessly letting his body flop against the concrete with each move. I tried to help her as much as I could, unsure where we were going or why. She dumped him next to the nearest wall then went back for Oleg, who was really shifting around now. If we had duct tape, we could've tied him up. He'd found enough strength to drag his lower body to the outside edge of the cargo area, too woozy to walk but his arms were ready to do damage to whoever might approach him.

"We need duct tape," I said.

Katarina didn't wait. She hurried over and without hesitation started punching the side of his neck. I'd never seen anything like it—the fixation, the repetition. She bypassed all other possible targets on his body—his nose, his temple—hitting just the side of his neck until he went limp. Then she dragged him all the way out to the old man, propped him against the wall, and opened the side door to the building. There was no lock—it stayed untouched thanks to a cluster of overflowing trash cans in front of it.

"One man each," she said to me. She meant how we'd be transporting them.

Nobody was around. No cars. No people. No lights on in windows. She started dragging Oleg down the small corridor while I did the same with the old man. My stomach spun. For some reason I couldn't get the image of the neck punches out of my mind, wondering how would she even *know* to do that. We came to a set of jagged steps, which led underground via a spiraling set of dusty stone steps descending along dusty stone walls, through which we dragged both men, down, down, turning, spiraling down, down, revolution after revolution, down, in a descent that just wouldn't end, down, until we reached a nasty-smelling area leading to a dirt-floor area. The walls were dirt. The air had dirt. We were deeply subterranean. She dragged her guy into a small room where she shoved him into the corner then propped him up, then took my guy from me and shoved him into the opposite corner.

"Try not to let them move," she said.

"What?"

On the far wall there was a stack of mattresses and some bedding. She picked up a pillow and pulled the pillowcase off, then slid the case over the old man's head before shuffling both of their bodies around to position each one to face me. She pointed. "This one's dumb. This one's dangerous." She went back to the mattresses and pulled a backpack up from the far side, which she unzipped and started looking through.

"Wait, what?" I said.

She took the gun out from the rear of her pants. The old man's gun.

"Wait," I said. "Which one's the . . .?"

She handed it to me. "Try not to use it. I'll get us a knife on the way back."

"Back from where? I don't understand. Which one's dumb? Where are you going?"

She grabbed what looked like a little piece of wire from the backpack and put it in her pocket.

"Where are you going?!" I said again.

"To get rid of the van." She opened the door.

"Wait, I don't even—"

She was halfway out when she turned back to give me an additional warning. "Whatever you do, no matter how you do it, do *not* let them talk to each other." Then she closed the door and left.

# CHAPTER 27

Alone in a minimally lit room with two unknown men lying unconscious in front of me and a revolver in my hands. A Smith & Wesson 45. That's what was printed on the side. I read and reread that little piece of writing about fifty times—as if it would inform me further. I don't know anything about guns. There were no chairs, so I sat on the mattresses. I repositioned the gun in my hand, several times, a hundred times, staring at the mess in front of me and saying nothing about it. Neither one of these two guys was moving but they were breathing. Oleg had blood oozing through his bandage on the hand that I'd originally stabbed but it didn't look fresh. I had to tie up the hooded guy, the old man. I had to. That was my thought. Between the two of them he was the one who wouldn't know I had a gun—because he wasn't able to see it. So he could theoretically wake up and charge at me even though I'd be yelling, *Stop, I have a gun.* He wouldn't believe me. He'd be blind. I needed him subdued.

Subdued with what, though?

We had no duct tape. The room had almost nothing in it.

I'd been functioning on pure shock, too overwhelmed by the lingering terror of combat to think clearly, but another type of rationality was returning and the rogue nature of all this was starting to seem very problematic. My brain went back and forth nonstop. *Shouldn't you just walk away and get help?* No, if you bring these guys to the police, they get a chance to report how *you* attacked them—with three witnesses against you, lying with their every breath. *That's not true—you can prove your side of it.* And how long would that proof take? You think these guys would leave you alone while you sat in a holding cell, waiting for a massive pile of reports to get sorted out?

Shoelaces.

After a while, the idea of using the old man's shoelaces occurred to me. If he needed to be tied up, that might work. I pointed the revolver in the direction of Oleg, aimed it somewhat, and stood up after what felt like a lifetime of forethought. It might've been ten minutes. I had no idea. I didn't make noise and Oleg didn't open his eyes or flutter them or anything, except his breathing pattern changed. You could hear it. You could hear every nuance down here. When Katarina left, I heard her footsteps for at least twenty steps as she climbed up the stairs, at least twenty before they faded from recognition. That's how quiet it was. I crouched down to undo one of the old man's shoelaces. I had to keep in mind I'd be operating within reach of Oleg and if Oleg woke up at this moment, he could lunge at me.

I had to set the gun down—which is the last thing you want to do but I'd already drafted a flowchart of tactical decisions in my head, already visualizing all the paths leading to my peril. The old man's hands lay limp across his lap. I put the gun down, slowly, over the course of thirty seconds, and started to bend forward even slower. I couldn't afford to let either of them hear me. There was a chance Oleg was faking it. You have no idea how terrifying it is to stare at a pair of closed lids when they're on the face of a violent person, fearing that at any moment his eyes might roar open, that he'll bend forward with impossible speed and shove you backward while his partner grabs your gun and starts firing bullets into you.

I undid the knot and slid off the old man's left shoe. Slowly.

I waited. I saw no reaction in either of them.

I quietly, quickly, extracted the shoelace, praying it wasn't too frayed to do what I needed it to do. I checked my gun—still there—took a breath, leaned forward, shifted the old man's hands slightly, then started to lay the lace gently across his wrists. He was limp, yes, but I didn't have the courage to position his hands behind his back. I *did* have confidence in the effectiveness of his hood—in that he'd feel the unseen tension on his hands and assume the binding was stronger than it really was. Smart, right? I got the string in position as best as I could with my limited knowledge of knots, wishing I knew more, then on a silent count of one, two, three—cinched it tight and quickly tied it then quickly grabbed the gun then scooted back toward the door as fast as possible all while aiming at Oleg.

No movement.

Neither of them.

The old guy hadn't winced or budged, and I felt a small sense of pride. I felt like I operated well, having done the best a regular person could've done under the circumstances. I sat back down on the mattresses. I stopped aiming toward Oleg. I now had a moment for some level-headed thinking. Because I hadn't killed anyone yet. If the police started to unravel this situation, I, at this point, was still a victim.

"Do you know who she is?" said Oleg.

His eyes were still closed. His voice came out of nowhere, almost giving me a heart attack with how clearly it rang out, almost causing me to react physically. He was lucky he didn't get shot just based on reflexes alone, because I did feel my index finger twitch.

We were all lucky.

I didn't respond. I didn't move.

"*Do* you?" he asked again, after a minute.

I was watching him, still trying to recover my lost breath. I didn't have an answer to give him, but more to the point, I didn't *want* to give him an answer. I didn't want to get involved.

"No?" he said.

I stayed seated, silently scrambling for a strategic response if one would be needed. I couldn't just let him toss up a paragraph of key information to his partner.

He started to open his eyes. He didn't register an ounce of surprise or bewilderment or fear at what he saw. He scanned the room a bit. I hated that he did this. I lacked the audacity to tell him to stop because if he persisted, I'd have no way to enforce anything, I'd have no way to demonstrate there were consequences. And he saw the gun in my hand.

"She's lying to you," he said.

He didn't stare at it.

"The girl," he said. "She's using you. They call her the Mistress of Lies, did you know that? Did she tell you about the Society?"

I showed zero reaction.

"No, right? She didn't. You are sitting there with a six-shot revolver in your right hand. You have me in direct sight. You have Ulrich covered with a pillowcase and his hands—"

"Shut the fuck up!"

He stopped. He didn't move.

I'd spoken too strongly—way too agonized. I sounded desperate. Fuck. I overdid it.

"She's a prostitute," he said after a minute, calmer now, continuing to look at me with his hands remaining in front of him.

I hadn't spoken up like a man in control. I'd spoken with weakness. You could hear it in my voice.

"She's assaulted at least three people from your bank," he said. "She burned the Goldman guy. Burned him alive. Did you know that? I'm sure you know that. You were there. She got you to help her. Did she tell you why? Did she entertain you with a story about how she has been mistreated?"

"Enough," I said, too weak this time. He'd informed his buddy about the layout of the room, spelling it out without even encoding it, brazenly doing it right in front of me as I sat there pathetically allowing it. I should've stood up and rammed his teeth in with the back of the revolver. He'd heard Katarina tell me not to let them talk to each other and yet he talked anyway. He talked right Goddamn in front of me.

"She tells everyone she was hanging from a noose and clients took turns fucking her while she choked," he said. "Do you believe this story?"

The old man hadn't moved.

"Ask yourself why she is lying to you," said Oleg. "She burned a CEO alive, would you agree? Yes. Yes, you would. She is doing the exact things that a psychotic female would do. For no reason other than she is angry at her father. Her father probably raped her six days a week. I mean, wouldn't you? Look at the face. That's a rape face—you can't deny this. So she was raped . . . and that is very sad . . . but does that entitle her to kill whoever she wants? She will kill you. She will certainly kill you next."

He studied my face. I'd played the best game of poker I could. I'd decided ahead of time that literally every word he'd say to me would be regarded by me as a total fabrication. I'd braced myself. I'd fortified my logic to withstand whatever cunning statements he'd make.

He nodded yes.

What he said just now was actually something I'd already been deliberating myself. When he said she'd kill me, he could see me flinch ever so slightly. He could see the pulse in my neck bulge slightly. I was sure of it. I was the shitty result of a shitty upbringing. I'd never seen it with such clarity until this week, this day, this purgatory. I'd learned just how much of a man I hadn't become. A thirty-seven-year-old boy. None of this mattered except that I was receptive to him.

He kept going. "Ask yourself why you're down here in a cave while she's somewhere else . . . leaving you with a traceable gun. She's framing you for murder, my brother. She's going to call the police. She'll come back into this room and she'll pretend to be your friend, don't you think? Then she will ask you to do things . . . do things to me and my friend Ulrich . . . so that you happen to do the specific things she already did to other dead men. Bah, voilà, then the cops waste time putting you on trial, connecting you to past events, and she gets the freedom to kill her next victim."

I needed to pistol-whip him unconscious. I needed to interrupt him. She was going to come back any minute. When she came back, she'd handle the situation. I had to trust that. She saved me once; there was no reason to believe from this point forward she wouldn't save me completely.

"Watch close . . ." he said. "When she returns, I'm going to ask her a question in front of you. One question. For you. You watch her. That's all I want. You have the gun. You have control. You watch how she tries to avoid answering my one question. She will avoid it, my brother, because she knows you will learn what she intends to do with you. With a single question, you are able to learn. You don't have to trust me, my brother. You just have to give yourself a chance to hear what you *deserve* to hear."

We didn't have to wait long to find out how I'd respond. Within a half hour, footsteps were audible again, the faint, rhythmic scuffle coming down the spiral stairs. I heard it. He heard it.

He started talking again, faster and quieter this time. "Listen, my brother, I have chased you and fought you. I am not going to lie to say that I am your friend. I am not. We tried to hurt each other, yes, but you listen, you *listen*, you have a chance to see the truth about her, you understand? So, protect yourself and make sure you get this chance. That is all. You make sure."

The door started to creak open. I pointed the gun at him. At Oleg. I did. Right at him. I also pointed it near the door. Right at the door. Back and forth. Both angles. Him. Door. Door. Him. Without rushing my arm. Because you never know what can come through a door. Back and forth. Because he was right. I did deserve a chance to hear the truth.

# CHAPTER 28

**K**atarina entered. Alone. I didn't point the gun at her. Not directly. I kept it aimed at the center of the room. She came in and saw that the old man's hands were tied, saw Oleg with his eyes open, saw the gun in my hand, how I held it slightly shaking, and saw that words were exchanged. Like a wilderness tracker who crouches to touch the warm terrain, she read the room. She read me.

"Where's the van?" I said to her.

She didn't answer.

She had her hands in her jacket pockets—possibly holding something hidden there. She was watching Oleg like a hawk.

"Where's the van?" I said again.

She looked over at me, then looked back at him. I felt my finger quiver, ever so slightly. It wasn't on the trigger, but it was near it, nearer than I trusted it to be. She stayed standing by the door as I did my best to keep the gun aimed at the floor. I thought of all the ways I'd stand trial in a criminal court for what was about to happen next. In a foreign country. Unable to argue on my behalf. In French. Did they even appoint defense lawyers here? What if no one other than me acknowledged the facts of what happened? Could I actually keep that gun from firing? I'm no killer—that was the key thought. I'm no killer.

I'm no killer. I'm no killer. I repeated it silently to myself, bracing for the inevitable.

I cleared my throat to ask her about the van again. "Katarina, where's the—"

With no warning, she marched across the room, hand emerging from her pocket with a kitchen knife, squatted in front of Oleg, and in one fast jab, poked the blade of that knife in and out of his throat, cutting him enough for blood to trickle in a dark cascade down his clavicle. He hadn't spoken. He hadn't even resisted. His mouth descended slightly as his hands fluttered up toward his chest in a vain effort to stanch the flow. She'd nicked him so quickly he didn't have time to raise his arms in defense.

"OH MY GOD!" I shouted the moment this began.

The old man started to squirm.

"OH MY GOD, WHY THE HELL'D YOU DO THAT?!"

She stood up then took a sideways step over to the old man, preparing to repeat the process.

"NO!" I said. "NO, NO, NO, NO, NO, NO."

The old man quickly tucked his chin down tighter, tighter, and tighter, curling inward like a human prawn, unsure where exactly her weapon existed in relation to him.

"NOOO!" I yelled as decisively as I could.

At which point she stopped.

She turned to look at me—to behold the desperate, frazzled version of me.

"You can't . . ." I said. "You . . ." I shook my head. Imploring her.

She stayed still a moment, contemplating me. I had the gun up but I still lacked the gall to aim it at her, yet I did have it up. She'd halted her activity temporarily, merely out of respect for how loud I'd gotten.

"You're not going to shoot me," she said.

"H-how do you know?" I said.

She nodded to Oleg to make her next point. "You should be aware that whatever this man told you—"

"We can't kill them."

"—is true."

She didn't blink.

"What?" I said.

She didn't stutter.

"What?" I repeated. "What he said is true?"

"I'm not here to save the world."

"What does that mean?" I'd been bracing myself for a series of convoluted denials from her, a series of contradictory brushstrokes that'd leave a grayish uncertainty on my mental canvass. Denials, rebuttals, counterpoints. I didn't know how to incorporate a flat-out *admission*. "Did you burn Evan Goldman alive?"

"Don't play their game."

"No, did you or did you not? It's relevant."

"What is relevant is that you survive."

"I just want to walk away. I can't sit here while you kill a defenseless old man, no matter what he did. I'm happy you saved me, I am. I'm grateful. I owe you. But I can't be part of . . . of . . . of . . ." I nodded to the unfinished act in front of her.

"You want to talk to him yourself?" She got up. She stepped aside. "You want to find out if he has a sufficient reason to be kept alive? A family? A nice dog?" She offered him to me. "Ask him."

The old man had stopped squirming. The hood over his head was hanging just tightly enough to trace out the contours of where he was looking—toward me—yet too loose for me see his expression. I got up. I slowly walked over to him, keeping my eyes on her, keeping my gun aimed at the floor. I took off the pillowcase.

His face was drenched in sweat.

"Ask him," she said to me.

I stood in his direct line of sight. "Why . . . did . . ." I started to say to him, "why did your friend come to my hotel room? Why did I find Oleg in my hotel room?"

The old man looked at her, then looked back at me.

I repeated my question. "Why did—?"

"You know who I fucking work for?!" he said with incredible conviction. "You will be lucky if they merely kill you. They will do things to your body you do not think chemically possible."

"What was Oleg doing in my room?"

He wiped his mouth with the top of his shoulder to remove some of the crusted blood. I swear, I thought Katarina was going to stab him right then. I still had the gun pointed away from everyone but there was a growing fear in me, a fear of my need to maintain some kind of order—some semblance of peace—at whatever the cost. "Once upon a time there was this diseased whore who started to kill things for fun," he said. "She came from nowhere important. Somebody peed in her mother."

He almost smiled. He let his words hang in the air, like a trophy.

Katarina gave the remark a moment, then crouched down in between his legs, which instantly made him shield his throat from her with his hands, flailing back and forth wildly in an instant conversion from smugness to self-preservation. "*Non!*" he yelled, thoroughly respecting her potential. "*NON! Ne le fait pas! Ne le—*"

She sliced his inner thigh.

An inch deep. Two inches long.

She made the incision through the fabric of his pants, which he quickly smothered with his hands as the blood started to exit from him relentlessly. *"Kurva! KURVA! Non,* you ugly dog! *T'es une connasse!"* Rattling off a chain of invectives, cursing her out in three different languages. She didn't reciprocate verbally. She remained there calmly as he hurried to use his pillowcase to tamp down on the wound.

"You need medical attention," she said to him unemotionally. "You are bleeding freely. If nobody is sewing this wound, you will die within approximately one hour."

The clock had begun. His age. His feeble body. His position on the floor. Everything was working against him.

"Now," she said to him, "why don't you do a better job of telling him what you know about me?"

"Are you insane?!" I said to her.

She turned to me. "After this I'm going to ask you a favor and I will need you to trust me because this favor is difficult." She pointed to him. "The best way for you to understand who they are is to understand what they *do.*" She leaned over to talk to him. "I'll make you a proposal, if you are accurate with your facts . . . and you say every fact you know . . . he and I will let you live."

The blood had come. Inexorably. His leg twitching. His demeanor changing. Panic setting in. Humility setting in. He looked at me, then looked at her, then looked at me, completely ready to state all he knew of her.

He cleared his throat. *"His name is da Vinci . . ."*

# CHAPTER 29

### In the Old Man's Own Words

*T*o know about Katarina, you must know about a man named Morgan da Vinci. To know about Morgan da Vinci, you must know about Katarina. They affect each other. I met Katarina for first time one week after her fifteenth birthday. Her mother, she doesn't have a lot of money, so the dinner for this birthday is only for a few of the neighbors and some of family, okay? Katarina is age fifteen, okay? One neighbor, he is a man who is owning a restaurant. This man tells the mother about a special job. He has small room in back of his restaurant with radio that is playing nice music. The mother agrees to allow Katarina to work a couple of hours each Saturday. The mother is making practical decision. No country has more practical mentality than Belarus. Katarina will have a nice job to do private dancing and make money for her mother and sister. This job is simple, okay? Maybe sometimes she will need to let some men do kissing to her, but is not dangerous because this is men from the family. Uncles. Cousins. Not so much strangers. On the first day of working, Katarina, she is going to this back room but she is refusing to dance. Men have paid extra to be in this specific room with this girl so for her to have hesitation . . . is . . . well . . . okay, this is a problem. One man tells her that maybe she can just put her

*hands to his pants. She say to him no. This man tells the res-*
*taurant manager. Restaurant manager tells mother. Mother is*
*refusing cooperation. Restaurant manager is telling me. Now I*
*am hearing about the whole situation for first time.*

*This restaurant manager, he offers me a standard price of*
*ninety rubles for introduction of mother to me. I see photo of*
*Katarina. This is my business. I pay. I tell mother Katarina*
*has opportunity to earn big money. I tell mother that everyone*
*is needing money: heating and food is expensive. I tell her that*
*this restaurant is full of disgusting men who have no money. I*
*say I have big opportunity outside of city.*

*The mother, she say no.*

*I tell you everything?*

*I say to mother, "We provide dream location and dream oppor-*
*tunity for your daughter. It is Paris. With big Paris money. This is*
*big job." I am telling to her, "Listen, your daughter, she will work*
*in big restaurant with celebrities and politician. Normally, you*
*pay relocation fee to Paris but we will be giving you nice loan."*

*The mother is agreeing as long as is no sex.*

*I tell mother, of course, is no sex.*

*I keep going?*

*I say, "Paris is best opportunity for her." I say, "Don't worry,*
*there is report about French thieves stealing passport and money*
*but I will protect her passport and I will keep her money safe from*
*greedy French banks."*

*Okay, so Katarina, she come to me private. Katarina, she is*
*crying. Katarina is begging me not to take her sister. She has a*
*sister. Not as beautiful. But nobody is as beautiful as Katarina.*
*She is believing her sister is next. She is saying, "My sister is very*
*good in school but I'm not so good. Please leave my sister alone."*

*I know Katarina is very good in school. I say, "Don't worry."*

*Katarina is sent to Paris. There she is given to Mr. da Vinci. Mr. da Vinci is her new employer. Mr. da Vinci is never introducing himself directly, but he is watching her and he is believing she has capacity to make big, big money. Okay? Okay, the first time Katarina gets in bed with a full-service customer, she is refusing to let this customer penetrate, which is a problem. She makes trouble and scratches this customer. Our staff are interested to punish her for this but Mr. da Vinci is unusual with her. He is saying no to any damage of her. Okay? Well, after additional week of these problems, Mr. da Vinci, he is proposing a more effective solution: I find Katarina's sister and bring this sister to La Jonquera in Spain. It was not difficult for my team. We can move girls when we need. The sister is now in La Jonquera. La Jonquera has big customer population, biggest in world. A telephone call is made. Anytime Katarina is saying no to a customer, the sister is given a client and we say to Katarina, "Your sister will now do what you refuse." Katarina is to be listening on phone while other phone is next to sister's bed. A man begins penetration of Katarina's sister. The sister is crying, so Katarina cries. Is good system. Is effective. Katarina quickly is cooperating with us. She is performing sex for customers and making them happy. Mr. da Vinci is good businessman. Customers are paying over five-thousand Euro for her. After two years . . . she is best source of revenue for . . . for . . . Mr. da Vinci. The rev . . . The revenue . . .*

The old man was feeling faint. He had to press down harder on the incision on his inner thigh to prevent himself from passing out as he struggled to keep speaking.

*The revenue is . . . is . . . good. We tell her she is slowly paying off her loan. We don't give her her money but this is the arrangement. Katarina is woman now. Is six years. One day she disappear. We are looking and looking and looking for her. We cannot locate her. Is possible we think she is trying to find her sister . . . even though she doesn't know where her sister is. Katarina is gone. Nobody knows what happened to Katarina. France is a good location for our business because France language is difficult for the girls but Katarina finds a way. She is disappearing for almost one year. Then one day I am told that Mr. da Vinci has found her. I don't know how. I don't know where. Mr. da Vinci isn't happy. Katarina is different and now Mr. da Vinci is different too. Everything is different. Katarina is going to be part of something new. She is going to be . . . pa . . . I am being honest . . . I am saying all the details . . . I am honest, you see?*

He looked up at her.

*I am saying what I know. I am not part of it. I was only called after the fire at hotel. So I am not . . . I am not in the . . . the . . .*

He winced in pain as he turned to me to finish.

*She was going to be part of something very dangerous. She was the beginning of a new club. This club becomes very successful for Mr. da Vinci. Nobody outside of club is knowing what this club is . . . but . . . but Mr. da Vinci is a good businessman. Powerful. I only know what they tell me they are doing . . . But what they are doing is . . . What they . . . are . . .*

# CHAPTER 30

He slipped unconscious, succumbing to his loss of blood despite trying as hard as he could to fulfill his obligation to Katarina. She knelt by him, genuinely surprised he'd passed out so soon. He'd been tamping down on his leg steadily, but his gradual loss of strength led to gradually letting the flow increase, which meant losing more strength, which meant a vicious cycle. She started tying it off, the leg. She took the shirt off the younger guy, Oleg, tore it in strips, then rapidly made a sort of rope, then tightened it across the top of the old man's thigh as tightly as she could. "Wake up," she said to him several times. "Wake up. Hey!" She slapped his face. "Hey. Or else you'll—Hey!"

He stirred. Slightly.

She turned to me. "We need elevation for his leg."

I didn't respond.

I no longer cared.

She started to reposition him, soon looking over at me and seeing that I hadn't moved. "Come on," she said to me. "We need elevation right now."

It wasn't the first time I'd heard about a life like this so it wasn't the *content* of his words that jarred me. It was his presence. Here. In the room. With me, near me—this wrinkly old guy had actually carried all this out, participated in it with his own bare hands, and now here he was, several feet away from me, his presence making it all so real.

"Adam!"

You fixate. You get so lost in how ugly it is that you fixate on the man and you really don't see the other person near you—the victim, the girl—and you forget to consider how the fuck she herself should feel about it.

She worked to retighten his tourniquet. "You're not going to help me?! Adam!"

"No."

"Help me!"

"I don't care about this man anymore."

"He will *die*." She backed away from him, seeing my obstinacy, seeing what she felt jeopardized her overall goal. "We need to get him to a paramedic or it will be impossible to keep him alive. I gave you my word. That I would keep him alive." She was growing frustrated. "It is crucial that you are trusting me. It is crucial because I'm going to ask you to do something and I need you to trust me when I ask you to do it."

"It's fine."

"It's not."

"It's fine. I'll do what you're asking."

"Khhhhh!" She scoffed.

"I will."

She got up and came over to me, then held her palm outward toward me.

She kept it there, her hand, outstretched.

"What?" I said.

I didn't understand but she wanted something from me. I'd just told her I'd do whatever she asked. I'd seen enough. I'd lost whatever motivation I had to argue over the morality of it. I'd spent most of my adult life making sure these sorts of grand decisions stayed simple for me. Not that I'd ever faced something this extreme, but the basics of it—right versus wrong—should never be complex or nuanced or tricky or layered or asterisked or annotated. There's either do you treat people well or do you not? Nothing between. But of all the undesirable places to shove a system-needing individual like myself into, the crevices of a sex trafficker's résumé were the worst for me to try to stay true to myself. What good could an old man like him possibly do on this planet? Reform himself? Reinvent himself? Do charity? If we sutured him up and sent him on his merry way, how many more girls does he scar?

"What?" I said again, staring at her open palm. "What do you . . .?"

Did she want comfort?

I reached for her, warmly. I wanted to hug her tightly, maybe kiss the top of her head. I felt numb, speechless.

"The gun," she said.

I looked down at it—the gun—still in my hand. She wanted to take it from me. I slowly started to offer it to her—the gesture alone being all the approval she needed before snatching it from me, clicking the release, popping the cylinder, emptying the shells, then snapping the cylinder back, and walking away.

"We're leaving." She walked out of the room.

I followed her without asking how we were going to get away with what we just did. I followed her without knowing who might find this place next. We were now in what felt like a hallway made of dirt. She dropped the empty gun just outside the door to the room, literally tossing it on the floor, then closed the door behind us. I couldn't conceive of giving up a weapon like that—I wanted to sleep with it under my pillow for a year—but I guess she foresaw whatever complication it'd bring. We were abandoning the old man in this room. Wasn't that murder? Should we care? She started leading me down the path for several minutes of silence, guiding us with an old flashlight she held up, taking us through a small junction where we kept going straight along a narrow, dark utility corridor. You almost had to hunch over as you walked.

"You sure?" I said to her.

In the first half hour, the walls we were passing were stone slabs. In the second half hour, our tunnel became more and more like the sides of a cave. Raw rock. Raw dirt.

"You sure?" I said again, wondering whether or not she had the right route.

She didn't answer. She had us hiking along a very gradual incline—seemed to be over a mile. We were no longer inside any kind of industrial structure. The thing felt medieval.

"What are we doing?" I said, knowing I'd get no response. "Hey!"

She didn't look back.

"I'm not following you anymore until you tell me."

"Lower your voice."

"Why?"

"Lower your voice. We don't want to be heard."

"Why?" I started to slow down. "Are there people down here?"

"Yes. And they're not friendly. We don't stop."

I stopped.

She turned around. "You have a simple question? You can ask me whatever you want to ask when we arrive."

"Arrive where? I have fifty questions. None of them are simple."

She came over to me. "You can ask me one—one quick one. That's it. We need to hurry to get up to street level before daylight comes.

The man who ran from us—the driver—he will tell who he needs to tell and it will be bad."

"Seven years ago you were fifteen. Does that mean you're twenty-two? You don't look twenty-two. Why are people chasing me? How did you find me by the van?"

"People are not chasing you. They're chasing me. Now that they know we are together, they will look for you and they will kill you."

"How do you know how to fight?"

"Be first."

"Are we in the Catacombs?"

"Yes."

"This is the Catacombs? Are there dead bodies? 'Be first.' What does that mean?"

"We have to go."

"Are there dead bodies?"

"Yes."

"How many?"

"A million? I don't know. Does it matter?" She motioned for us to move forward. "We have to go."

"A *million*?"

"The whole city is built on top of caves. It's . . . how do you say . . . . the, uh, uh, *calcaire*. The rock. It's very strong." She pointed to the rock all around us. I was nervous in tight spaces in general, but to be in a tight space surrounded by a million corpses? "We have to keep moving. We have to protect ourselves from the homeless here. They are territorial."

"Did you have something to do with the burning of Evan Goldman?"

She knew this was one of my crucial questions. This stopped her. I didn't have to grab her arm to hold her in place. She took a good, long look at me, calculating what I had the capacity to hear. "If I told you that he caused his own death, you'd say I'm lying."

I couldn't exactly spell it out—why I'd agree to help her, why I'd agree to involve myself in something so antithetical to the comfort of a lower-class kid now in an upper-class life. I chose to believe she represented my best path to legal redemption and that any help I provided her was justifiable under the lens of the law. I chose to believe that. "I'd say you were lying, yes."

"So . . ."

"So . . .?"

"So let's not have you think I'm lying. I won't say anything about Evan and you can believe what you want."

"Why can't we go up to street level here?"

"It's too soon. It's safer for us to move down here. We are going to visit someone. When we get there, we can prepare for what's next and I can explain to you how you can give me what I need."

"And what is that?"

She turned around and continued up the path. She was done talking.

"And what is that?!" I yelled.

# CHAPTER 31

A half hour later we stood at the front door of a top-floor apartment in the north section of Paris. The Catacombs have hidden exits all over the city, which meant we could minimize our usage of the city streets by maximizing our time underground. We emerged from the caves to go up a stairwell into the night air, taking care to stay hidden, going cautiously at first, then hurrying over to a tangled row of scooters parked on the sidewalk where Katarina took out a short piece of wire from her pocket, a bare strip of it, then searched for one of the older-looking scooters. When she found a decent one, she ripped off the panel that covered the front, yanked up a cable leading to the ignition switch, followed that cable with her hand until she arrived at a little white plastic thing, then stuck her wire into that plastic thing to jump the circuit while she pressed the ignition.

The damn thing started up.

She drove us a quick half mile to the apartment building we were in now, to the aging but gilded door that we now stood in front of. She knocked loudly. "Let me talk," she whispered to me. "You don't talk."

She knocked again.

We listened. We waited.

When we heard some movement inside, she knocked a third time in what seemed like code. A slow repetition of quiet taps. That's when the door cracked open, a little, not fully, and we saw the face of a woman appearing in the vertical strip of darkness.

"*Non*," she said as soon as she saw me.

I recognized her eyes before I heard the voice but the voice confirmed it all. Mathilde—the lady from the shop.

"*Non*," said Mathilde, who looked just as unhappy to see me as I was to see her. "*Ici? Lui? Non. Non, non, non.*"

The two women then mumbled a long, heated argument entirely in French, where I understood nothing except "*vingt minutes*"—twenty minutes—the quantity of time Katarina kept repeating, which was apparently her only bargaining chip, as in whatever we were about to do here, it'd take only twenty minutes, and "*confiance*"—trust—as in people like me weren't to be trusted but let's accept this. Mathilde then gave in and we entered her midsize over-decorated multibedroom Paris flat, where she flicked on various lamps to illuminate various amounts of gaudiness. Leopard-print curtains. Candelabras. Candles. Filigree. Velvet. A home shat straight from the bowels of Versailles. As they moved to the kitchen, they talked even more quietly—clearly not wanting me to be part of their decisions—so I forced my attention toward the window, toward the skyline beyond the balcony, to check what part of town we were in. I was ready to help her, Katarina, I was, but that didn't mean I trusted who she trusted. Where were we? She said we'd arrived in the eighteenth arrondissement. I needed us to be near the town center where I had a better chance to do what I personally needed to do. The signature rooftops leading up to Montmartre and its distance to the Eiffel Tower told me I'd have a ways to go for all that. The city was unlit, so it was at least past 1:00 a.m. I noted all this while pretending to admire the view outside but found myself distracted by what was right next to me, just across the room from me—the vision of our enigmatic, long-limbed, high-cheek-boned warrior in soft lighting, hair down, pacing back and forth—wondering to myself what in God's name fate had in store for us. She hadn't finished arguing with Mathilde, but in the midst of whatever they were debating, she began preparing the bathroom for me. *"Donc je ne vais pas continuer à te dire,"* she said to Mathilde, *"ça me fait rien,"* then she ushered me to the shower, gesturing for me to take off my clothes, which was something that was to occur right in front of her.

*"Alors,"* Mathilde said from the next room. *"Je comprends le situation entier."*

"Non.

*"Oui."*

*"Pas de tous. Non."*

*"Tous que tu m'as dit, et inebrealbment, t'es foulle."*

*"Non!"*

*"OUI!"*

*"NON! TU NE COMPRENDS RIEN!"* Katarina held out her hand for me to give her my shirt while yelling out the rest of whatever debate they were having, *"Tu préféres rester une marionnette!"* She'd probably seen a hundred men get naked so I just did what she asked as she handed me some gauze, pointed me to the mirror, still arguing, then returned to the living room, where she and Mathilde then switched to English for whatever reason—maybe because Katarina knew it'd give her the upper hand—I had no idea.

I got under the nozzle. I got under the warm water, which, my God, felt surreal. There's nothing like it. The steam, the heat, the isolation, the immersion in a hot shower, and it was only here that I understood how damaged the side of my upper back was. Had she seen that? Is that why she gave me so much gauze? The cut was much deeper than

I thought. My wound had reopened under the water and blood now circled the drain. Craning my neck around, I could sort of see part of the gouge in the mirror. A newly cleaned wound looks anatomically incorrect—you're missing a piece of you. The barbs of the bottom of that fence dragged open a sizable rip midway up the back of my shoulder. I exited the shower, keeping the water on as I toweled off while standing close to the door so I could hear as much as possible.

"Because I don't want to justify myself," said Katarina.

"Oh, la, la—"

"Just give it to me!"

"There is no way to justify this," said Mathilde. "This is a bad choice."

"Yes, and it's *my* bad choice! And you can't keep from me what is mine!"

"Yes, I can."

"Where is it?"

"*Je ne l'ai pas.*"

"I said tell me! Where is it?!"

I heard a lot of physical commotion out there: books being tossed, drawers slammed, doors opened, doors shut. I heard Katarina, frustrated, pacing around, banging around, while Mathilde followed her, trying to reason with her. "We agreed together on how we would deal with someone like him and this was never part of the plan."

"You don't even know the plan!"

"I know you bring this American here. He will help you connect to other Americans. I'm not stupid. I know what you are trying to do."

"Where is it?! No, you don't. I'm trying to break free."

"He looks weak."

"Stop."

"He looks like he is a partial man. He cannot protect you."

"You promised me it was mine. *Tu n'as pas me dire des choses comme ça! Il est ma meiulleir chance de réussir!*"

"*Pour faire quoi? Pour provoquer ta putain de mort?* I'm not giving it to you. I never agr—"

"WHERE IS IT?" They could be heard approaching the bathroom, rapidly, both of them coming in here before I could duck back from the knob, barging in, seeing me there, guiltily, the shower still running, as Katarina started searching around me. "Is it here?" she said to Mathilde, kneeling down to check behind the back of the toilet for whatever it was.

"Talk to her," Mathilde said to me. "Tell her."

"Did you pack it in the wall?" said Katarina.

"Help her understand," said Mathilde.

"Leave him alone."

"Tell her you don't care for her," Mathilde said to me. "Tell her she is trusting you to help her but in the end you will betray her."

"Don't listen," said Katarina, turning to me then back to Mathilde. "Did you spend it?"

"She doesn't like you," said Mathilde to me. "She never will."

"He's *helping* me. Where did you hide it?" She then turned to explain to me. "She has eight hundred euros that I've kept here for two months, which is *my* money, which is money that I need."

"You are committing suicide and I will never let this happen! Voilà."

This was what stopped Katarina from searching. She lifted her head up from the bathroom cupboard to confront Mathilde directly. "So you *do* have it."

They both went quiet.

"So you do have it," said Katarina again.

"*Non.*"

"You said never 'let' this happen. So you have it?"

Mathilde didn't answer her but after a moment Katarina suddenly rushed out to the kitchen, leaving Mathilde facing me.

"She is not who you think," said Mathilde before heading down the hall in the other direction to pull a particular book from the top of the shelf of a bookcase while across the apartment on the far side Katarina continued searching in the kitchen. I could see both of them. Mathilde opened the book and extracted a clump of bills, fifties, looking like maybe eight hundred, which she carried over to the fireplace so she could hold it over a cluster of lit candles on the mantel, then stood there, facing the kitchen, waiting.

Katarina turned around, stopping midsentence as she caught sight of it. "Where would—"

They were now glaring at each other.

"No," said Katarina.

Mathilde looked at me. "This girl means more to me than my own life. She is thinking I will let her return to a man who will cut her into pieces." She looked at Katarina with her verdict. "*Donc*, I refuse."

The gap between them, roughly twenty feet, was too wide for Katarina to cross in time to prevent anything. She could only plead verbally from a distance. "No!"

"Da Vinci is clever. He *wants* you to come to him. He wants it."

"No."

"He is waiting to drown you in front of the world."

"If you burn that money, I will find a way to get more. I am resourceful. I can take care of myself. You know this is—"

Mathilde lit the wad.

"NO! YOU—NO!"

Torching the entire €800. All of it, sending Katarina slumping down to her knees in tears, almost to the point of pulling her hair from her head. It'd been horrible to watch. The act was ravaging both of them. Mathilde was equally gutted and could only murmur to herself, "How else can I keep you alive?"

Katarina stayed hunched over in a ball for a bit, then abruptly got up. "I'm *trying* to stay alive." She walked straight out the front door.

So that Mathilde was now staring at an empty living room.

"She doesn't mean it," said Mathilde to no one in particular—to the house, to the walls, to the floor, to maybe me. "This girl has been betrayed by everyone, and now me. She is trying to stay alive? This is a lie. And if she is telling you that you have a chance of staying alive with her, you are already dead."

# CHAPTER 32

Katarina waited for me down in the courtyard. It was several minutes after 5:00 a.m. and the city would soon be active enough for us to disappear within its busy chaos if that were indeed what she wanted us to do.

"Are you okay?" I asked her, taking my time in approaching the low brick wall she was perched on.

She didn't respond.

"Are you . . . uh . . ." I couldn't see much of her face. She might've been teary eyed a minute ago but she seemed to have wiped away whatever emotion had been there. I wanted to put my arms around her but didn't know how to initiate something like that with someone like her. "Are you disappointed?"

She nodded somewhat.

"About the money?"

"No."

"No?"

"Money? No. Money can be replaced." She nodded toward Mathilde's flat. "What is disappointing is her. She is old, she is beautiful, she is real, she is the only person I admire. But she is scared. Like a mouse in a jar. And this is not how to live."

"What is the thing you're going to ask me to do?"

She had yet to look up, still seated on the wall.

"You want me to go to Amsterdam," I said. "Okay. To do what?" I had certain comforting things I could say to her, wisdom gained not just from a career in monetizing other people's crises but from decades of personal frustration, prefaced with a *Listen, Kat, my grandma used to say* before rattling off helpful anecdotes. But I hadn't earned the right to comment here. "To help you get in front of him," I continued answering my own question. "Da Vinci."

I deeply resented my ineptitude—a lifetime of lacking confidence, faking it nicely in all areas, never feeling secure in the face of any adversity. Any.

"And you can't do that on your own?" I asked.

"No. I don't know who he is."

I almost didn't understand the sentence. Of all the steps she'd mapped out for herself on her journey, I never imagined she hadn't traced the most fundamental one. She didn't know who he was?! We were searching for an unknown man amid untouchable men inside an impenetrable group?! "You don't? And you think I'm someone who can find him?"

"Your convention is in Amsterdam," she said. "There is a train from Gare du Nord at 7:35 a.m. From what I know, he is very difficult to find in most situations but tonight . . . tonight is a night of the Society. And he will be there."

The Society.

I'm not into conspiracy theories—I don't believe two people can keep a secret, let alone ten, let alone ten times ten—but I'd started hearing rumors several years ago about an exclusive gathering that operated well above the law. Credible rumors. Jokes. The Society. The Guild. The Prism. Sometimes you heard it called "The Group." Always vague and forgettable, the names. You'd have no chance of asking around about something like it precisely *because* everyone had heard at least some generic, fanciful version of it. So, no one actually knew anything that mattered, and this only made people spew out speculation, which left you drowning in misinformation. Yet as much as it sounded like something impossible to penetrate, my doing so, if it could be done at all, happened to coincide with the only path that was starting to look morally correct for me—exposing the wolves I worked for. Whether it was digital records or cellular logs or emails or straight-up eye-witness testimony, I knew I had to speak up. Which presented a problem for me in that I had zero confidence I could convince *myself* my plan would work, let alone convince someone else—someone like her—that I knew what I was doing.

"So, here's the thing," I said to her. I'd have to assure her that the office building security staff would allow me inside, that I somehow wouldn't land us in jail, that I could get myself to her train on time, that I wouldn't imperil what she had to do. I'd have to tell her I'd seen something deeply incriminating within my firm and needed to obtain it before they started straight-up deleting my accounts. There were rumors of other companies involved in underage shit and extortion that, until now, I never thought would intersect in the elite circles of a bank like mine, yet at those stratospheric levels of power, does anything *not* intersect? As much as my scant evidence might be laughed at by fellow colleagues—C'mon, Adam, seriously, this shit?—it was at least a way to shine a light on certain backroom conversations no one thought a peon like me might overhear. I began to outline my plan for her. "There's something I need to do before we leave Paris."

Before I got halfway through describing it, she cut me off and said okay.

# CHAPTER 33

"**N**ine minutes total," I told her. "Two minutes to get to an empty desk. Two minutes to log in. Four minutes to download files. One minute to leave. Out the door by 7:01 a.m."

We had to be precise.

We arrived at 6:44 a.m., setting up across the street from the front door of the bank building. I'd decided to come from the opposite side, unlike the last time when I ended up ambushed. Very few employees had gone in and out in the eight minutes we stood observing the door. I checked the café to make sure I saw no one problematic—no Oleg, obviously, and nobody *looking* like Oleg, and no police. If certain people were trying to predict where I'd be next, this building represented the most logical choice, but I had to take that risk. I walked up to the front entrance with Jenn's employee card ready, doing what I could to ignore the skepticism of my thoughts—how stupid this was, how much this wouldn't affect the big picture, how I wouldn't ever find anything, how it was possible Jenn had already reported her ID missing—at which point I looked down at the card. I hadn't thought of that until now. *What if she'd already called it in?* They'd immediately deactivate it and I'd be scanning a dead magnetic strip. I'd be scanning a strip that alerted the security guard by lighting up his control panel with small blinking lights that said call the military. *No, relax, you're just collecting files. Your own files.* I held the card up, clutched it at the ready, as I approached the entrance.

The door opened up on its own.

Right in front of me, before I even tried the handle, the door opened up. A security guy was holding it open for me, having seen me coming. *"Bonjour, Monsieur."*

"Uh . . . *Bonjour.*"

He didn't question a thing. He let me in. Let me pass. Maybe he saw the company logo flash on my card, maybe he respected my freshly combed hair, maybe I looked purposeful enough, I don't know. Whatever the case, he didn't think twice about what I could be doing there. Because who breaks in to steal files at 6:53 a.m.? I didn't even need to swipe the elevator panel. The lift was ready, and I took it unimpeded to the third floor where a smattering of early workers were at their desks typing, too drowsy to raise their heads over the cubicle walls when my elevator chime went off. What I needed was one of the "temp" desks, these temp workstations that had been assigned for the week, ten of which were on one side of the building, the rest on the other, all set up for my team. I sat down in the farthest one.

Within moments I'd know my fate. Sweaty hands, sweaty brow, I slid Jenn's card into the desktop ID scanner and waited. The beep normally lags three-quarters of a second behind the insertion of your card, the time needed for the signal to travel through to the satellite network and back. I swear to God, today this lag, this lag in particular, felt like eleven years. It was dizzying, just that small increment of time, the light finally going green as the company logo appeared on the screen just above the log-in box, showing the username—defaulting to Jenn's—which paved the way for the next pivotal moment.

LOGIN: Jennifer K. Graham

PASSWORD: _____

Would her card allow a different log-in name? The one I was now inputting?

LOGIN: Adam L. Macias

PASSWORD: ___* * * * * * * * * * *___

I typed in the new entry. I closed my eyes. I hit return. I opened my eyes. The home screen instantly came up. Dear God, I was in! Every tab was now present, every option and, most importantly, my email inbox along with the expense sheets of everyone on our team. At exactly 6:56 a.m. I'd just hit the Holy Grail of corporate weaponry. Three minutes remained. I had to work fast. I did keyword searches for "entertainment" and "hospitality" in my archives and expense logs, calculating I'd get a decent number of hits, maybe a hundred, maybe a little more—a search that ended up penetrating into the content of the attachments to bring up any and all documents with those keywords in them. Any. And all. Bringing up a total count of fifty-one-thousand one-hundred seven.

"Fifty-one thousand?" I whispered.

Gotta be some gold in *that*. The status bar started to crawl along horizontally as my download began, as a lady from the far side of the office was wandering up from behind me.

"*Bonjour*," she said. "*Est-ce que je peux vous aider?*"

"*Bonjour*," I said, trying not to look up at her.

"*Est-ce que je peux vous aider, Monsieur?*"

I nodded hello. I half waved. She was asking if I needed help.

"Sir . . ."

I kept looking at my screen.

"Sir, what you are doing?"

"Me?"

"Yes. What are you doing?"

"Yes." I kept working. "Uh. Thank you. Yes. Yeah, good."

"*Non*." She stood at the edge of my workstation. "*Monsieur . . . Monsieur!*"

I pointed at my screen as good-naturedly as possible. "These summary sheets . . . are, uh . . . *Ces numeros . . . sont . . .*" Trying to pretend like I was thinking of the word in French, watching the status bar continue to crawl. "Have you seen the backlog? It's crazy how much work they're . . . um . . ."

She looked around to see who she could summon over to us, then turned back toward me. "You should not be here, sir."

"I'm just doing what's called post-debrief retrieval, yeah. I'm, uh . . ." The batch wasn't complete yet—78 percent. "I know it looks . . ."

"*Au secours!*" she called out. She yelled toward the other coworker down the aisle. "*Au secours!*"

"No, listen, lady," I said quietly, urgently, desperately, "if you ask for security, they won't just call security, they'll call the police, and when the police come, it will not be good for anyone here, including your—"

"*AU SECOURS!*"

She saw right through everything I threw at her, belting out her words like she'd just found a dirty bomb in a school yard. The files finished uploading and I yanked out the USB flash drive at the exact moment that a security guard was emerging from the stairwell on the far side, a guy who, from twenty yards away, took one look at my face and hit a button on the wall next to him—the alarm, the fucking alarm—which started a siren that rang out through every corridor, every room, and every hall in the building.

# CHAPTER 34

The lady stood there, in the middle carpet, eyes full of disdain. "*Restez là*," she said to me, instructing me to stay in my seat while the security guard hurried down the row with his hand on his holster.

I wanted to curse her out.

There was another coworker in the distance, coming over to help. I pushed my chair slightly closer to the window, pulse racing, unsure if I should get up to run or stay and negotiate, unsure what the statistical best choice of escape would be, paralyzed with the uncertainty of it all. *Go, Adam, get up.* I was now officially late. From the second-story vantage point, you could see that down on the sidewalk below there was a guy standing on the street corner who didn't seem like he had a reason to be there. The security guard halted in the middle the aisle near me. Did these people actually think I was armed? What did their memo about me *say*? That I'd be dangerous? I looked at the exit ten feet away, calculating the odds of making it.

I got up.

"Excuse me," said the guard.

I walked toward the side exit in the opposite direction.

"Excuse me! *Monsieur*," said the guard. "*Arrêt!*"

"STOP HIM," yelled the lady.

I then ran out the exit, down the stairs, rammed open the outer door, and ended up on the sidewalk just across the street from Katarina, who hurried over the moment she saw me, already well aware how complicated this was about to get for us. The alarm was blaring outdoors.

"We need to go the other direction," she said, pointing west.

She could've bailed already. She could've been long gone. The alarm was piercing. How surreal—to be on the gorgeous streets of central Paris with its historic architecture and design while major turmoil was about to go down. The fact that it hadn't gotten ugly yet gave a false hope, a slight hope, that you and the girl—just you and her—might make it out alive.

"Sorry if I ruined this," I said to her.

"No. The noise might help."

She was noting how the guy, the same guy I saw from the window, the one positioned on the far corner, seemed equally perplexed by the new situation. If he *were* one of da Vinci's guys, which she seemed to think was the case, he was probably unsure how to handle the two of us—given that several police cars had to be on their way.

Katarina started to lead us down the sidewalk. Up ahead, two other men, built and dressed just like the first guy, started heading in our direction. Da Vinci's men looked like any normal people you'd pass on the street except for one specific trait. The eyes. The eyes were overly focused. These guys paid *too* much attention to what was around them—that's how you knew. Katarina abruptly pulled me down a random side street. We could hear police sirens in the distance as we rounded the corner to find yet a *fourth* guy, facing away from us, waiting for us to come from the other direction. The streets are so randomly aligned here, you can't tell what's the geometric opposite side of any one particular block. You can't. This fourth guy happened to be on a motorcycle. A Kawasaki. Triple 750. A vintage machine whose details I'd be paying infinitely closer attention to in the ensuing seconds.

"We need his bike," said Katarina quietly.

"What?"

"Get ready."

"Wait, what?" I already knew it was happening. "No, no, no, are you kidding?" Dreading it. Cringing from it. Not just the inevitable fight it'd entail, but wondering how the hell we'd survive riding the streets if they were swarming with police. What we needed wasn't a stolen motorcycle but the chance to duck into a building—or a hole—or duck back into the catacombs. That felt correct.

But she'd already started to extract a small, black item from her pocket, leaving me behind to stride up to the guy, get close enough to him to begin, then grip him by the back of his collar to yank him downward so she could hold that small item in his eyes and spray its contents directly into him, relentlessly.

Mace.

The guy contorted violently back and forth to shake off what couldn't be shaken. How much urban lava actually went on him, I couldn't say, but she unleashed at least half the can, which was enough to scorch anyone.

And he didn't go down. He torqued himself backward to grab her. He was that fast, that agile.

"Get his leg!" Katarina yelled to me, receiving his first kick. "His leg!"

Which I couldn't catch.

I'd snapped out of the temporary shock of watching all this and lunged forward to help her, unable to snag anything within the tornado of limbs. I kept fixating on the thought that we were just seconds away from the police rounding the corner, along with the mobsters coming from the opposite direction. Our small street was hidden from the direct view of the majority of the neighborhood residents but we weren't out of *earshot*, and her yelling at me felt like the most raucous noise ever. "GET HIS LEG! GET HIS LEG! GET HIS LEG!" she shouted. She had to mace him a second time, which was when I caught hold of his knee, gripped it, and tried pushing it upward as he kicked at both of us to get us off him. He grabbed her hand as she was spraying and pushed the nozzle away from him, pushing it in every other direction but his own, so it squirted *everywhere*, in a massive cloud all around us, a grenade of airborne pain, forcing my eyes to crimp inward like they'd been bathed in hot acid.

As for her?

Blinded.

She'd been in the epicenter of the second blast, maintaining her grip, but she couldn't see anything now. On instinct, she launched herself backward so that the two of them rotated backward to hit the pavement, where he landed on his head, where he instantly went limp.

The concrete was our greatest ally, knocked him out cold.

And she remained blinded.

I'd already begun to move the bike onto the road, out from the crevasse of space between the parked cars, kickstand tucked, rolling it into position so she could hop on and drive us away before the cops would come. And, yes, they were definitely coming. By now our screams had echoed across half the facades of the eighth district, so we had to move fast. Katarina started pushing me forward along the seat toward the handlebars, as she threw her leg over the back *behind* me.

"Go," she said.

"Go?"

"Go now!"

"What do you mean?!"

The bike rolled forward before I was ready for it as her momentum propelled us farther out into the street. "I can't see," she said. "You have to drive." Her eyes were absolutely gushing with tears, locked shut. Her skin wet and red.

"I don't know how to . . . how to . . ."

She didn't care. "JUST GO!"

Limitations weren't allowed. We could hear the police sirens arriving at the front of the bank building now—three cars would be my guess—in addition to any bikes that pulled up. I didn't know a thing about motorcycles.

"*Arrêt!*" The police were emerging from around the corner. "*La bas! Arrêt!*" The first cop to see us started shouting to the other cops around him.

I'd ridden twice. Twice. The first time was my dad putting me on a dirt bike, then grabbing me by the hair to pull me off it when I saw how inept I was. Second was my college roommate—he tried to teach me how to shift from first to second in a Target parking lot. I started the engine.

"You have to help me shift," I said to her.

She was wincing from the spray, too agonized to function. I looked down at the handlebars. One of the levers was a brake grip, the other, a clutch—I knew that much. And the opposite handle rotated back for gas. I think.

But which was which?

"*Arrêtez-vous!*" At the opposite end of the street the first police car had rounded the corner and the driver was shouting at us. "*Ils sont là!*"

"*Vos mains!*" shouted another guy on foot. "*Regarde les autres!*"

You press the clutch. First gear is down. Second and third are up. I revved. Loud. The engine echoed throughout the concrete canyon.

Our guy on the ground, the one whose bike we were stealing, started to twitch back to life—his brief bout of unconsciousness coming to an end. I looked in each direction, letting the bike creep forward, letting out the clutch slowly, trying to let the natural idle carry us forward, all while I did my best not to lose the blind girl draped across my back. I'd gotten us lined up to jet down the street.

And then the engine stalled.

It sputtered out cold. The cops on foot shouted to the cops in the car on the far side of us. They wanted their fellow officer to veer into a diagonal stop to block our route.

"Stay calm," said Katarina.

I started the bike again, then revved it again, then slowly let out the clutch, slower this time, slower, overcompensating with a monstrosity of RPMs, promising myself, promising it profoundly, that if I got shot at, even if the ground split open ahead us, or a meteor struck the road, that no matter what, no matter *what*, I absolutely, positively, one hundred percent would not let that engine stall again.

"I trust you," said Katarina.

# CHAPTER 35

**W**e fishtailed as the bike lurched forward, then sputtered, then found its own trajectory that rocketed us through the upcoming barrage of parked cars, which flew past us—six of them in succession—barely missing contact with us before the fender of the seventh nicked my leg as I then leaned the opposite direction to balance us out. Just get to second gear, Adam. That was all I lived for as I stared at the speedometer written in kilometers, not miles, knowing that if I could shift to second, I could get us to 40 mph, which would be enough, which would be inhumanly fast in the twisted Parisian maze that lay ahead of us. This town was one giant, crooked grid with every intersection bent in one of six gruesome angles on the compass: left, more left, hairpin left, right, more right, hairpin right. There wasn't a stretch of even two consecutive blocks where you could go straight. The train station out of Paris was called Gare du Nord. Fifteen minutes away by car, ten minutes by bike. Northeast of us. That was our destination.

"You good?" I yelled to her.

I'd driven us three full blocks before I took the risk of glancing back at her. You simply can't take your eyes off the road for more than a millisecond. I lightning-quick peeked back and happened to see behind her what we were contending with. Two cops. On motorcycles. Lights lit. Coming fast.

"We need a route," I yelled.

She didn't say anything.

She also didn't say to give up. She also didn't say I couldn't make this work. Her eyes were useless. She had my chest gripped so tight, her fingers were knifing me. How the hell would we walk *into* the train station with bike cops behind us, bike cops who were gaining on us, who had me thoroughly outmatched in skill?

"Hey! We need a route," I yelled.

I couldn't slow down for any turns. I couldn't because I didn't trust that I'd be able to clutch back up to second gear again. The parked cars lining our way were impossibly obtrusive, nipping at us left and right, at both my mirrors. You can't imagine the claustrophobia you feel when you go triple the speed limit in a place where the slightest spasm of your wrist alters a destiny.

"Hard turn coming!" I yelled.

We banked sharply. I kept the front wheel aimed slightly away from the turn—counterintuitive, but that's what does it. I was going to get her killed. I knew it. I opted for whatever choice of streets had the most gradual, most open-angled intersection—anything under ninety degrees spelled doom, anything wider gave us a chance. At 60 km/h on the dial, I'd taken us way past my personal threshold. If even a pebble hit us wrong, we'd flip. If someone opened a car door wrong, we'd flip. I caught sight of a cop car, blue lights flashing one street over from us, heading down a parallel course. The driver was on the verge of finding the optimum alley to cut me off, so I dropped down from 45 mph to 35 mph—all speculation, those numbers, I divided the metric gauge by point-six—then turned left again. The fastest route to the Gare du Nord would require using boulevard de Magenta, an insanely high-volume street where morning traffic routinely comes to a crawl.

I rounded the bend to catch sight of just how tightly its vehicles were stacking up in front of me.

"Fuck it."

Those cars were slowing down to a stop-and-go speed but the lanes had just enough room in between those cars for us to keep going, so I steered *through* that traffic, lane-splitting it at full speed, slicing our fate wide open. I never slowed down. This would become my one weapon against the cops.

How do you defeat superior competition? You change the rules.

Katarina never questioned it. Survival was no longer our central objective. My priority was to outpace them to the train station at any cost—any. Every car up ahead was coming at us ferociously fast, every ten feet represented a new opportunity for pulverization. I felt my stomach drop. The cops in my mirror stayed visible but their size began to shrink as their distance grew and my insanity paid off. Another stagnant clump of stopped cars ahead had formed a massive barrier in front of us with the two lanes in my direction both coming to a standstill. A bus had crossed in front of us and stopped, gridlocking everyone in our direction. The only way to keep going would be if I did what was inhuman.

"Katarina . . ." I said.

I felt a swelling deep inside my chest, my father's rant about me never amounting to much having reared its ugly head.

"I need you hold still," I said to her on the remote chance she might shift her weight and send us tumbling.

She didn't budge. She gripped down. The bus was looming fast, lodged in the middle of the intersection along with everything else that had come to a halt as I swerved left into the opposing traffic.

# CHAPTER 36

A horrifying storm of lethal metal came at us in an onslaught of Citroëns, Volkswagens, scooters, trucks, bikes, buses—their oncoming 20 mph against my 40 mph netting us a dizzying 60 mph. It became surreal, this moment. You'd think the fear of death would dominate your mindset, but it wasn't like that at all. Your entire world is distilled down to one single, isolated, purified, simple task.

Steer.

You have a specific set of physical moves to execute with each of your two hands, and that's it. Your job is to steer. Nothing else exists. I swerved precisely three times. In quick succession. I hadn't checked behind me yet. We'd amassed a swarm of at least three police bikes and two cars and all of them had gotten back on track, including one guy who drove parallel to us, all while I was now aware of a massive wreck—someone hitting someone—somewhere—but didn't know which direction to look, having heard only its elusive echo, until I saw that the damage was being done in *front* of me. The police car on a parallel course had cut over too hard and spun to collide with a truck, both vehicles cutting across our path, presenting me with a ghastly dilemma to resolve within a split second. If I avoid the truck, I swerve toward the cop car, meaning I really only have one viable route, which is to aim for the middle of the chaos, praying that if I'm meant to stay on this earth and keep fighting the good fight—both of us—Katarina and I—I'll be able to split the difference.

Moments like these are the ones that define faith—your faith in yourself, your faith in physics, your faith in the spiritual justice owed two people who refused to back down. Seven-tenths of a second had elapsed. We were currently heading toward nine tons of actively moving steel. I gunned the RPMs well into the red, steering toward a head-on collision with the slight hope that those cars up ahead were about to not be there.

# CHAPTER 37

"You can't beat a rigged game, no matter how much you cry about it." This was what he said to me on my eighth birthday. My dad. He had me standing next to his armchair, standing there trembling, after he'd just knocked two of my teeth loose. "You have to understand who you are and what . . . what . . . what your limits are." With a sixth or seventh beer in hand, his lectures rarely didn't wander onto the topic of society as a whole. "False hope from your dumbass mother is only gonna make you think you can be somebody big . . . when the reality is you can't win a rigged game." He was talking about my violating an elementary school lunch policy but it was a warning that'd infect my self-confidence for years, the best part being just how many times as a professional adult I touted the value of a debt investment to a client who'd remain oblivious to the fact that my words of wisdom originated from a perpetually drunk, biweekly-abusive dad. And for the first time in my life, here, now, Paris, on this bike, I was doubting him. I'd achieved it intellectually in the past years, but I'd never *felt* it. I never *felt* he was wrong. That's the strange cure that a 60 km/h trip through a blocked Parisian intersection will provide. I saw the fissure lines in his grip on my neck and it flooded me with conviction. I drove that motorcycle full speed through a gap narrower than five feet between three oncoming bumpers, and we fucking cleared it—cleared both tires—with the back treads evading contact by a matter of inches—slicing through the intersection diagonally back into the opposite lane. So we covered the expanse of the nastiest gridlock in Paris in under nine seconds while the men directly behind us—the first two biker cops—got absolutely walled in by the cross traffic. Gone. Everyone in my rearview mirror—gone. Allowing me to veer toward the final stretch of road between us and Gare du Nord. I was now just two blocks south of our final destination.

Which put me in front of a very problematic individual.

Up ahead, one last mafia member had managed to cut off our path. It wasn't the cop in the car who'd outdone me, it was one of the da Vinci guys, doing so out of sheer malice. I could see his determination from two hundred meters away. He must've crisscrossed the opposite route, the north-south street, and found a hairpin turn to get himself lined up with me. I'd already softened down to 25 mph having eased off the gas, still in second gear, still facing the possibility of eluding him on the wide sidewalk.

I didn't do that, though.

I didn't veer away from him. I gunned it, accelerating to 5000 RPM toward him, the tach popping instantly, the speedometer climbing. 25 mph. 28 mph. 32 mph. *You wanna come at me, you dead bastard?!* He gunned his bike and screeched forward to head down the tiny street toward me—the two of us going head-to-head. An urban joust. I didn't just accelerate, I lined up with him; when his bike went slightly right-center of the lane, I swerved slightly right-center of the lane; when his bike inched back to center-center, my bike inched back to center-center. *You wanna play?* I leaned forward, leaning *into* his approach. *YOU WANNA PLAY?!* With his third attempt to swerve, getting back to his original course, I swerved too, thereby signing our contract in blood, communicating to him with scant distance left between us that I didn't *want* us to pass each other, I didn't *want* the happy ending; I wanted the collision.

This was how I stole their game.

Be first. Her words. I could see it register in him—realizing I was a hundred percent willing to end it all. From a hundred yards away, I saw him see it. Hyperawareness. 38 mph, 40 mph, my speed climbing, I'd hunched low enough to get half my face below the handlebars so he was seeing nothing but dilated pupils. Fifty-five yards apart, forty-five, thirty-five—at catastrophic net impact velocity.

And he quit. With twenty yards of gap left, the span of less than three-hundredths of a second, he screeched and ducked to the side. He didn't test me. He *knew* his only chance of remaining alive was to brake and bail, skidding, going horizontal, tumbling toward the sidewalk as I sped past his wreck, a stranger even to myself, having undergone the brief but permanent baptism of the streets. I knew only one thing for certain—I was no longer bowing down to the rigged system my father swore I'd bow to. I eased off the throttle, finally, steering us around the last two turns to get us to the entrance of the train station. Katarina couldn't have been aware of all that had just happened. Her fingers remained fully dug into me.

"Gare du Nord," I announced to her.

"At the side," she said. "Park at the far side on the right."

We pulled up next to several other bikes and I led her by the hand as we walked in through the side doors and pushed our way through the crowd. Train stations in Europe are slammed in the summer—acres of people in every shape, size, and color, heading in different directions. The large clock on the wall read 7:27 a.m., meaning we were two minutes late for the final boarding call. Her face was a flood of tears, still stinging from the mace, which was a key factor she was about to exploit.

She turned to me to give me the instructions. "This has to be exact," she said. "Don't question what I'm about to tell you. Just do what I say, is that clear?"

She nodded toward the row of high-speed trains we were queuing up for. Massive. Sleek. Built like bullets.

"I go through the gate first," she said. "You wait sixty seconds. When I get to the last car, you then go directly to the gate staff and you say that your girlfriend has both of the tickets. You point at me all the way down the platform. You need to cry. Can you cry? You point and you are crying and you say, 'She has both of the tickets.' Is that clear?"

She headed for the train.

I didn't say yes. I didn't say anything. My fingers were shaking. I had slurred speech. I was *amped up*—my body having soaked itself in adrenaline. I turned around as instructed to end up facing the giant station clock where I was to watch the second hand tick through a complete circle. Sixty seconds, she said. It hadn't occurred to me to ask how she herself would get through the gate. I kept my eyes fixed in the opposite direction as told, which meant I was now catching sight of several of the gang members entering the front of the central station area.

"No," I said to myself.

They had to know there was a strong chance we were going to Amsterdam—that we'd be heading for an Amsterdam-bound train. They were walking toward the TGV lines. They were walking toward me. Halfway through my one minute, I'd lost track of the second hand on the clock, too inept to remember if I'd started my count at twenty after or forty after, too wired with adrenaline to track even sixty stupid seconds. That's how busted my brain was. The mob guys were coming, yet it felt too soon for me to initiate the role she'd laid out—because she might not have her end of the ploy in place.

I spun around. Maybe too soon. I faced the direction she went. *"Attends!"* I bellowed out to the staff of that train. *"Attends!* Hey!" I couldn't risk waiting any longer. I hurried to the gate. "Hold on!" Hustling over to the guard just as he let the last passengers through. "Wait! Hold the train! Hold the . . . !" I pointed to the far end of the platform. "She's got both of them!"

*"S'il vous plaît, Monsieur!"* said the guard for the third time. "Stop!"

"She's got both our tickets. Up there!" I pointed to Katarina. I called out to her. "Hey!"

Way down the track but not yet all the way down the track, Katarina was heading toward the last open car. I'd come too soon. She hadn't gone far enough to be realistically out of my reach. She could theoretically be summoned back if they took a good look. I glanced behind me. Da Vinci's men had temporarily disappeared from view. They could be anywhere. I didn't see them by the gates. I didn't see them in the crowd of people checking the info board. Were they talking to security? Raising my voice one more time would mean attracting attention from everyone around. "Sir," the guard said to me, "you need to—"

"YOU HAVE BOTH TICKETS!" I yelled as loud as I could.

# CHAPTER 38

Way up near the front of the train, she turned around. She'd kept walking until she was close enough to engage the main conductor on the far end of the platform, then, several key seconds after she'd heard me yell, she turned around and made a big, exaggerated, demonstrative gesture of telling me to hurry up, waving for me to "just come through," then turned away.

I did my part to look frustrated by this, which wasn't hard. "She has 'em," I said to the guard. "My fiancé. She has both our tickets."

The gate guard was holding me in place, yet the majority of the train cars had sealed their doors. Katarina then turned briefly to wave her arm to coax me to hurry as the conductor near her started arguing with her to get on board alone. The guard next to me, my guard, the gate guard, looked at my face, scrutinized my reaction, then looked toward her, scrutinizing her, then looked back at me. You could see it—the gears turning as he took a professional glance at the throng of passengers lined up for the next train—already a mess—then took an additional look at me, weighing the extent of whatever migraine I or my supposed partner represented to him, estimating just how much I might brutalize his workday even more, sorting through the logistic conundrum that Katarina had masterminded.

"*Allez, Monsieur,*" he said to me. "*Allez.* Go."

And waved me through.

"Go," he said. "Hurry."

I sprinted. Katarina saw it, then disappeared into her car while I raced toward the forward conductor, who was now angrily shouting how I needed to race even faster. The ruse worked. I couldn't begin to imagine how many permutations of trial and error it'd taken her to figure out the timing of something like this—hiding in Europe for a year, hiding in plain sight, dodging sex traffickers, weaving in and out of bureaucratic loopholes—but it worked, the ingenious tempo. She had to know exactly when the first notes of chaos would begin and when the last opportunities for exploitation would end. I boarded the train and sat down on the plush seat she nodded for me to take. The men from the mob? They could be anywhere. They could be in possession of tickets. They could be bribing the other conductor. They could be on board.

"Toward the window," Katarina said to me quietly. She was motioning for me to turn my body so I'd be turtle-shelled away from the aisle, as in, more difficult to notice. I couldn't picture da Vinci's men getting aggressive with the station staff—not in public—not without creating a commotion—but at this point, how could I be sure? The train started moving within minutes of us getting on board, with us now seated in a four-chair arrangement, facing an older couple we'd soon learn were from Finland. Katarina leaned over, speaking even more quietly to tell me, "The train stops in Brussels and Rotterdam. We go to the food car when it does. Separately. We wait in the bathroom, then we return to our seats. Separately."

"Separately. Got it."

"For summer trains . . . half of the time . . . the conductor will not approach you."

She sat back.

I sat back.

Half of the time? The train took a brief crawl through the city, then we revved up to two hundred miles an hour through the countryside. You didn't sense it, the speed. *Half* of the time? Whenever the door between cars would open, my anxiety would reignite and my mind would return to wondering when exactly they'd be coming for us. The staff. The law. The conductor. The mob. The diverse array of people who hated us. Katarina showed absolutely no signs of fear while I sat there in growing awe of her. Of what she could do. Stealing glances at the profile of a girl who'd just been maced yet uttered not one word of complaint, who continued to navigate an escape for us after being ravaged by a maniac, after being strangled the night before by another maniac, long after being strangled for years, in fact, while maintaining the illusion of normalcy for the nosy old couple across from us.

"You need to calm down," she whispered to me. "You keep shifting around in your seat. People will notice."

"I'm sorry. I'm trying to convince myself to stop."

"There's nothing else we can do right now."

"You're not worried about them being on this train?"

"Yes. I am."

"I know I'm not the one they ultimately want, I get it, but I also know they believe I'm helping you and that maybe before, they only believed I could *lead* them to you, but now that they've seen us together, they're assuming you convinced me to help you destroy them."

"Stop thinking so much."

"I'm sorry, I'm trying. You're able to control your thoughts. That's great. Myself, I'm constantly overthinking."

"No, I do the same. But that does not mean it is good."

"Yeah, it's . . . uh . . . There's . . . At . . ."

I was trying to figure out the next thing to say, some kind of insightful remark, but nothing seemed appropriate, and the longer I took to come up with a reply, which ended up being quite a while, the less confidence I had in one. Every thought I wanted to share felt so disjointed, like I had no respectable rationale.

"I didn't know my company was corrupt when I started, just so you know." I spoke up after forcing it out of myself. "You might wonder why I would *continue* to work there. The short answer is I'm a fucking coward. The long answer is I'm a fucking coward and I can blame my dad and my complicit mom and the Mexican Cession of 1848 but I actually don't wanna blame anyone. I want to move forward. And to move forward I have to pay the bills because nobody likes a guy who borrows bus fare. So I'm working for corporate machinery that I know is corrupt and I hate it, and, actually, if we can be honest, I should say that I no longer work for them."

"Your parents were bad?"

"My father."

"What did he do to you?"

"Everything. Nothing. He drank."

"He hit you?"

"Sure, why not?"

"That is bad."

"You can choose for it to be hard or you can choose for it to be a stepping stone. I don't want to feel sorry for myself. I don't want to meet people at a cocktail party and say this cheese is amazing because, by the way, my dad beat me on a weekly basis."

"Why do you care what people think?"

"No. Yeah. I don't know. My mom made okay money as a nurse. She calls herself a failed painter. What she really failed at is choosing my dad. My point is . . . my family . . . is . . ."

"For me 'family' is a lie. I don't owe my mother anything. Just because she is blood, I don't have the obligation to bleed for her. There are rodents who leave their babies for snakes when attacked. Sacrificing them to live. She is this."

She stopped talking for a couple hundred miles of passing scenery, and that prompted my mind to go even further along all the wrong directions, conjuring up fears and doubts, both rational and not, that served only to reduce my ability to do what we needed to do. I hadn't wanted to tell her all this shit about myself, to confess it, purge it, but my cortex was riding this bizarre surge of fear and I felt a biological need to trust her. Yet there was something growing within my consciousness, a splinter in my thought process, which maybe I'd been drowning out with empty rhetoric, and I honestly wasn't sure if it could be left alone anymore. It was *the* thing I needed to know about her and I went back and forth a thousand times deciding whether mentioning it would destroy us or not. Yet I had to risk everything. "I need to ask you a question . . ."

# CHAPTER 39

I waited until we were somewhat settled into the journey to bring it up. Her eyesight had improved. She'd slept a little. It was a question I'd been saving and as soon as she looked over at me, she saw how serious I was about to get.

She sat up. She seemed ready for it. "Before you ask me . . ." she said, "you should know that I want things to be okay for you . . . so I'm going to tell you whatever you want to know . . . but you should understand . . . that once you hear my answer . . ."

I might not be able to walk away legally.

That's what she meant. She knew where I was going with it. I'd aided and abetted a potential criminal and I'd done it unwittingly until now, until, enlightened by whatever she was about to say to answer my question, I'd be irrevocably liable for any awareness obtained. She watched me as I processed her little caveat. It's staggering how gorgeous she was—the awe she struck in me. To look at someone like her. To *be* looked at by someone like her.

"Why do you need my help?" I said.

She waited for the rest of it.

"Why me?" I said.

She seemed perplexed. *That's your question?*

"Do you really know nobody else in Amsterdam?" I said. "Girls you worked with? Past girls? No, that's not my question. Who else can help you?"

She shrugged. She shook her head.

"No one?"

"No one I trust," she said.

I made her describe her most recent contacts. She hardly remembered anyone, and when she did, it'd be a one-word stage name of a fellow prostitute—Astral—or the vague title of a place she used to work—Decadent Splash—Pleasure House—some club before that—a rear unit of a shitty apartment building with the big, burly bodyguards who checked in on her.

"I think you should know," I said, "I'm not trying to walk away. I'm not trying to get out of it. What I'm doing is . . . I'm taking a stand. Which sounds overblown. But right now, today, in Amsterdam, the heads of every bank will be at a big table and they will finalize, *finalize*, a $4.8 billion stimulus loan, and if I can expose a piece of the corruption . . ." I pointed to my USB flash drive. "I mean, can you imag . . . ?"

I quieted down.

A guy in a knit cap had come into our train car at the Brussels stop and sat down across the aisle from us. He had other open seats to choose from, several that would have meant decent spacing, but, for some reason, he took the one in a crowd of three overweight Nordic guys and their equally overweight backpacks, across the aisle from us. I didn't notice him until he stood up again on the pretense of going to the bathroom. I didn't know if Katarina noticed either. She and I talked more quietly, more intimately. I leaned in. She leaned in. Her knee pressing against mine. Our faces just inches apart.

"Now," she said, "why don't you ask me what you really need to ask me?"

I had to breathe for a bit before crossing my own faintly drawn line of morality. "Da Vinci . . . When you find him . . . when you're in front of him . . . what exactly . . . ? What exactly . . . ?"

". . . am I going to do to him?"

I nodded.

She didn't speak immediately but she also didn't take as long as I thought.

"Save him," she said.

"Save him."

"Yeah."

"You mean that in some kind of poetic . . . poetic sense of . . .?"

"If you ever met Morgan da Vinci, I doubt you'd think of him the way I do."

"Okay. Well, yeah, okay, that makes sense. The thing is . . ." I had my rebuttal to this, built up, rehearsed, revised, for hours. "You want me to penetrate some ultrasecret, dangerous prostitute club, but how? Me? What is this club? The Society? All I know is there's our convention in Amsterdam. That's it. That's all I know."

"Are you in love?"

"Excuse me?"

"Are you in love?"

"Am I? What?"

She wasn't joking.

"With Jennifer," she said.

"Jennifer?" It wasn't simply that the question came out of nowhere, it was the way she asked it, with no animation, no inflection, no emotion.

"Are you in love with her?"

"What does that have . . . ?"

"Is she in love with you?"

"No."

"You are fucking her?"

"No."

"You are not fucking her?"

"We've had the opposite of sex. For eight years. We're best friends. She says this to me. 'Best friends.'"

"She says what you expect to hear."

"No."

"She is waiting for you."

"No. For me? No. To do what?"

"I don't know."

"No. Why in the world do you care?!"

"Tell me how we can get to her."

"What do you mean?"

"Tell me how she is vulnerable."

She didn't want gossip, she didn't want the details of a schoolyard crush. What she was asking for was intel.

"What leverage do you have over her?"

"None," I said firmly.

"She has a weakness."

"Not her."

"Everyone has a weakness."

The guy in the knit cap had gotten up to get something from his luggage. It occurred to me that anyone around us in any direction could be part of the convention in some auxiliary way, even the old couple in front of us. The husband could be a tax attorney. So could his wife. What my company did in Paris was lay the ground-work for the much larger nest of transactions that would get inked in

Amsterdam. This involved hundreds and hundreds of people all over Europe.

"I will propose something to you," said Katarina, undeterred by the threat—leaning closer, her leg incidentally pressing even deeper now into mine, with part of our upper bodies now touching, the gorgeous warm pale-gold skin of her forearm feeling shamefully sensual. "If you help me meet him, I will stop hiding. I will let the police know whatever you need them to know to clear your name."

"You'd do that?"

She nodded yes.

I couldn't tell if she was lying. I couldn't tell if she was telling the truth. I couldn't read her. I'd analyzed a thousand people in a thousand high-stress situations, negotiating countless price points. She was one of the few human beings I had no gauge on. Could I trust this? I barely agreed with the principles involved yet even if I did, I still had several very fundamental unanswered questions. Even if she responded to me openly, how could I know she wasn't just telling me what I needed to hear? I had no objectivity. All I had was a sickening feeling she was going to be dead soon, perhaps by the end of the week, and what was starting to haunt me, I mean haunt me to the core, was that she seemed so alone. Even her close friend—that lady—Mathilde—as hard as Mathilde tried, you could see this helplessness in it, this fear that no matter what Mathilde did, she could never hug this girl tight enough. Sure, this was me reading too far into shit I didn't know, as usual, amplifying it as I amplify everything, but you just felt an overwhelming need to hold this girl, to draw her close and shield her from the bleakness. Because she was the type of female who didn't get sympathy from very many places. She wasn't just pretty, she was oppressively so—to the guys who craved her, who recognized they'd never have her, to anyone who resented the infinite privilege they projected on her, and to those who outright wanted her dead. And here she was, next to me, a matter of days or hours away from extinction.

"Look," she said, speaking to me out of mercy, seeing just what kind of disordered state I was dragging myself further into, "just assume the worst about me. There are questions that don't have the answers you want, so just assume the worst. That way when the time comes for us to say goodbye, you won't have any hesitation."

# CHAPTER 40

The train staff didn't bother checking all the people who were on board. Indeed, during the entire ride, Paris to Brussels, Brussels to Rotterdam, Rotterdam to Amsterdam, they simply didn't have enough employees to verify anyone's ticket in our section. Such was the chaos of European summer travel, legendary for its charming mayhem. Katarina mapped out a path through the station that would bypass both the passport security and the ticketing gates, prescribing the exact level of pandemonium necessary for the officers to be distracted as we avoided detection. None of which ended up being needed, as the deluge of travelers began overwhelming the gate team with their constant onslaught.

"Don't slow down," said Katarina to me. "Don't speed up. Walk exactly the same as everyone around you. Look around at the buildings, laugh and be normal, but don't make eye contact, understand?"

She saw me scanning right to left, left to right, robotically. She saw how fixated I was on the fear that they'd follow us off the train.

"Don't do that," she said. "You can't be this obvious."

The train station opens up directly into the heart of Amsterdam, putting you in the city center from your very first step. We dove into the throng of beautiful, young, vibrant people from all over Europe, the faces and energy you only dream of seeing as an American kid—everyone with a sporty backpack on, or neon-colored luggage, students torn straight from a study-abroad brochure. Spain. Greece. Sweden. Italy. I didn't acknowledge any of it. No eye contact. No connecting. Nothing. Smile. Keep walking. Be forgettable. People were staring at Katarina. Even in a sea of the most alluring faces imaginable, she stood out. And this meant anyone could catch sight of us. She had us hold hands.

"You're not seriously going to walk us through broad daylight, are you?" I said to her.

We were heading into the middle of a district called Leidseplein.

"Everyone can see us," I said.

"We are going to wash off."

My first inhalations of Dutch air were coming at the all-too-familiar pace of pure trepidation. In theory, the crisp oxygen of a climate like that of the Netherlands should snap you into a useful alertness. In theory. I couldn't help but see flashes of dangerous faces everywhere, in every corner: phantoms darting in and out of—no, borrowing, like transient demons, borrowing the bodies of the general public. "Wash off?" I said to her, unsure I'd heard her correctly, thinking she might mean wash with soap somewhere, rinse, smooth out our clothes somewhere, fix our hair, which I'd partially done already on the train, but she meant something much more figurative.

She meant the Anne Frank museum.

We crossed out into the bus area, through the bike racks, past the lightning-fast bike lane, onto the sidewalk. I kept my eye on the station behind me, trying to catch sight of whoever might be following us. I was hoping she was looking for a place for us to duck into—for refuge—but after several blocks she abruptly tucked us into a long queue of people in line outside the Anne Frank museum. She started talking to the random person ahead of us. She was cutting in line. She was telling a story to justify it. She said what she had to say and then somehow we were now situated ahead of two Scottish ladies.

"None of da Vinci's men can follow us in there," she said to me quietly. She nodded to the metal detectors in the doorway to the building, run by a busy crew of security guards who had high-tech wands and gear. "Their weapons won't get through."

A museum like this, renowned for statements about oppression and resilience, was a convenient target for attacks, so security was strict enough for us to purge ourselves of layer one, whatever that layer might be. She told the main guard that someone ahead of us has our tickets and had gone in, which was her go-to ploy, but the guard said we couldn't enter the actual Anne Frank house without confirmations, which felt like a defeat, but he also told us we could wait in the museum's cafeteria, and according to Katarina, that was just as valuable. We'd still be going through the metal detectors for it, so the thugs—if there were any—there had to be—would still get culled.

This was washing off.

The visitors inside the center were eerily quiet and somber. Most museums echo with at least *some* murmurings. This place was relentlessly silent. "I don't get it," I whispered to Katarina. "Since you're so good at penetrating tights spots like this, why don't you penetrate da Vinci's club using the same, I don't know, same stuff?"

"I've only been to his event once," she whispered back. "I never actually got invited as a guest. Females aren't guests. The problem is that the invitations are sent anonymously, and they don't give out the address until the last moment."

"I still don't understand. So you want me to follow . . . some of my coworkers . . . and . . .?"

"Your coworkers will not get invited."

"But they know about it?"

"No."

"No?"

"I doubt it. There's a password."

"So then . . ." I was beyond lost. "How do . . ."

"You're going to need to bend your rules."

It was confusing, thoroughly. I dreaded whatever that meant, knowing for quite a while that it was coming. The route leading outdoors took us past giant photos of little Anne—bright eyed, earnest—an indomitable spirit no one could stifle—where Katarina found a chance to pickpocket a silk scarf right from the open purse of a random lady near us, nobody here anticipating such a thing. Then she coaxed the guard in the back to let us outside through an emergency door on the pretext of me being sick, which wasn't hard to fake—I looked dismal. She put on the head scarf like a '60s starlet and we kept our faces down as we hurried to the far side of town on foot, taking a half hour to get to a place called something like Koninklijk Palace. This was it. This was the site of what would be the well-televised handshaking of all our banking VIPs and various heads of state. The place was straight-up posh, and even though it was located in the middle of the city, there was a massive police presence roving the streets. We had to find a strategic spot at a busy corner where we could stand unnoticed and watch who was coming in and out of the palace gates, where I could—yeah, fuck it, here we go—persuade her to change her approach.

# CHAPTER 41

"Let's multiply this situation out," I said to her, "just to analyze it. It's a way of analyzing a decision if we multiply it out, repeating the hypothetical of making this same decision over and over. Okay, so what if every girl does this?"

"Does what?"

"What if every girl in your position reacts like you?"

"Then . . . that's their choice."

"Nine-millimeter feminism. What if every girl who learns about what you're doing becomes inspired to be their own ticking time bomb? Ready to explode the next time a man comes near her?"

"Okay."

"Rips his dick off?"

"Yes."

"Cuts his face?"

"Yes."

"That would get her *killed*."

"Good."

"No. You don't think they deserve better? These girls—who'd get beaten dead if they tried what you're trying? You don't think their life is worth living?"

"Trust me, these girls are not living. Are you ready to go inside?"

I gave it thought, I did, thinking maybe I wasn't seeing my own arrogance here, that I simply had no idea what it was like to have a vagina professionally entered two times a day, that maybe I'd do the same thing—explode. "I'm not sure how you want me to approve of what we're about to do."

"I don't need you to approve. I need you to search."

Koninklijk Palace was a problem. The moment we arrived at the entrance, the situation was exactly the letdown I hoped it wouldn't be. The main seminar for Euro Mutual was underway but it was behind locked gates that were behind additional gates—security having increased tenfold thanks to all that'd happened back in Paris. On that note, regardless of how much I didn't approve of Katarina's methods, there was no denying the impact they had—she'd had—on an international level. Right in front of us, every inch was locked off, locked down, highly monitored by security and staff.

"It is about rank," she said, starting to undo her head scarf, incidentally exposing her neck to me, briefly exposing her scar, without intending to, as she wadded up the fabric and slid it in her pocket. "About who has the highest rank in your company."

"Rank?"

"Who would it be?"

"In terms of power? A guy named Gerald Merck."

"Then we use him."

"Gerald—is not going to want to help us."

"It doesn't matter what he wants. Once we isolate him in a room, we change his mind."

"I'm not part of shit like that."

"We need his cooperation. This is how it works."

"Yeah, that's the thing I was trying to say. That's the whole thing. Not with me."

"Unfortunately—"

"Not with me. Okay? No torture. I'm not part of that."

"Do you know what these men have done? To a hundred girls? You talk of multiplying."

"So, what, we're about to *waterboard* a CEO?"

"Do you understand what they will continue to do? I'm not talking about the past. I'm talking about what's *to come*."

"This is what you mean by 'bend the rules'?"

"You have a morality. You lived by it, yes? You lived by it *until now*, until you are beginning to see a new side of the world for what it is and you see that your morality . . . it no longer solves this type of problem. Your morality cannot keep you alive. Yes, I'm saying that the rules should be broken. Yes. Why? Because the way they treat girls like us is broken."

"I just don't—"

She suddenly shoved me against a wall, grabbing me by the shoulders, embracing me with her face right up close to mine, while whispering aggressively, "Laugh."

"What?"

Her lips were up close to the side of my head, her body pressed into mine, very much the way a real couple would look, granting her the position necessary to peer around the edge of the wall so she could look at a particular sedan parked near the gate of the palace without drawing attention to us—because inside that sedan were two particular men.

"Keep laughing," she said to me.

I laughed.

The mob guys were here.

I swear, you could spot the breed a mile away. Once you'd seen one, you knew what to see in the others. Not the clothes, not the skin, not the age. Again, the eyes. Their preoccupation. They overwork in relation to what's around them. And right now those eyes were overworking in our general direction.

"Stay normal," she said. "Keep laughing."

I kept squirming, my pulse racing.

"Stay normal," she said.

"Did they see us?"

"No."

"Then we have to leave."

"No. We are deciding what to do."

I did have an idea, which I'd already rejected—based on a lack of confidence in it—in the idea itself—in me—in human civilization—despite my recent overconfidence in my heroics. I'd built myself up back there on the motorcycle in Paris, merely hours ago, achieving some sort of warrior's serenity wherein the threat of death didn't paralyze me, then I returned to the normal me, realizing—humbly—rationally—that I'd let myself think I was far more effective than I really was.

She was about to extract that idea from me.

"What is your best possibility?" she said.

"Best?"

"Whatever you have—what is your best possibility of doing it?"

"A guy. Who I haven't mentioned yet. I didn't mention him because I wasn't sure if, uh, if we'd, uh—"

"Who?"

"His name is Nikos Dimopolous. He's the only son of the tenth-wealthiest family in Athens. He just lost his father. He inherited everything."

"And he's a participant?"

"Well . . ."

She took another look around the edge, checking while listening. "Yes? Yes, he's a participant?"

"Maybe."

"You can make use of him?"

"I-I-I don't know. We can't access him here but where he's staying . . . He might be at the Dutch Intercontinental Hotel, I think. *Maybe.* That's where we put our top prospects. But he's not easy to, uh, to . . . He's an introvert, okay? I doubt he'd ever go to an event like da Vinci's thing but he's easy to isolate if we—"

"Okay. You go to him. You go right now."

"Okay. Wait, without you?"

She'd decided it. She'd already turned her attention to the next phase. The two men in the car hadn't gotten out yet.

"Hold on," I said. "He might not—"

"That's the direction of the Dutch Hotel." She pointed to the opposite side of town. "You can go there and wait for him."

"Yeah, but then—"

"The way the invitations are sent out is unpredictable. There's a confirmation at some point and maybe a delivery at some point but it is never the same twice. You are going to need to convince this person to involve you and you cannot let him know what is going on. Just get the info. Nothing else. You need to be unseen. You cannot be followed by da Vinci's men."

"I don't even know if the—I said tenth-richest family in Athens but I'm not—"

"That's not what I'm focused on."

"I know but—"

"You said you thought of him already. You thought of him. This means you had a reason. This means there *is* a way to make it work. Look at the driver." She pointed to the younger of the two thugs. "This man's name is Hugo Mesrine. He is the one who drove his motorcycle at us."

"Him?"

"Take a good look."

"Okay, yeah, okay. I don't understand."

"Stay away from him."

"You're not coming with me?!"

"No. Your job is to be unseen. My job is to make sure you stay unseen."

I tried to hold her hand so she couldn't pull away but she was going regardless. "You're going *toward* his car?! How are you going to avoid him?"

"I'm not going to avoid him."

## CHAPTER 42

She didn't wait for me to talk her out of it. She headed directly to the enemy, walking in plain view where he could see every step she took, where I could see too, which was terrifying to witness. And when she got close enough to force them to react, she made a hard turn and walked past them, disappearing behind the building so that these two guys hurried out of their sedan on cue to follow her around the corner. Jesus. It was on me now—to do all this—to recruit Nikos—to complete her next step—without understanding what that even involved. There was no guaranteed way to approach someone like him in isolation and it had to be in isolation.

Think.

My best bet was to use the valet desk of his hotel instead of the main lobby, where there were too many entrances to wrangle at once. At the valet he might be alone even if it was for a half minute. It took three hours for that to happen. At the Dutch Intercontinental Hotel, waiting off to the side of the driveway for the conference lunches to end—waiting without being awkward about it—I finally saw a particular black SUV arrive and, thanks to the backseat window being down, saw Nikos inside. A lucky break, or a controlled probability—you take your pick. You got your chance, Adam. He saw me and immediately had his driver stop.

"Whoa! What?!" he said. "Whoa, whoa whoa, hey, man!"

"Whuttup, man!"

"You're here!"

"*You're* here!"

Sales 101. Assess the mood of your prospective client. He had open body language. Was leaning forward slightly. Dilated pupils. Eyebrows raised an eighth of an inch. Rubbed his fingers together. Laughed too hard at any vague opportunity to laugh. I had a solid shot at coercion because my mark was genuinely happy to see me.

"Yeah," he said. "You good?!"

"I'm good."

"Cool because, yeah, cool, I mean . . . I heard, uh . . ." He didn't know how to say it. "That you'd . . . uh . . ." He was about to run down my list of SEC violations, arson, larceny, trespassing, civil disobedience, traffic violations, foreign assault—how I was wanted by international law.

"It's all true," I said to him.

"Hahaha."

"All of it."

"Hahaha. What is?"

"Every word."

"Of what? Every . . .? Wait. Are you serious?"

"Thug life, homie."

My statement was a shock on its own but what was really rocking him was the *way* I stated it—half joking, half not, half real, half colored with levity. I gave him a self-assured, jovial affirmation, which was the absolute last thing he expected from someone delivering news like this.

"I'm not here to deny any of the shit you heard, man," I said, looking him dead in the eye. "None of it, but, c'mon, whatever they told you about me is mostly pranks and paranoia, that's all. That's what my firm faces every day. When you're good, you're the target. The only thing that matters is I have a history of making clients a fuck ton of money."

"Wow."

"Our team has no idea how to conduct itself in a bedroom but . . . we do know revenue."

"Hahahahaha. Nice."

I'd hit him with the slogan.

"Nice," he said again.

"I mean, would I be standing here if any part of it was serious?"

"Hahaha. No." He needed to see me shrug it off, that's all.

"Any of it? No. You going up to your room?"

"Uh, yeah, *yeah*, the guys wanted to go to lunch. They just finished the presentations on stimulus-debt financing. Not bad. Here lemme . . . uh . . ." He got out of the SUV. "I was gonna head upstairs to take a shower."

"Just presentations? Just lunch?"

"Yeah. Why?"

"That's it? Just that? They didn't let you guys get magical?"

"Magical?"

"Seriously no?"

"Magical?"

"Yeah. C'mon, what's the number one thing you want out of this town? Out of Amsterdam. What's *the* thing you want here?" He'd arrived here at my request, to have the time of his life at my request. I had to find out what he knew about the da Vinci event—if they'd contacted him, texted him, sent him the wax-sealed invitation written in virginal blood. I had to do it quite carefully.

"Uh . . . a girlfriend?"

"No. No, no, no. Not that." You couldn't risk scaring him in case he felt the invitation had to be kept secret from peasants like me. "C'mon, man, no, every city has hookers, even Wyoming has hookers. No, I owe it to you . . . to introduce you to . . . the one thing Amsterdam has that no one else can top."

"Okay."

"Van Gogh."

"Van Gogh."

"The museum."

Katarina had suggested it. And based solely on his face, I saw how much mileage this would get me, which wasn't much. Sales 102. I figured it was a one-in-ten shot that the museum alone would entice him—which it didn't—so now, facing the 90 percent reality, I'd have to use the rest of the pitch.

"You're gonna visit the Van Gogh Museum on magic mushrooms."

"Oh."

"Yeah."

"Oh . . . uh . . . I don't . . . uh . . . I don't . . ."

"It's epic, my friend. Nowhere in the world can you do what you're about to do."

"I don't really . . ."

"Safer than coke. Proven."

I absolutely cringed at the prospect of getting high in the midst of all that was going on but it'd mean without a shadow of a doubt that I could control my mark, which itself was crucial. He'd need me to coach him through the drug and I'd thereby have him mentally pliant with it. I could handle the dosage better than he could, I could manipulate him, I could distract him, and then I'd sneak his phone into my possession.

"Super safe," I said.

"And . . . And . . . uh . . . you'll do it . . . with me?"

"Of *course*! Of course! You need a shepherd and—sounds corny, but this is the one drug I know—someone who can guide you through it and make sure you have the ideal environment. It's all about the environment."

"Yeah, 'cuz I don't want to end up with a massive head trip."

"You won't."

"Like, seeing dead giraffes in a tree."

"That's a rumor. That's acid. Totally false. This is calm."

"Yeah?"

"Super safe."

"Cool."

"It's documented."

"Cool." He was gradually convincing himself. Gradually buying in. And the more we talked, the more I realized this was the only option that would work for my objective. "No, yeah, cool. Cool, cool. I'm interested. Like when?"

"When?" I checked the clock mounted by the valet station, making a big show of doing so. "Maybe in about half an—Whoa, it's already two? It's two?! Wow, man, like now. It'd be now. Are you free? The museum closes in—We'd just be in time, if we went now."

"Cool. Okay, yeah."

"Yeah?"

"Yeah, I'm free."

"Nice!"

"Totally. Let's go." His smile got big again. He was into it.

Our conversation had inadvertently led to us on a stroll all the way out to the main street. I'd accomplished the initial goal of separating him from whatever asinine activity the rest of the team had arranged. The next step would be to babysit his phone, which would entail mak—

"Nikos!"

"Yo, Nikos!"

"Yo!"

It came from behind. They came from behind. They. Them. The hellos. The exchange. I turned around to see Trevor and a young man named Dustin Green hurrying to catch up with us.

"Yo."

"Hey."

"Whuttup."

"Nikos."

"Hey!"

We all traded greetings. They must've emerged from the lobby where they had to be waiting to corner Nikos like I'd cornered him, only just now spotting him heading into town without them, heading into town with, that's right, me, of all people.

"Adam," said Trevor, in a general acknowledgment of my presence, a hundred wrong reactions scrolling across his face—victory, defeat, rage, confusion, enmity, loss, casual friendliness, fear. "What're . . . you . . . uh . . .?"

"Sup, man." I bro-hugged him, big and loud, pulling him into me uncomfortably close so that I could get right fucking in his fucking ear and rapidly, angrily whisper to him, "I'm here to close the sale of this kid because no one else can do it and you fucking *know* this to be true so I'm trading you half my commission because you're gonna say yes to whatever the fuck I'm about to propose, out loud, right now, or I destroy any chance *anyone* has with this *billionaire* and leave you standing around holding nothing but a warm cup of dog shit." I pulled out of the hug. "Big Trevvvv."

He stood there wide eyed.

Me—talking even louder now, friendlier, bigger, as if I adored every moment of our four-man bro-gasm. "Trev knows the market inside out! A math whiz!"

"Uh . . ."

"Oh!" I pointed to him as if I'd just now remembered the following, "Oh, hey, man, is it cool if I give Nikos back to you in about, uh, two hours? I promised him I'd show him the only unique thing Amsterdam has to offer and I don't want to let this nice young man down. Yes?"

Trevor couldn't figure out how to react.

Neither could Dustin.

Everyone looked at Nikos.

"Yes?" I repeated to Trevor.

"Th . . . uh . . ." he said.

"What's the only unique thing in Amsterdam?" said Dustin.

I pointed right at Trevor, ignoring Dustin. "Say yes, man. Say yes to winning in life."

"The Van Gogh," said Nikos.

"The Van Gogh?" said Dustin.

"On mushrooms," added Nikos.

"The Van Gogh is overrated," said Dustin.

I was looking right at Trevor and continuing to smile. "You good with it, man?" I didn't care what came out of Dustin because no one cared what came out of this social toilet hole, but Trevor . . .? Well, Trevor was a factor.

"Uh . . . well . . . I, uh . . ." said Trevor. "Yes."

"Okay."

"Okay!" said Nikos.

"Okay."

And I thought he'd arrived at the end of his sentence but he was only halfway through it.

". . . I'm in," said Trevor.

"You are?" said Dustin.

"You are?" said Nikos.

He nodded.

"Cool!" said Nikos.

"Don't listen to Dust," Trevor said to Nikos as an aside. "Museums are full of girls. He doesn't like girls."

"What?" said Dustin.

"You don't like girls?" said Nikos.

"I like girls," said Dustin defensively. "I like girls more than anyone else here."

"He doesn't like boys either," said Trevor, putting his arm around him like a scrawny little brother. "Dustin's what we call a lactating, nonrepeating semi-male."

Dustin Green. The only reason Trevor kept him around was because Dustin worshipped him. Wanted to be him. Memorized him. Trevor stood two-point-four inches taller than me and four-point-a-million inches taller than Dustin. Trevor had pecs, biceps, quads, abs—all his profile pictures featured abs—his commercial teeth, the latest shoe, plus a two-hundred-dollar haircut. "Let's take the Escalade," he added. But the man truly didn't know how to sell. He didn't. He'd never bothered to understand the most basic tenets of closing a deal and now he was inserting himself into a labyrinth of sales nuance he barely comprehended on the best of days—let alone this day—the dagger in my gut being that at any moment, any, he could misinterpret the smallest detail and unwittingly derail the entire operation for both himself and certainly for me. At any moment.

"Great," I said. "Great. Yeah, no, perfect. Great. It'll be the four of us."

# CHAPTER 43

Nikos didn't want to spend any of his dead father's money but he felt an obligation to act wisely, to act responsibly, to act manly, to participate in man things, and to demonstrate that manhood. It all emanated from guilt buried deep in the recesses of a frightened outcast of a child—never to be recognized by someone as oafish as Trevor Manning. Trevor closed $23 million in sales last year; I closed $104 million. I don't note this difference in an attempt to brag—those numbers sound *way* more impressive than they actually are—we as a team barely made 7 percent of 1 percent of it as profit—I grossed under a $100K last year—but the gap between Trevor's performance versus my own weighed heavily on him. He thought sales was about the sales*man*—loud, handsome, slick, be the scratch golfer, win the tennis match, tell the best joke. He didn't understand it was about something far more humiliating.

The mood of your buyer.

"Six caps and eight stems," I said to our group.

I had open a wax-paper bag of Amsterdam's most average dose of magic mushrooms—Tree of Life was the brand—held up for my small audience to see. The four of us had just emerged from the nearest coffee shop—the local name for a drug dispensary.

"It's poison," I told them. "Literally. Your body tries to eject this poison, and in that expulsion comes a heightened sense of color and sensation, and, dear Lord, when you put yourself in front of a van Gogh on this shit?" I held up the pouch. Mixing exaggeration with facts was within the standard sales coercion process. "They're gonna taste terrible at first, like chewing on an old shoelace, so we drink OJ as a chaser." I jiggled the small carton of orange juice we bought. I considered faking my own consumption of the drug, I really did, slipping it under my tongue to spit out later in some lucky bush, but that was before Trevor arrived. Being around him and Dustin—I couldn't risk faking it. The potential loss of trust far outweighed whatever upside some sobriety might offer, so I gambled that I had enough general terror pulsing through my veins to keep me mentally alert, which was reckless on my part, I know, but I had a *feeling* it'd work, and feelings are everything in this dance.

"How long does it take to kick in?" asked Nikos.

"Half an hour."

"Half an hour? Will it hurt?"

"You might barf," said Trevor.

"Seriously?"

"It's no big deal. It's trophy barf."

"Seriously?"

That part sucked, the nausea, but in a group setting it's less daunting. "Don't worry, man," I said to Nikos. "I'll make sure your dose is small."

"No, no, no," he said. "Nothing small. I want a solid hit. I want it fully legit. I mean, don't you think?"

"Totally, man."

Nikos didn't believe he had any friends. Shy, rich, isolated, not the best-looking guy in a room, not actually bad looking either, didn't dress well or style his hair well—yet he drastically needed to be liked. He was trying, struggling, gasping to find a social buoy, and for whatever reason, he regarded me as someone decent. Maybe it was that he saw the same struggle in me—a guy desperate to fit in, desperate for the external approval I'd certainly never located within myself. Or maybe it was us sitting on a bench right now facing a picturesque T-junction on the famed canals of Amsterdam, easily visible to anyone in any direction, which wasn't my smartest choice militarily, but with a newcomer like Nikos you had to set up a gentle ambiance. Plus, I had to make Trevor believe I was serious about closing a sale and not hiding an ulterior motive. Drug usage went against everything Trevor knew about me. Alcohol as well. He knew I only drank to close deals. Thus, in his mind, from his frat-boy perspective, watching me devour two caps and two stems of Tree of Life in front of him was the visual evidence needed for him to confirm the only thing that mattered—that I wanted the commission as bad as he did. It was the only motive Trevor could trust.

"This tastes like fresh urine," he announced to everyone, chewing up his dose, as we all began to do the same, gnashing it in our teeth.

"It's awful."

"It's so awful."

"This tastes like homeless-people feet."

Within minutes, we'd devoured enough of it to send ourselves over the clouds and on into the Promised Land. My mom was the one who'd inadvertently taught me the ins and outs, having dug up a bunch of psilocybin articles in *JAMA* in a sad quest to justify her rising chemical dependency, so I knew the alchemy well. The thirty-minute walk to the museum from the canal was the perfect physical stimulation to bring us to a quality high. The key was to look like I was having the time of my life while forcing my brain to stay excruciatingly alert. Focused. Hyperaware. While stalking Nikos. And his phone.

Within the hour the four of us were strolling through the museum lobby. Nikos would be getting the text soon. *The* text. Soon.

"Nikos," I said, waving him over to the rear of the gallery. I hadn't found an opportunity to talk to him without Trevor until we finally stood in front of the paintings. "Nikos, man, you good?"

"I'm so chill," he said, smiling.

"You good?"

"Yeah, man. I'm happy. I'm really just happy." He pointed the row of pieces in front of him. "Drop knowledge, man."

"The art?"

"Vince."

"Vince. It's all about texture with this guy. The brushstrokes." I pointed it out. "A van Gogh is almost as much a sculpture as it is a painting. See?"

"Cool."

"See it?"

"Yeah."

"Here. Stand in front of this one over here." I moved him in front of me. Guiding him like a little brother. "It's called *Wheatfield with a Reaper.* There. Okay, there. Good. Okay. You'll never forget this. Watch." I had to make sure it looked like we were talking about what was on the wall—in case Trevor was keeping tabs. He and Dustin were on the other side of the exhibition room, chatting up two honey-colored young women from Madrid. "You should be seeing heavy contrast right now. Like someone messed with your TV contrast."

"Okay."

"Look at the fields. The grass. Slow. Just . . . Slowly . . . Look at it."

"Okay."

"It moves."

"Yeah, it . . ." He let it resonate with him for a moment. "Holy shit. Yeah."

"Right?"

"Holy *shit*."

"It's like you finally see what he meant for you to see. This isn't a painting, man. It's a pulse. He captured life without skewering it on some frozen urn."

"For real."

"And once you see it, dude, you'll never unsee it. Never. Even sober." He was enthralled. Loving every moment.

"Told you, man. The Dam."

"The Dam," he said.

We bumped fists. "Did they hit you up? About coming to the club tonight?"

"The club?"

"Yeah."

"The . . .?" He searched my face for a moment, searching for an awareness in me.

I gave it to him. I looked right at him. Fully communicating it.

"Oh, whoa, *you know about that*? Yeah, yeah, I'm so glad you *know*. I'm waiting for some kind of text, I think. You know about that?!" He was flooded with a joyful relief, almost taking out his phone to show me his screen, as in I had to stop him so that Trevor wouldn't see this. "I'll show you as soon as they send it." He wanted to prove to me he was part of the "in" crowd, thinking they'd invited me and not him. "They're supposed to send it during the next maybe two hours, right?"

We continued the stroll. I was trying to focus on his phone while tripping on the drug a little harder than I expected. I managed it well but I thought the time was 3:15 p.m. and didn't realize that *two hours* had gone by. When I finally checked a clock, it was 4:40 p.m., sending me into a drug-infused obsession over every ensuing minute.

4:41 p.m. Nikos listens to me worry about the time.

4:42 p.m. Nikos has to puke.

4:42 p.m. I tell him it's normal to puke, it happens to everyone.

4:43 p.m. I volunteer to help him to the bathroom but Trevor steals the opportunity. Despicable, I know—the fact that we argued over who gets to do this but, hey, Sales 103, with $800 million at stake, you're willing to help a billionaire vomit.

4:44 p.m. I'm in the lobby on my own. Waiting. Trying not to pace.

4:45 p.m. I see a girl who looks like Katarina standing near the gift shop.

4:46 p.m. That girl is now right in front of me. That girl is Katarina. Katarina doesn't look good. The closer I get to her, the more I realize she is, in fact, very, very far from good.

# CHAPTER 44

I was already panicking even before knowing whatever it was she was about to tell me. "What're you doing here?" I said to her in a hushed voice.

Her presence had to indicate our plan was changing, a plan I was already struggling to keep up with. How could I take on something new? How did she even find me?

"You okay?" she said.

"Yeah, yeah, yeah, I'm okay, I'm okay. Are *you*?" It was a mixture of emotions, actually. Keep in mind I was already falling for this girl while sober. To try to resist kissing her now, drugged, reality swirling, as she hovered closer and closer to my face, while she looked more imperiled than ever? Not a simple thing. "Are you?"

"Do we have it?"

"The invitation?"

"Yeah."

"No."

"Okay."

"No. Jesus, how could I have it already?! I thought you said it comes later!"

"It's okay. It's okay." She looked around the lobby, then looked back at me. "We need to leave now."

"Leave?!"

"Try to relax. You're moving around too much."

"What do you mean?"

"We need to leave. Try to stay still."

"Why? Where's those guys in the car? Did you follow them?" I looked around, thinking I might actually spot the one she called Hugo. "What happened?"

"The situation changed."

"How? What changed? I don't have the invitation yet. I'm close. It's happening tonight. I just need a little longer, maybe about an hour—"

"We don't have an hour—"

"What're you talking about?!"

"Shhhh, please." She held me by the shoulders for a moment, which allowed me a random glance at her fingers. She'd kept her right hand discreetly down by her side until now. "We need to go. We can't stay here."

"Tell me what happened."

Her knuckles were pink and swollen—speckled with blood. She'd done something significant. Of all the low-probability outcomes that went our way, she clearly encountered something that didn't. She was taking my hand to lead me out.

"No." I yanked away from her. "This has to get done."

It was a little too demonstrative, my movement.

Which drew attention to us.

Which she didn't want.

"I'm no longer asking you to do it," she said.

"We can't back down. I saw what these people can do. I saw everything you wanted me to see and I can't unsee it and I'll tell you something, I'll tell you something, Katarina, I don't *want* to unsee it.

Because what I know is that this is right. This." I pointed to us. "Us attempting it. We have to do what's right."

We stood there, sizing each other up. She probably couldn't recognize me at this point. I looked different. I *sounded* different. To whatever degree I'd forced my cortex to operate beyond the inhibitions of a drug that wanted to flatter my brain, I'd also, by accident, not very eloquently, instilled in myself a relentless sense of purpose. She saw it, she had to, or maybe *I* saw it and she saw that I saw it—my bold rejection of any suggestion that we didn't have control.

"We gotta do what's right," I said. "We *do* have control."

"Fine." She abruptly put a crumpled wad of cash in my hand. "Meet me at Beguine Courtyard before it closes."

I looked down at it.

She'd given me €600. "It's safer if it's on you."

"I don't underst—"

"Beguine Courtyard."

She didn't say bye. She just walked out the door, disappearing into the crowd loitering outside, just as I turned around to see Trevor and Nikos emerging from the restroom, hoping, *praying*, that neither of them saw who I'd been talking to.

# CHAPTER 45

I played it off as smoothly as I could. We traded random jokes, huddled up as a foursome, laughed at everything, laughed at the absurdity of what we were doing, laughed at Nikos—who looked better now—then made a plan.

"I'm so fucken' starving," said Nikos.

I put my arm around him, buddy to buddy, knowing I had to stay deep in character and play the game harder than ever. "Then here comes the best part."

Fifteen minutes later, a kilometer and a half away, we were seated at a small Italian restaurant at the corner of Leidsekruisstraat and Lange Leidsedwarsstraat. I tried to get situated to his right so I could view his cell phone the instant he might take it out, maybe even steal it and run, a fleeting thought vetoed immediately.

"Food tastes biblically amazing on mushrooms," I said to Nikos.

"Like *amazing*," said Trevor. "Like, for real. Like, your colon's getting tongued by a tiny herd of virgins."

I didn't ask any of them if they saw Katarina. I didn't want to draw attention to the possibility of it—in case they simply saw me talking to the back of what was to them a random tall female. I had about two hours to get to the Beguine Courtyard, that meant two hours to wait on the infamous text, if Nikos would even get invited, which was a workable amount of time except that Trevor invited additional people, who'd be arriving any minute. "We should get Mathieu and Jerome and all them."

"From the team?" said Dustin.

He was having three of the other sales reps join us—reps from the Paris office, reps who knew exactly what my current status was within the company. It was the power move on his part—Trevor's—he'd already started messaging them by the time our waitress was serving us our pizzas, personal-sized, one to each of us, perfectly dripping with perfect cheese.

"This is delicious," said Nikos.

"You seriously won't let me get you a pro?" said Trevor. "What's your preference? Redhead? Brunette? Blonde? What do you like?"

"Me?" said Nikos.

"Seriously, what's your flavor? Fifty euros gets you twenty minutes here but that's street-grade. For us? For you? At the royal price range? I know where we can buy girls hotter than any living creature you can imagine."

"I don't know, man, the whole prostitute thing . . . feels . . . feels . . ." Nikos shifted in his seat.

"Feels defeatist? Not at all! Y'know, if you're a cripple, the Dutch government gives you vouchers to get laid? They give you twelve sex vouchers a year if you're disabled."

"Do they like it?" said Dustin.

"Who? The cripples?"

"The hookers."

"Do the hookers like the cripples?" said Trevor.

"Yeah."

"What the fuck kinda question is that?"

"It's gross," said Dustin. "When I think of touching one . . ."

"You think about touching a cripple, Dustin? Maybe you're the one who should be accepting the vouchers?"

Nikos laughed.

Trevor laughed.

I tried to laugh but I could barely get it out. Their world was nauseating. No wonder Katarina was ready to plunge a dagger in the back of all mankind.

"No," said Dustin. "I like girls way more than any of you do."

Another hour of this drivel went by. I couldn't partake of it but I had to try. Maybe it was the chemicals in me, or the fatigue, or the emotional turmoil I felt in every neuron, but I had to play the game despite the constraints. My attention kept drifting to the TV screen mounted on a wall in the opposite restaurant—a newscast. The significance of it wasn't apparent to me right away but it was in my field of view and I kept glancing at it for no reason other than that it was there. It was replaying a random clip—a grainy video clip—of a recent criminal assault. I must've been hallucinating because it looked like the camera had zoomed in on a young woman with the same exact face as Katarina—same clothes, same hair—and whoever she was, the caption was saying she maliciously beat up a guy in broad daylight, possibly with the same bloody fists I saw on my own Katarina. And the city was putting out an alert.

"Christ," I whispered to myself.

Was this what she didn't want to tell me about?

I leaned over to get a better look at the screen to see if the police knew she was Russian or French or something else dangerously indicative. I wasn't totally stupid. I knew I was running around town on a pretty hopeless mission on behalf of a young lady who was, by any normal application of logic, setting me up, while I sat at a table surrounded by juvenile delinquents who'd—

"What're you staring at?" said Dustin.

The other guys kept talking as Dustin turned around in his seat to take a look at whatever he'd caught me looking at, not in a friendly way, not out of an amused curiosity, but as a competitor hoping his colleague might make a fatal mistake.

"Nothing," I said to him, sitting up, straightening up, trying to keep the rest of the group's attention away from the TV. "You guys, uh . . ." I broached the only topic that could work at this table. "You guys, uh—Hey, if you guys wanna know the best way to meet a girl in the Netherlands, like the actual way to meet a local girl in a genuine type of courtsh—" Which was when Nikos got a message on his phone.

## CHAPTER 46

Within a span of ten seconds, the tenth-richest kid in Greece was checking his invitation, reading it, rereading it, clicking his phone off, then putting it back in his pocket, having seen what he needed to see. Jesus Christ, I almost didn't catch any of this. With Trevor having announced additional buddies coming from the home office to join the four of us, I'd been so preoccupied with getting out of there as quick as possible that I'd almost missed the whole reason I *was* there. Nikos made no mention to anyone what he read but he did take a seriously long look at it, holding his screen just below the edge of the table to do so, while I let the current conversation wander wherever it was wandering. Did he receive an address? A code? Contact numbers? What did he just see?

"Hey," I said to the group, raising my glass.

I had to control his response to it yet absolutely couldn't risk doing anything in front of Trevor.

"Cheers to sex at any price," I said, feeling the pressure coming to a boil, "including the golden price of zero." Katarina said to meet her at Beguine Courtyard—how long would she be able to wait there if she were trying to elude cops as well?

"Cheers!" said Dustin.

"Cheers," said Trevor. "Sex at any price."

We were on our third round of Ouzo. In honor of Nikos, who also raised his glass. "Cheers!"

And I knocked over his bowl of soup.

I lifted my glass outward in a sweeping motion so it bumped his bowl upward and fully spilled it in the most natural way possible all over him and all over my own arm.

"Shit!" said Nikos.

"Shit," said Dustin.

I'd been eyeing the geometry for the past two hours. "Sorry, man, sorry, sorry, sorry," I said. "Sorry, sorry, sorry, wow, fuck." I handed him a too-small napkin for him to uselessly try to blot it out. He and my forearm were now drenched. "Wow, I'm really . . . Here . . ." I knew the soup was thick. I knew he'd need to rinse off.

"Uh, okay," he said politely. "No worries. Don't . . . uh . . . The . . . uh . . ."

He sat there at a loss until I pointed to the restaurant across the terrace from us. Its bathroom was closer to our table than our own, which would be slightly awkward both socially and logistically but I'd been masterminding the idea for nearly an hour. I escorted him out of his seat while Trevor and Dustin laughed at how dumb we looked, then I led us to that bathroom.

Nikos was a lot more agitated than I thought he'd be, mostly because of how drugged he still was, which made me wonder just how drugged *I* still was and how I'd lost track of how dangerous the environment had become.

Once inside, we were rinsing off.

"Sorry, man," I said again, genuinely.

"No worries."

"It's all over your shirt, man. Sorry. Not sure it'll come out."

"No worries. Yeah. No, no."

"Did they finally, uh, text you?"

"It's fine. Yeah. What? Oh, uh, I don't know."

"Don't know what? Did they text you?"

"If I'll go."

"What?"

"Yeah. I don't know if I'll go."

"Seriously?!"

"The shit creeps me out, man. It's like . . . It's like all these details about what to wear and how to enter and . . ." He showed me the phone, I knew he would. I'd engineered every minute of the afternoon, every risk, every perversion of value, to lead to this exact moment. He held it up and I casually took it from him, casually looking at the address, so I could casually memorize the hell out of it in a single glance.

". . . and what?"

No matter what happens from here on out, Adam, you *memorize* what's there.

"I don't know," he continued. "Is this, like, a masquerade?"

I was reading it—a bizarre description of what seemed like a masquerade. "Wow . . . that's . . . uh . . ."

"What?"

"I don't know."

"What?"

"It's . . . Yeah . . . Probably . . ." I did what I could to keep my thoughts unspoken. "I don't know." To increase the confusion on his part, to enhance my value to him as a shepherd.

"You want to go together?"

"Together?"

"Yeah."

"Uh . . . sure, man." Jackpot. I gave him back his phone, trying to commit the address to memory, formulating the best way to keep him hushed up from this point on. "Sure. But don't let anyone know you shared it. These things are super exclusive. They want you to come but don't let anyone else know. Especially Trevor. Trevor is a talker. Not saying that in a mean way. It's just . . . something like this is *the* opportunity for you. Big. And if the people who run it find out that you talked to other people about it, they'll ban you. They won't even *tell* you they banned you, they'll just leave you outside the door."

That seemed to impact him more than all else. I saw it—the loss of inclusion. That was it. I saw it in the forlorn face of a child standing outside a picket fence. He certainly had a useful quantity of issues, this kid. He looked down at his torso—the pastel-colored wreck I made of it.

"I look ridiculous," he said.

"Nah."

"I can't go out in public."

"No, man, seriously, you're good. I'll help you. You were gonna need a nice suit tonight anyway, right? That's in the text, right? Formal attire? So here's what you do. This'll be great. Here's what you do. You take a cab back to the suite, you order an Armani, I'll show you how . . . There's an account we use . . . You wash up, you get dapper, *you tell no one*, you meet me in your lobby in, let's say, three hours, and we go. Sound good?"

The details were coming together. Ninety percent of sales is proximity: where you are in the room, where the mark is. I managed to get Nikos out of sight from Trevor's posse merely two minutes before it got ugly. Across the street, you could see that the coworkers, Mathieu and Jerome and whoever the hell else, were arriving. We couldn't have timed it any tighter. Scary, in retrospect. I hustled Nikos out the other side of the restaurant to a smaller street and got him in a taxi without the others seeing any of it. I closed his cab door and watched his car disappear before walking away from the whole circus entirely. I'd finally seen the TV screen up close. The news showed iPhone footage of an "unidentified young woman" trouncing a guy near a bridge. She must've been in the thick of it—Katarina. The female in the video grabbed his wallet and the video went to a freeze-frame with a hotline number written across her pixelated head. Apparently, the best image they had was a blurry mess but it was definitely her in the '60s scarf. I counted up the wad of cash in my hand. Six-hundred forty euros. I already knew she wouldn't be showing up at the courtyard. I could sense it long before it'd become real. I'd go there anyway, to the location, and check for her but I already knew I needed to resort to a very, very dangerous plan B.

# CHAPTER 47

Katarina mentioned that she knew another prostitute living in Amsterdam. She mentioned her name on the train. I spent the next forty-five minutes of my walk trying to remember that name. Amber, or Aquarius, or something with an "A." The only thing Katarina told me about this girl was that she had Bible-verse tattoos and worked at a brothel called—I think—Decadent Splash. I needed to be smart about all this. It was doubtful her street name would still be the same after this many years but maybe her *brothel's* name wouldn't have changed. I gave it a twenty-percent chance.

Katarina and I agreed we'd meet at Beguine Courtyard but this was before her low-resolution face went public. Beguines is a women's-only commune dating back to the fourteenth century. That's what I learned reading the little plaque fifty-five times in two hours. She wasn't there when I arrived. She wasn't there when I wandered around. She wasn't there when I stayed in the middle of the square, waiting, pacing, circling around to the far side, checking the perimeter, returning, rereading the plaque, pacing some more. I walked one last lap around the place, increasing from deep panic to desperate panic, before heading to the front of the police station in Centrum. This was the closest precinct to the bridge where her fight had been videotaped. I stayed across the street from the precinct entrance as I took a good, hard look at my future. She could be somewhere else or she could be in there, in a situation where I might be able to vouch for her somehow.

I didn't go in.

I tried to force myself to go but I couldn't. In order to do what we came to this city to do—for her sake—I had to prioritize the minimization of risk, and I couldn't imagine a scenario in which I walked in there and didn't get arrested. *You're a coward, man.* True, I told myself, but if she *wasn't* arrested, my only hope of finding her would be to go find Astral.

"Astral."

Her name was Astral. It hit me out of the blue. She mentioned meeting an Astral. I had that much to get started on before discovering that, God help me, Decadent Splash wasn't where you'd assume it should be. The red-light district is surprisingly small. You can walk the entire grid in twenty minutes—back and forth, checking every storefront—twenty minutes. Luckily, it only took two random conversations for me to learn that Decadent Splash is actually a *houseboat* located somewhere else called the Borneo-eiland. A half hour later I was in a much less crowded part of town near the wharf. Empty lots. Empty docks. Very few cars or pedestrians. The ideal setting for me to be murdered. What had seemed cowardly an hour ago now felt outright insane.

I found the houseboat.

"You go up to the door, you ring the bell, you ask for a blow job," I told myself.

That was the plan I made.

"Mention oral and say you want it from someone edgy, like with tats. Like, Bible tats."

Stupid—but that was how I could ask for her without asking for her. Or I could just ask for her. I'd have to see how it goes. Most of the sex in town is tightly regulated to protect the prostitutes, allowing the prostitutes to run prostitution with no middleman. Most. But a house-boat way out here? Could easily be under the rule of a thick-neck, gold-chain-wearing roid-rage Russian mobster who might recognize me as a known enemy. Who might have a spiked baseball bat behind his back.

I rang.

The door opened.

An attractive jet-black-haired young woman answered.

"Hi," she said.

"Hi. Is this Decadent Splash?"

"Yes."

"Great."

"Do you have an appointment?"

"I do."

"Under what name?"

"Astral."

"No. Your name. What name are you under?"

It was one thing to get myself in front of her—Astral—if she were even here—if that were even her name—a girl whose level of allegiance to Katarina remained completely unknown to me. It was another thing to successfully recruit her once I found her. I'd have to go all in.

"What name are you under?" she said again after I took too long.

"Da Vinci."

I said it. She didn't seem to process it at first but when she saw my unflinching gaze, my deadly conviction after putting it out there, her mental echo of my answer must've confirmed the severity of her new predicament—I'd said the thing she never wanted to hear.

Her face went cold. I didn't nod in affirmation. I stared her down until the silence was ripe enough to drive home my next step.

"I'm not going to repeat myself," I said with the right amount of merciless eye contact to resolve her pressing question: Is this guy actually part of that world? She could choose to doubt me and she knew the risk of doing so. "I'm here because he's making it possible for me to be here."

Her eyes scanned the empty dock behind me to see if there were others.

I motioned for her to let me in, adding one assurance that'd benefit us both. "You're not going to be part of what's about to happen."

She nodded okay.

She brought me in, pointed down the hall, then let me head for the last door at the back of what felt very much like a boutique—surprisingly clean, surprisingly bright, almost cheerful. I'd never entered a brothel before. I didn't even feel good in strip clubs—something about a dark interior covered in man fluids and shame, the way the girls are perennially annoyed with you, resentful of every part of you except your ATM card, giving off that vacant stare while they gyrate against your wallet. No one wins in a strip club. And this place felt even weirder. I knocked on the last door down the hall.

I waited a minute.

I knocked again.

The Prostitute Possibly Known as Astral opened up. She must've been with a customer—I couldn't see for sure because she held the door open only a crack. She had a soft voice. Shy. Sweet. She was wearing a blue silk robe and, yes, there were foreign words tattooed on her chest along with what was recognizable as "Proverbe 27:17." I felt my breath vacate a bit.

"Yes?" she said.

"Is your name Astral?"

"Who are you?"

"Is your name Astral?"

"Why? I'm with someone. How did you get in here?"

"We need to talk."

"I don't know what you think you're doing, but—"

She'd started to close the door but I put my fist against it. Commandingly. Getting right in her face. Preparing to deliver the following words and have them sting with each letter: *I'm here for Katarina Haimovna and I will make your life way fucken' worse if necessary, so let me in.* "I'm here for Katarina Haimovna and I will make—"

"Wait."

She put her fingers up to silence me.

She leaned in, bringing us closer. "I meet you in ten minutes. Tell Sabrina you will have King of the World."

"What?"

"Go."

"Tell . . .?"

"Tell the girl who is letting you in. Sabrina. Black hair. Tell her you are getting a hand job at the end of the dock. Is King of the World. I will meet you in ten minutes."

I couldn't think fast enough to respond.

"You will trust me," she said, closing the door.

# CHAPTER 48

She came outside carrying a folded picnic blanket. She had on a big pink hoodie and looked fifteen years old in it, coming over to me at the end of the wharf, standing there, looking around, then leading me, us, even farther out along the water's edge onto a small wooden dock where we didn't say a single word to each other until we got all the way to the end of it.

"Here," she said.

She'd usurped my role as the aggressor.

"Now is okay," she said.

Coming to a place this secluded felt like another patented bad move on my part. She had us standing at the very end of the dock, where she wrapped the large picnic blanket around the two of us.

"We need to make sure we are far from the house."

"Okay," I said. Half the thugs in Europe scouring the city for me and she wants to stand out in plain view. Nobody *seemed* to be watching us, but for all I knew, everyone was.

"You tell me all the things you want to tell me. Maybe as fast as you can. You go."

I was more than a little hesitant.

"You go," she said.

I could be unloading key info on someone who'd use it against me and maybe against Katarina—pouring gasoline on a lit match. After all, Katarina explicitly stated that no one she knew in this city could be trusted. Nevertheless, I spoke and spoke fast, summarizing what I could, focusing on how I might meet da Vinci and that there was no way I'd meet him unless I had additional resources. I did everything I could not to mention my own angle in all this, which had morphed over time, becoming somewhat of an Oedipal urge to destroy the throne both on a personal level and worldwide—the sort of hate-my-drunk-dad cliché that might drown my point in front of someone so relentlessly pragmatic.

"What additional resources do you need?" she said. That was her first question. Her accent was thick—Hungarian or Romanian, maybe Czech.

In a matter of minutes, I'd come to understand the essence of what was going on with her, as in how I might have a chance of winning her over.

"Yes, right," I said. "I need resources but . . . first . . . I gotta ask . . . uh . . . Is there tension between you and Katarina?"

"Tension?"

"Tension . . . like, uh . . . Fight-argue? Fight-fight? Fighting?"

"No. It is her who is having tension. Me, I am liking her. She is not trusting of me."

"Ah, okay."

"She does not trust me because I am weak."

"You?"

"Yes."

"No. You're weak? How?"

"I have a son."

A son?!

"They take him when he is six month," she said. "They say they are to keep him safe. They allow of my talking to him on video phone. This is how I know he is alive. I do this for maybe it is one year. It is hard but it is okay. Then there is some bad month where I do not earn so much money. They start to canceling my opportunity to talking with my son. They say I do not make enough money. They say I must be more sexy. So I try. I am more sexy. I have good body." She lifted her bulky sweatshirt to show me her torso. "Good. Is nice? One day I talk to my son on video but the connection is bad but I see I am watching *old* video but because he is so young I cannot know if he is to interacting with me. Yes, you understand? Interacting. Was this in the past, I am asking. This video. Is very hard to know because he is young. I start to believing my son is not okay. I ask for proving he is okay. Proving?"

"Proof."

"Proof. I ask for proof of my son is alive. They tell me work harder, work harder. I work harder but then is maybe two months is passing and I say no. I say I need to see *proof* and then they send to me a new video. In this new video, he does not talk directly but I do not see this video before so maybe I think maybe he is okay . . . I think . . . Yes. But is the only video I see."

"How long ago was that?"

"Eleven months."

"Eleven *months*?!"

I shouldn't have said it like that. Fuck me. I knew it was harsh the moment it came out, a reaction that could *not* possibly soothe her frail little universe. I mean, Christ, she talks to her kid every week then goes eleven months with no contact? She had to know, right? Even without me blurting it out, she had to.

I tried to smile nicely.

"Do you think there is chance he is still alive?" she said.

What do you say?

What did she need to hear? If I tell the truth—Your son is fucking gone, Madame—she tumbles into a full year of despair, locking herself up in mental exile, commits suicide, and society moves on. If I tell her he's alive, she remains in the grip of a tyrant, long, long, long after I exit her life.

"You seem to understand these men," she said. "Do you think he is still alive?"

"I mean . . ." So I told her the only thing I could. The only thing I genuinely believed. "I don't know . . . but what I *do* know . . . is I trust Katarina."

She stayed with that for a second.

We both did.

"Yes," she said. "I trust Katarina."

"Yes."

"I am wanting to help you." She looked up at me. Decisively. "I will help you."

The whole time she'd been talking I kept telling myself to stay mercilessly committed to the mission at hand—da Vinci—and not get swayed by the fact that, Jesus, was I about to be regarded as some teen mom's savior? Because she wouldn't just be doing me this as an idle favor. I mean, when it comes to protecting a threatened child, whoever represents your one chance of saving him becomes someone you deify.

"Okay," I said.

"Yes."

"Thank you."

"Yes."

"Do you want . . . uh . . .?" It occurred to me. "Do you want me to give you proof that I am with her?"

"No."

"No?"

"You call her Katarina Haimovna. Nobody know this name. Haimovna. This mean if she tell you, she is trusting you. This mean *I* trust you."

That was it. Apparently full verification didn't matter to someone in her position—already teetering on the abyss, peering down at the unthinkable. I mean, even if, hypothetically, from her point of view, I did harbor ill will toward her, what the hell did she have to lose?

"What do you need?" she said.

"It'll be dangerous."

"Yes, I know. What do you need?"

"I . . . uh . . . I need . . . I need you to help me be someone I'm not."

# CHAPTER 49

Morgan da Vinci changed his name. He used to refer to himself as Voltaire, then Morgan Voltaire, then M., then V., then just John. Prior to that he was Archimedes, then the Eastern Minister, then Atlantic Exports, Inc. Prior to that was anyone's guess. The guy prided himself on relentless anonymity. "I am any of you," he said to someone somewhere at some point, appearing at private events only when masked and only when everyone else was as well. According to rumors, it was his humble size and benign demeanor that kept him from being recognized. Regardless of what anyone thought, this was the man who controlled the men who controlled half a trillion dollars of Western commerce. With a silk fist.

To get near him, I needed to be someone substantial.

I needed to be Nikos.

Astral helped me rent the right limo. We did it in Jenn's name, under Jenn's business account, using Katarina's stolen cash. Astral met me at a tram station called C. van Eesterenlaan, and, wow, she was dressed to kill. Straight up. If anyone had been watching this girl leave her house today—she clearly looked like she was heading off to please a very high-end client. I didn't recognize her. Gorgeous. High class. Curved. Breathtaking. I no longer worried about the con we were about to run on Nikos. Little Astral would do the trick.

"Ready?"

"Ready," she said.

In the limo she and I quietly went over the parameters, reviewing what little info I had to go on. She didn't say much—agreeing with me that any chauffeur I hired was bound to be networked, watched, checked, scrutinized, monitored, bribed—to relay snatches of any info overheard to whoever was paying for it. All we could do was keep our voices hushed.

Once we pulled up to Nikos's hotel, I had the valet desk call the phone in his suite—some eight times—before he finally answered. I told him we needed a half hour to drive to the site. I told him it was already getting fun.

"Cool, man," he said. "Cool, okay, be right down."

I was dreading the outcome of each of the many, many things that could go wrong tonight but what I feared most was Trevor somehow showing up. I sat in the back of the limo facing forward, sitting across from Astral, who'd elongated herself in her skin-tight cocktail dress that had strategic gaps for side cleavage as well as a lethal slit up the left leg.

"This event isn't that old, is it?" I asked her. "This . . . this Society?"

She'd only heard vague rumors. "No, the event is new."

She didn't believe da Vinci was still alive but if he *were* still alive, she, too, would want him dead. I asked her if she had the dust ready to go. She did. Nikos got in, looking much better than his usual bland self. Tailored Armani suit, purchased, measured, snipped same-day. Hair groomed by an in-suite service. Clive Christian cologne. Such is the luxury of a nine-zero bank account. He slid in next to Astral, animal mask in hand, which was the one item the Society had delivered anonymously to his hotel.

"Hi," he said to her.

"Hi," she said.

"I'm Nikos."

"Astral."

"Wow." He seemed happy with her. He turned to me. "Hey, man!"

The stretch SUV was spacious enough for the three of us to comfortably open a bottle of Armand de Brignac, a crucial element in the plan—my entire future hinging on it—my entire future hinging on everything, really—the limo, the champagne, the tux I rented, the fourteen-centimeter YSL shoes on Astral's feet, her dress, her laugh, her eyes, and, of course, our dust. It was this particular dust that would spill surreptitiously from a simple bracelet she wore. During round two of the champagne, she'd let her hand casually hover over his second glass. Not his first. People pay attention to the first. I had to hope that nobody would know how to roofie better than a girl who'd *been* roofied. In fact, on cue, without a hitch, she let her bracelet happen to dip into his glass, while pouring him another sloshing amount of Brignac, then handed him the result while making sure to say something distracting. "Cheers to the hottest new guy in Holland." Looking directly at him, smiling. Her marksmanship flawless. For all he knew, she was a featured prelude to the elite services ahead.

He was giddy, laughed, drank, chatted her up. My presence must've helped his confidence. Somehow her flirtation felt more legit to him with me there, like he'd met a girl who was genuinely into him because, hey, your buddy in the corner isn't telling you otherwise. Rohypnol takes thirty minutes to slow you down, sixty to put you under. In the initial phases you simply feel drunk and, in Nikos's case, quite truthful. He slid over to whisper to me loudly, as if Astral couldn't hear him, "Dude, this is the first time I've felt really good about myself." He patted me on the back. "Seriously, man, thank you."

"Cool."

"You're a good guy. No, I'm really excited about tonight. You were right."

We were drugging him to keep him from leaving the SUV, which, of course, made me feel like a certified asshole even before he'd begun gushing out that gratitude. Once he finally fell into a full stupor, Astral held his thumb and pressed it against his phone button after checking to make sure the driver remained busily driving. Nikos's customized entry code would be texted to him in whatever final text he'd get, which would occur maybe fifteen minutes before the scheduled arrival time. So I had to keep that phone screen active until I saw that code.

"Is he good?" I said. I gave him a test pat on the shoulder.

After twenty minutes, he was fully inert.

I convinced myself I was doing him a favor, knowing he'd probably never forgive me. "You don't want to be part of this, man," I said quietly to the side of his head.

The limo stopped at the Hotel Oosterdok, where I'd found a decent suite a few blocks from the wharf, having reserved it under Jenn's name. She'd kill me for doing so, but, realistically, it'd take her at least a week to discover anything. All over town various conference guests were checking into various hotels using her corporate account. The cash our company dished out was staggering, so my grabbing one small suite with it would take *weeks* for anyone to trace. We drove around town in a giant circle for forty-five minutes, then told the driver our pal was passed out. Astral helped a random valet walk him up to our suite. Nobody in there suspected a thing—not with this arrangement, an incoherent guy guided by a cute young lady—the staff merely chuckling. I watched her disappear around the corner with my limp billionaire under her control. She didn't wave back to reassure me. She could soon be doing *anything* to him up there. He'd wake up knowing nothing about her, not even her name. That's if she even stayed. She could do what she wanted and leave him in shambles.

I'd just placed all my trust in my ability to judge her.

"Sir," said the driver.

I let the chauffeur close my door and sat deeper in my seat. I read and reread and reread and reread the oddly brief street address in the text messages, then called it out to the driver as he put the car in gear.

"Mercury, 65 Dokken Lane," I said to him, sliding my animal mask on, staring at my warped reflection in the window as the city began to pass across it. My name: Nikos Dimopolous.

# CHAPTER 50

They asked for the code. I thought there was chance they wouldn't but the hostess up front explicitly wanted me to say it to her. She then typed this answer into a mobile computer screen while I stayed standing in front of her. She'd greeted me in a skin-tight pants suit in front of two massive men in tuxedos. I figured there was a small chance this info was linked closely enough to Nikos's identity to red-flag anyone who seemed or looked or even sounded different from him, but I also figured he and I had a similar physical build, with him being an inch shorter, so that any—

"Can you please step to the side, sir?" said the hostess.

"Why?"

"Please, if I could have you step to the side. Thank you."

"To . . .?"

"Thank you, sir."

"Sure." I moved. "Sure, sure, yes."

She started radioing someone on her headset, getting them on the line for a private conversation. About me? This was merely the foyer of the club and she wasn't letting me enter? There was no way I could be stopped here—that's what I told myself. No way, no, not after going through what it took to get into this room, not after having come this far. The "Mercury" address, the first address I'd given the driver, had

led us to the outskirts of town where we saw literally nothing, no buildings, no cars, not even a windmill. My limo just idled on the side of the
road as I debated a possible wrong turn with my disconcerted driver,
until a beautiful blonde on a *bicycle* randomly rode up to his window,
out of the blue, appearing out of nowhere—she was the "Mercury" of
it, I guess—and told him a second address, which sent us back to the
middle of town, the *middle* middle, I mean literally the middle, and I
got out and walked through a swarm of tourists through a shopping
plaza to get to the front door of what looked like nothing more than a
nondescript, unmarked hole in the wall. I was let in and escorted up a
dank flight of stairs, which brought me here, now, in the foyer, trying
silently to rally myself—There's no way you don't get in, Adam—trying
to focus on what Katarina said about combat—her response when I
asked her how the hell she wins so many street fights—"Learning
what to do is easy," she said, "with just an hour on the Internet, you
can learn anything, how to cross a border, how to make a knife from
a coin, how to make a bomb in a kitchen, or kick someone dead. You
just need the will."

The will.

She spent a year running from angry men. She had that. The will.
Did I? Would I?

"Thank you for your patience," said the hostess. "Please allow me to
accompany you to the main hall."

The nice young lady then led me—just the two of us, no guards
anymore—into the main hall.

I was in.

The real decor started to be visible. Maybe they'd staggered each
participant to arrive at a different time? I don't know. Whatever the
case, the previous room was a front. Once you were through the hall,

you saw that you were walking into something nearly palatial. White fur carpets running along marble floors between lavish pillars. Gold trim. All that.

I was in.

"You have a really nice smile," the hostess said to me. She'd turned around just coyly enough for me to behold her profile as I followed her. "Tonight's theme is the Alpine Moon. You can touch me in any way you choose." She stopped at the gate. "All front rooms are open to you. You can touch any woman here in any way you choose."

She stood in front of me. Open to me.

"Okay," I said.

I'd been in a number of strip clubs throughout my life, been in a number of posh bars—I'd never ever seen such carte blanche direct accessibility to a female. It wasn't just *what* she said, it was the *way* she said it.

"Thank you," I said to her. I didn't touch her. My hand quivered at the prospect of almost stroking her shoulder in some kind of awkward, creepy, platonic way. I didn't let myself do it, though she stood there at my disposal. And, yes, she stood there for what was as long as I'd wanted her to. "Uh, what are all the rules? Like . . . the stuff I can't do . . . or can't . . . y'know, as far as . . .?"

"I just told you the rules."

"Okay."

She stayed in front of me.

"Okay," I said, "I guess I'll . . ." I motioned for myself to continue heading in, and headed in.

She returned to the front reception area, after which two silver-plated gates opened for me, and the world got a whole lot darker and hotter. This was what a billion dollars gets you. We'd all seen what a million got you. We'd seen the douche brigade sitting courtside at any Laker game. Fat old dudes who looked like they punched a wall with their face next to dainty, little LA eights. That's what a million got you. *This* place?

"Hi," said an evocative voice beside me.

I turned and nodded a hello.

"I'm Athena East. I'm here to quench your deepest thirst." She was one of the cocktail waitresses. "I have several scotch options available. A 26 Macallan. A Glenfiddich 37 and a Dalmore 64 Trinitas. I have other options as well. Just name your one need."

"My . . . uh . . ." It occurred to me I should've slid my fingers up the crotch of the first hostess. It occurred to me she *expected* me to do so, and it occurred to me that when I didn't, she turned around and reported to her superiors that I was an impostor. I held Athena's lovely fingers in mine. What would an unfettered rich bastard do here? "You look ravishing."

"Why, thank you, Nikos." She smiled. "When you want me again, just glance in my general direction. East. I'll start you with a 26 Macallan."

She returned to the server room.

I'd meant to kiss her hand. I didn't. I'd stayed where I was. "You're already in," I mumbled quietly. They'd already let you in. "Stop acting like you're not." And here it finally, *finally*, occurred to me to even check if there were other males in the room—my only objective, right? I'd gotten absurdly distracted by the regal interior, by the women, how built to sexual perfection they were, the bizarre way they carried themselves, convincingly genuine—like they weren't "arranged" to be near you but genuinely found you entrancing. It nearly blinded me to the presence of the male guests. There *were* male guests. And, just like me, all these gents wore dark suits and dark masks, hunkering down in the dark periphery—most of them surrounded by several females each. A third server brought me a glass of scotch with a huge cube of ice in it—her statuesque body perched on a pair of strappy leather boots. Even though these women wore masks, their gazes still pierced right to the soul of you. "Just do it," I muttered to myself as I left yet another one of these ladies untouched while every other guy in there was groping them like lap dogs. "Blend in, Adam, get this going, get it done, get out. C'mon, blend in, blend in. Get it done." I had the emails. I had the leverage. I had low odds of succeeding in here but for whatever those odds were, for whatever two or three opportunities I was about to get, I had to make them count.

I scanned each man's face. I skipped past anyone blustering loudly. Nobody thriving on anonymity would do that. Who seems like a da Vinci in here? The Korean man near the pillar? Maybe. The two Persian guys talking to the three girls in latex? Maybe. The pudgy guy one-on-one with the brunette? Doubtful. He's loud. The red-haired man sitting at the small bar?

Him?

I went over to the row of bar stools near the guy with the red hair. I put my drink down and pretended to need a napkin. He wasn't talking loud enough for me to fully eavesdrop, but he was chatting up a friend and I heard two odd words get said, "republic" and "swan," in a somewhat intriguing context. I looked toward the other side of the room. There was one other candidate for me to check after this one. I almost recognized him as a Catalan banking CEO I'd seen in the news, just based on his laugh. Could be him. Jordi Carreras. The masks we wore hid half our features, but the *laughs* came through, which was when I heard the red-haired guy say something about "interior acoustics." None of what he talked about stood out on its own but there was a vibe to him. A tone. He seemed regal. He was the only guy in here who *seemed* like a da Vinci. Poised. Like a duke from some place historic. I leaned forward, pretending to get a better look at the gin bottles.

"Sir?"

He'd just started another anecdote and I must've been staring.

"Enjoying the evening, sir?"

A man's voice was coming from my flank. I turned around to find myself next to a new guy—masked, shorter in stature, possibly some sort of usher—definitely looking like he was deployed by a hidden security team.

"Uh, sorry," I said to him. I stood upright, moving away from the shelf of gin.

"Sir," he said for the third time.

"Thanks, yes." I turned to try to head in the other direction.

He remained facing me.

"Yes," I said. "Thanks."

He wasn't leaving. In the middle of the ocean, swimming with the sharks, I'd lasted ten minutes.

"Thanks, I'm great," I said. "I'm . . . uh . . ." I knew I should've acted with entitlement and not as my usual obsequious self.

"Sir, would you be so kind as to follow me?"

# CHAPTER 51

The usher was leading me to the far side of the main floor to a door that was somewhat hidden behind a dark velvet curtain. I followed him without protest, wanting all this to look as casual as possible to everyone else around us. On the off chance I *wasn't* about to get ejected or castrated, I wanted it to look like maybe I was being shown the restroom or a special buffet. I already felt the scrutiny of the others—their attention on the one man being led anywhere by *any* staff member. If the ruse was over, if I were identified, this little guy would either be turning me over to the police—a bad thing—or he'd be turning me over to the staff to deal with me in house—a *terrifying* thing.

"Have you been to one of our gatherings before?" he said with a fairly polite tone. "Or is this your first occasion?"

"I . . . uh . . . I always feel like I'm new."

"We saw you standing near the bar somewhat confused as to protocol. We began to wonder if maybe this wasn't the most suitable area for you." He then pulled a tall, heavy velvet curtain aside for me, bringing me face-to-face with a large bouncer who took a look at me, took a look at the usher, then opened the door for us to let us in before shutting it behind us as we then entered a long, dark sconce-lit corridor. "Is the general temperature satisfactory?" said the usher, motioning for me to follow him.

"Uh, the . . .? Yes."

"Good. Comfort is important for what is next."

"Those curtains are great."

"They're soundproof."

"Soundproof."

"There was a torture device used in sixth-century Athens called the Brazen Bull of Phalaris. Do you know it? It's metal statue of a bull that is hollow inside. The sixth-century engineer Perillus built it for Phalaris, constructing it with internal tubing very much like that of a brass musical instrument. When you imprison a man within its bowels and you slowly heat the shell of this statue, the man inside will begin to scream, which is of course vulgar, but the tubing serves to *channel* his sounds in such a way as to shape his anguish into luscious musical notes. It is, in fact, an expression of civility itself, one might say."

We arrived at a heavy wooden door with wrought-iron hinges and a wrought-iron door knocker.

"I would liked to have heard such a symphonic masterpiece as this one thousand years ago," he said. "Wouldn't you?" He grasped the door knocker. "Perhaps, if we as a society were to bend our intellect toward the abstract, we could say this device conducts the voice of God, no? Regardless, can you imagine the sound it produces when you encapsulate a *woman*?"

He knocked once and within several seconds two bouncers opened the door, looked at the two of us, approved whatever was about to happen with me, then stepped aside to let us enter a very strange room.

"Please . . ." The usher gestured for me to enter ahead of him.

There would be a lot to comprehend in here. I could spend the rest of my short life trying to describe it but let's just say that the first thing

I saw—the only thing that would really matter in the grand scheme of things—was a naked female chained to the floor.

"The beauty's in the process itself," said the usher. "For what is most intriguing in terms of your own artistic union of musician and instrument is not *that* you can make her scream within this device, but your choice of *how*."

# CHAPTER 52

Every man in this room wore the same type of face mask—a wolf or a jackal. Not many of them were talking, and those who did talk were doing so in hushed voices. Yet the mood here was lighter than in the main hall, almost like a sporting event.

"This represents something new for us," said the usher.

In the middle of this room was a rustic bed next to a rustic trunk next to a stone fireplace. The walls of a log cabin surrounded us so that you had a half circle of about maybe fifteen anonymous spectators just like myself, relaxing on plush benches as if we were all in a sort of rustic theater, and center stage, chained to the headboard of the bed on a long leash, was our woman.

None of which was the most disturbing part.

It was the *window*.

On the far side of the room was a giant window facing directly toward the general public: a massive floor-to-ceiling piece of glass contorted into a twisting cone, set street level with the main square of Amsterdam's city center, in front of tourists and locals, who were everywhere, *everywhere*, coming right up to us, passing us, hovering near us, *using* us—women adjusting their makeup in the reflection, guys smoothing out their hair—everyone walking by with absolutely no idea what was in here, oblivious to the fact that fewer than four inches away from their noses a girl was about to wish she were dead.

"Fear not," said the usher, seeing me see this. "Even if the people outside were to shine a searchlight beam of a billion lumens at us, point-blank, they'd see nothing of what is inside. The glass is one-way. Zero transmittance. Bulletproof."

I began to understand that not every guest of the Society would be invited back here. The main lobby contained the secret party everyone *thought* was the secret party. This room housed the true taboo.

"We call it the Chamber of Harmony," said the usher. "None of the women who are brought in here are compliant. In fact, we've gone out of our way to select *only* females whose sincerest wish is to remain untouched in this way."

He smiled.

Organized rape.

"Quite something, isn't it?" he said.

In the city center.

They weren't selling sex, they weren't trafficking indentured workers through financial coercion or extortion. They were simply providing public rape. No legal ambiguity, no room for interpretation, just forced sex in public.

# CHAPTER 53

One of our fellow spectators was getting up to walk from his seat down to the stage area, taking off his jacket, stretching his arms, stretching his neck, stretching his shoulders as he went. He had just finished chatting with his buddy, looking slightly nervous about what was to come, as if it were his turn at bat. His cohorts were giving him words of encouragement. "You've got this, ol' boy." "C'mon, chief." "Out of the park." "Tallyho." Pep talk as he took the plate. "Contact, buddy." This guy, now jacketless, walked over to the wooden trunk and opened it. From there he picked out a hatchet, upon which there was a surge of laughter and applause—everyone in the room getting giddy.

"You can't . . ." I started to say to the usher.

Can't what, Adam? Are you really gonna dispute this shit? If you run crying to the main lobby, the usher signals the bodyguards to have most of your bones broken within seconds. There was another wooden door by the fireplace, a smaller one—maybe they'd stashed an entire army of guys back there. Who knows? You have no idea how many additional guards could come after you, man.

". . . You can't . . . uh . . . surpass this, my friend," I said to him, smiling, trying to sound as awed as I could. "Can't be surpassed. Magnificent work."

The jacketless man put the hatchet down and picked up a knife instead, as he continued browsing through the tools. The girl remained as she was when I first entered: mortified. But it was a growing mortification. The trunk had several items inside and as he reached for each one, some guys booed, wanting the hatchet, and some guys cheered, wanting something new. He'd held the knife for a few seconds, then traded it for a whip, then fingered a leather belt, then showed the girl he was now considering a grappling hook, then a net. The girl backed away. He showed the grappling hook to the crowd. The girl ran from him as far as she could go until her chain yanked taut, snapping her at the neck, at which point the crowd cheered louder than ever. This was when the red-haired guy entered the room. *The* red-haired guy. Coming in unnoticed by the other spectators. He moved minimally. He swirled the ice in his drink minimally as he watched the jacketless man, who'd picked up a set of metal claws meant to resemble animal paws, get into position. The red-haired guy then made his way to the railing at the perimeter to watch from the shadows, where he remained unnoticed by everyone else in the room except me.

Except me and the usher, who was noticing me notice him.

"Indulge me if you will," I said to the usher. "You spoke of the . . . the ultimate expression of civilization, yes? So if I'm hearing you correctly . . . and if I'm observing the topology of it . . . this window was built to funnel the screams of the young lady almost like an orchestral horn, sculpting them into a musical cord . . . which . . . allows . . . *fosters* . . . the plangent . . . Let's say plangent . . . cry of submission . . . And when this cry is channeled through a . . . Let's call it a technological feat of man . . . it in effect . . ." The jacketless man tossed the pair of claws to the girl, apparently for her to wear. She hadn't lost consciousness. She stayed where she fell on the floor, with a massive window full of unwitting tourists as the backdrop to the scene, as the claws landed on her midsection. I wish I were back on that motorcycle. The crowd started to yell at her to pick up the claws. To get into the fight. She couldn't move. The people outside the window kept passing by with no clue what they were merely inches from. I would've swerved head-on into the Paris traffic and just ended things cleanly. "Are you then suggesting," I continued to say to the usher, "that our greatest collective accomplishment is to *color* the anguish of humanity? With the expression of music? Is that what da Vinci is suggesting?"

"Da Vinci," he said, as if I'd broached his most beloved yet vexing, controversial topic, coming closer to me to tell me what he could. "First of all, I'm one of the few men who's ever looked Morgan da Vinci in the eye and knew to whom I was speaking. Everyone else on earth partakes of an illusion. They've imagined him as an insidious set of muscles, blessed with a fist like Theseus and-and-and-and a *swamp* of ink for a soul. In reality, Morgan is as ordinary as you or I. He's the cooperative man you talk to at a bus stop, who stands next to you in line, who shops, and strolls, then goes home and cuts open a beauty queen."

He searched for a response in me.

He laughed.

"Or maybe I tease you, yes?" he said, as a pleasant expression crossed his face, as I'd definitely bitten into his appetizer. "No, you're missing the intention. It's something much more pragmatic. One needn't traverse the mountains of technology or spirituality to mine the precious stones of which Morgan da Vinci speaks."

The girl put one of the claws on. The guys cheered. The jacketless man started to shift back and forth on his feet, dancing like a boxer circling another boxer, the spectacle looking absurd—with the girl just standing there, cowering on her leash, having zero chance of fighting.

"In this small room we have sixty-three percent of the most powerful men in Europe. They are the hammer with which nations shall themselves shape. Now, I ask you . . . the male desire to destroy . . . Can you really allow the *intrinsic* male desire to destroy to remain unchecked in a group this influential?"

I glanced back at the red-headed guy. My options of escape were limited. If he was the grand master, it made no sense why he'd summon me back here. To intimidate Katarina? To let Katarina know what he was capable of?

"No," I replied.

"No," said the usher.

To bait her?

"You cannot allow it, my friend," he continued as the jacketless man started twirling the hook over his head in a circle. "Men *need* to brutalize women. It is our most fundamental sexual desire. In all of us. Young. Old. Rich. Poor. Anglo. Moor. We want to strike them down. Bleed them. Choke them. Not *permanently*. No. No, no, no, what we crave is that fairy-tale fracture of the time continuum wherein we do all that we wish—be you Zeus, be you Jesus, fingers curled upon the neck of Mary Magdalene—defying the laws of entropy itself—and have it instantly restored to normal in the embers of our aftermath." The jacketless man swung toward the girl's leg, letting the hook fly freely to snare his prey. "Herein, we have created a catharsis. For, without this outlet of expression, eighteen trillion dollars of power goes unchecked."

The hook snagged her flesh. "Unnnghhhaaaagghhhh!" The girl howled in pain as the jacketless man yanked that hook upward so its prongs dug into the front of her shin meat. "Nnnggggahhhhh!"

I couldn't help but watch for the invisible sound waves as if I could see that scream radiate toward the window instrument, which then channeled that sound through its small, flutelike opening so that the pedestrians heard something. You could see them hear something—a few of them looking toward us in baffled delight, some of them beginning to take pictures of that window. Selfies with it. Videos of it. The jacketless man pried the hook off the girl, then undid his pants—the arousal evident.

"Please," said the girl, making her one desperate plea, squinting into the spotlights at us. "Please, my name is Lily Volkova, please help me if you can do anything. Please, God!"

The crowd cheered. They cheered loud enough to drown her out as she tried to futilely talk over them, motivating the usher to talk louder as well. "Sex is not 'one' of our fundamental human needs; it is *the* need. Every other impulse we have is self-preservation. Sex is the only desire that's self*less*, the only means by which we offer part of ourselves, our seed, as a gift back to civilization." To whatever degree the girl had been contending, she gave up entirely. Despair. Frustration. Pain. The jacketless man grabbed her by the hair and held her head upright against the glass, as she offered no resistance. "Mainstream media has lied, my friend. Copulation is not an act of love." I looked over at the red-haired guy. "It's an act of war. A war against erosion."

I looked back at the usher.

If you're gonna go down, you might as well go down swinging.

I marched forward into the light, onto the stage, directly toward the treasure chest to grab the hatchet—the crowd cheering upon seeing my intrusion—as I moved the jacketless man aside, who didn't protest, being both shocked and exhilarated by my presence—in fact, giving me a fraternal nod—for all he knew, it officially wasn't his turn anymore, as indeed nothing in here seemed scripted—and the crowd got even louder as I then marched directly toward the girl, who saw me coming, saw the blade of the axe in my hand, saw the look in my eye, and froze as I stood right over her, towering above her upper body while she cowered against the glass. I'd lined up a trajectory that she had to believe would split her forehead wide open and put her out of her misery, and I raised the weapon high enough over my head to generate as much force as I could possibly deliver.

# CHAPTER 54

I swung the blade down directly into the glass—five-inches to the right, three inches north, about six inches total from the top of her tender head—into the window, into the slight concave area, into what I estimated would be the weakest structural point of the pane. And that blade hit its mark fucking dead-fucking-on-target.

And cracked nothing.

"Nooooooo!" the girl screamed.

She screamed so hard and uncontrollably, you'd think I actually split her skull clean open. The crowd roared with applause, having no idea that I *didn't* touch her. With my back to the majority of them, no one in the room could see that my eyes never locked on the girl or any part of her. Everybody thought I'd missed her, or that maybe I wanted to scare her first, to intimidate her with my physical might. I wasn't paying attention to these men. I just wanted the hatchet to crack the glass the next time I hit it, and after I ever-so-briefly fingered the nick above her head, sizing the depth, noting the angle, I hauled back and swung the whole thing again, this time with more desperation, aiming to hit the same gash again, same spot—the girl screaming rabidly, the tourists outside hearing it all as pure music.

Wham—coming within millimeters of the initial gouge, splintering part of the window into a light dust.

With no crack.

The horizontal dome was freakishly thick, built not only to secure the sounds of the interior but to withstand, who knows, an errant pedestrian, some drunkard punching it, a stray car? Bulletproof? I swung a third time, even harder—insanely hard. I thought the bones in my hand would break I hit the damn thing so hard. The crowd cheered again but a few of them were starting to grow unsure as to whether or not I'd actually *missed* this girl. "He's cracking the glass!" someone shouted. The girl had slumped down, believing her life had already ended, crying, gushing tears. I hit it again. I hit it again. I hit it again. More and more guys started to feel the potential of the glass cracking as I checked my target for a fifth impact. They had to know the odds of me rupturing their sacred membrane were zero—I'd known it after my first contact—but, c'mon, you pit your theory-based confidence against the real-world prospect of you as a billionaire potentially getting caught?! Caught for a broken window leading to your organized-rape session?!

Pandemonium began behind me.

In stages.

At first it was one or two guys. "Security! SECURITY!" I swung again, hitting with precision again. Then all hell broke loose—the collision course between two desperate forces. Men who had everything to lose, leaving. Men hired to protect those men, trying to enter. The wealthy elite couldn't get out fast enough and the bouncers beyond the door couldn't get in to save them, bottlenecking at the small entrance. Some of them saw the maniacal look in my face and none wanted to be the *one* guy to come get me, to risk injury for the sake of the rest of the group. They were fighting with each other to stampede out. I swung again, a sixth time, powdering the previous incision ever so slightly—the whole process, from first chop to now, taking maybe fifteen seconds to complete—just fifteen seconds for me to test their barrier, for me to foment what had blown up behind me. Anarchy.

For the first time I looked down at the girl. "Don't move," I said to her, as I adjusted my stance, looming directly over her.

She quivered just before I then let the hatchet sail down in her general direction.

To split her chain in two.

It succeeded thanks to pure adrenaline. She lay there wide eyed in confusion, looking at the undone tether, then sped off like an animal, in a crawl-sprint-stumble, through the rabbit-hole exit by the fireplace. Nobody was paying attention to her. The members of the Society were fleeing. Their bouncers were finally pushing through and they'd have me dead in under a minute. I'd originally wondered if it'd be the red-haired man or the usher who'd be the first to topple me but both of those gentlemen were the first to vanish.

I ran for the rabbit hole. I had to kick and kick to get the little door open because she'd shut it behind her, but I kicked hard enough and ducked through the hatch then ran through a series of turns where I found her scurrying ahead of me, stumbling to a stop when she saw me. I still had the hatchet in my hand so to her I must've looked like the Antichrist. She was cowering at the far end of the hall as I approached her, scooting herself backward, which put her in the arms of an elegantly dressed older lady, who began clutching the girl steadily in place. The house madame?

"Stop!" screamed the lady, directly at me. She had to be the madame.

I should have flung my axe into her face—a tomahawk—for having deployed *any* of her girls into this shit, not just the current one.

"Where's the exit?" I said to her.

They had to have a service entrance, where the slaves and maids entered from whatever cargo truck they came off of.

"Where's the exit?" I repeated.

I looked at the naked girl she had in her grip. Lily Volkova. I remembered her name. I went over to grab her. Lily. Dragging Lily. Dragging her with nearly zero compassion for the very life I was saving. *You fucking come! You come whether you like it or not!* It was unreal, the misplaced anger I felt. We could each hear the commotion in the distance—the voices down the hallway growing louder, growing in number. On the manhunt.

"Let's go," I whispered to Lily.

"HE'S HERE!" yelled the madame. "HE IS WITH ME HERE!"

Lily didn't budge and I gave up. I ran. I had no idea how to win. At any of this. I arrived at a T-junction—to the left was a large kitchen where I could see people bringing glassware to a washroom, to the right was nothing in particular. I ran right. I could see one lone guy remaining ahead of me. "She's got a bomb!" I shouted to him. "They fucking let the bitch back in and she has a bomb." I might as well yell the most confusing thing he could hear from me. He had to know about Katarina, right? He had to be on the lookout for Katarina. When he saw me running at him, he couldn't decide fast enough if my words were actua—

*Sklurge.* I sank the blade into his clavicle.

At a sixty-degree angle to the horizon, splitting open the marrow of his collar bone in a single slice, I swung well. I almost missed him entirely—such is the messy momentum of adrenaline. I should've hit him eighteen more times, one for each year of that girl's young life. I should've carved her initials in his neck. I scurried out through the next door in utter self-preservation, having no idea where this might lead me, walking directly to the middle of the tourist heart of Amsterdam—a street corner lined with clubs and bars—quickly slipping off my masquerade mask along with my bow tie, quickly becoming unremarkable to meld into the throng of rambunctious drinkers.

Go. Calmly. Walk, walk, walk. Go.

The route to the Oosterdok Hotel wasn't long but it wasn't simple either. I didn't hear police sirens in the distance. I listened. I didn't hear them. I had to cross through a lot of crowds, so I just kept going. The cops ride bicycles here and they ride fast. I'd grown terrified of the sound of sirens in the past three days. Prior to this week I'd never noticed them—someone else's problem—but now every sharp sound around me became police or police dogs or the shouts of a da Vinci bodyguard. I kept going southwest, directly toward the hotel, just wanting to get clear of the crowds. Yet what had I even accomplished back there? Was da Vinci even present? The red-haired guy at the bar—he stood out. He seemed like the most prominent person in the equation. The other guy, the one who laughed like Jordi Carreras—too flashy. I should've run to the lobby of the club and buried the axe into the red-haired guy's spine, almost like marking lumber for a future cut. Look for the man with the chipped vertebra. I didn't do that though, did I? I did nothing. So, congratulations, Adam, you now have no idea who da Vinci is and everyone in Europe is looking for you.

By the time I reached the driveway of our hotel, I almost wished his men *would've* caught me. I couldn't think straight—instead of entering the lobby, I walked around the block twice. I had no idea if this was the right way to elude someone, but I felt compelled to do something—the misfiring synapses of a man in over his head, a man in panic, still replaying the moment his axe bounced off a window, dwelling on the myriad of better ways he could've handled it, saved her. That girl's name was Lily. Nearly every alternative action I came up with now was more effective than what I'd actually done for Lily. I walked to the edge of the hotel's delivery entrance to get a look at the exterior of the room we booked for Nikos—second floor from the top, two windows over. I could see a light on but no other clues. Nothing felt secure about it. What should I expect up there? For all I knew, I could be entering a hotel suite full of policemen, guns drawn. Nikos could've demolished the room in an understandable rage. He could've beaten up Astral. Astral could've beaten him. She could've left with his kidney in a bucket of ice and I'd be walking in to find him lying in a bathtub, looking up at me, waiting for me to explain why I'd let him down, or I could be knocking on the door of an empty suite—everyone having fled the country.

I held the hatchet inside my jacket—I still had it—held there all bulky and awkward, as I entered the lobby. Whatever was about to happen up in that room, this time I was going to be the one to initiate it. Be first. The moment you see trouble, you be first to act. You swing without hesitation. You swing first. The elevator arrived on my floor. I walked out. I arrived at my door. I listened. I knocked. I listened. I waited. I heard footsteps inside. I gripped the hatchet.

# CHAPTER 55

I watched the peephole go from light to dark then light again, then I heard the latch click. I readjusted my grip on the hatchet, clutching it just inside the front of my jacket, feeling my heart rate triple as I saw the door open.

Katarina. Once again she was standing in front of me. Blankly staring at what was in front of her. Ingesting my general appearance. She didn't say anything for a moment, likely taken aback by the fact that now *I* was the one whose hands were covered in blood—blood on my collar, blood on my lapel, blood on my shirt, bloody-red dampness on my pants. I'd caught sight of myself in the hallway mirror—I looked disturbing. She slowly led me into the suite, never once taking her eyes off me as she brought us to a standstill basically in the middle of the room.

We were alone.

"Where's . . . uh . . .?" I started to say, looking around, not seeing anyone, not seeing Nikos.

There were trash bags in the corner. Food had been ordered, the bed was slept in. Other than that, there was no sign of anyone else besides Katarina.

"Where's Nikos?" I said to her. "Or Astral?"

"Astral can't stay out of her house for very long. She has to sleep there each night."

"Where's Nikos?"

"I don't know."

"You don't *know*?"

"We should, uh . . ." She pointed to my jacket.

"You don't know where he is?!"

"Your shoulder."

"He was with her! With Astral! A girl who *told* me you don't trust her. You yourself said you can't rely on her."

"Astral wouldn't hurt him. You should sit down." She was trying to get me to sit on the bed. "Your shoulder."

"He trusted me. Maybe you don't understand what that means but I feel an obligation to him." We pulled my jacket off.

My upper body was covered in blood. Drenched. I felt no wound but since most of it came from under my jacket, I was beginning to realize it might not be just the blood of a bodyguard. It might be mine.

"Is it bad?" I said.

She'd begun examining me, moving her head around to get the best lighting from the dim, moody lamps. She had me sit on the edge of the armchair. Nothing about the room felt right—the lines of the interior looked distorted, the colors felt surreal, the horizon felt tilted. It was her, Katarina, the way she was looking at me—that's what made it all so different. Her bizarre disposition transformed the details around me, the way an imploding star might bend gravity around itself, warping every view in the vicinity.

She wasn't asking me the key question.

"Aren't you wondering?" I said to her.

"Wondering what?"

"If I met who we needed to meet."

She didn't seem anxious to know. She took her time before formally asking the question, doing so more out of protocol than anything else. "Did you meet Morgan da Vinci?"

I wasn't going to lie but I was going to hold part of it back. I'd already contemplated doing this on the walk over here. I wasn't sure when I'd see her again but seeing her now, I knew my initial suspicion could be considered a real possibility—that, yes, she could be setting me up. Here. In this room. How did she get herself inside? To the hotel? How could she evade the Dutch police?

"I don't know what I found," I said to her. "I got escorted away from one particular guy. He was at the bar."

I looked up at her to discover that she was pointing to my shirt sleeve. She meant for me to unbutton my cuff. There were two main reasons to proceed cautiously around her. One, as soon as she had what she needed from me, I'd be expendable to her. Two, having seen what these men were capable of, I couldn't in good conscience *help* her get back to them. Christ, that'd be profoundly irresponsible of me—not to recognize that an abused woman could form a pathological need to be in the presence of her abuser.

"And you?" I said. "Were you arrested? I saw your face on the news."

"They detained me."

"Did you escape?"

"No."

"Is Haimovna your real name? How did you escape?"

"The police received additional footage that showed it was self-defense." She helped me slip half the shirt partway down my right arm, letting herself get close enough to where I could feel her breath on the back of my neck.

"Who did you fight?"

"One of the two men in the car."

"Is Haimovna your real name?"

"Haimovna was a Russian girl who tried to assassinate Lenin."

"Lenin?"

"Was he European?"

"Sorry?"

"The man you met at the bar. Was he European?"

"I overheard him bragging to some girl. You can't bank on what a guy brags about to a girl but I think he might've been an architect of it."

"What did he look like?"

"Reddish beard. Early forties. Tall."

"His voice is high?"

"Slight accent. A high voice, yeah."

"What did he say?"

"He described something about republic and swan. I didn't hear much. Do you know who he is? I got escorted away from him. He was bragging about building something, I think. I don't know. Is he an actual architect?"

It didn't feel safe, any of this. Her explanation of the new video footage seemed too simple. She took my hand and led us to the bathroom. She had me lean forward against the rim of the counter, then picked up a small towel and got it wet under the faucet. "He was in Paris," she said. "He was on the rooftop terrace. I didn't know he was an architect." She kept making eye contact with me in the mirror, lingering a moment longer than what felt right as she began putting the towel against my wound, lightly but directly, which hit my tissue like a sledgehammer. She was different around me. She dabbed the area one last time, then, with the blood cleared, took a better look. "There's a piece of metal in you."

She walked back out to the living room to go to the minifridge, opened the door, got one of the vodka bottles, a Carbonadi, opened the ice bucket, took out the ice tongs, then pointed to the bed, wanting me to go to it. I hesitated at first, then sat on the corner. Again, she looked at me for a while. She unscrewed the cap from the bottle, then started dousing the tongs with the Carbonadi, then walked over to the edge of the bed, soon standing close enough to me that her bare leg was up against mine as she inspected the rest of my wound. To access it better she shifted herself onto the bed so that she could kneel there behind me, taking a moment to adjust herself until she seemed ready for what she was about to do.

"This will hurt," she said.

# CHAPTER 56

When even just two-percent of you wonders if someone is about to end your life, the rest of you becomes very effective at intensifying that suspicion regardless of how rational the other ninety-eight percent of you stays.

"I think I'd . . . uh . . . rather just let the wound . . ."

"Breathe deep," she said.

She got herself in better position, kneeling even closer to me, placing her hand on my neck to keep me still, then, without any additional discussion, did the thing.

"GhhhhhaaaAAAAaaaaa."

She fucking did it, as I yelled my ass off, as she continued to demolish my shoulder in what was merely her first of several forays, making me contort in utter agony as she dug the teeth of the tool deep into the most sensitive, broken tissue imaginable, continuing and continuing and continuing the ungodly excavation, doing it much longer than I thought I could withstand—every stroke, the bite of a carnivore dragging its canines across bone. I knew she was being as gentle as she could. I knew it. I saw the smooth stroke of her arm. Her cautious, delicate focus. Yet at the same time, I was about to lose consciousness.

"Breathe," she said.

Teetering on my last connection to reality.

"Breathe!"

I breathed.

"It'll end soon," she said in the midst of the tumult. "You're doing well, okay? I'm just working on one last part, okay? Breathe."

I think I forgot what joy felt like. I was millimeters away from the most exquisite female I'd ever seen and nothing about this intimacy or the life I led felt joyful. I let my eyes stay shut. This is what sleep deprivation leads to—an eternally foul mood. You can't get happy. You can't even picture what happy looks like.

"Stay still," she said.

She did one last excavation—digging and digging—and found whatever shouldn't have been in me, dragging it from the clutches of my inflammation. It hurt like pure hell—wickedly enough to make the room spin, and then, possibly done, she got up to get a towel and held that towel against me, securing it by using the belt from a bath robe. A makeshift bandage. A makeshift adulthood. She was done.

"Try to stay still, okay?"

"Okay," I said.

"I mean it."

"I'm sorry."

"Sorry?"

"Yeah."

"Stay still. For what?"

"I'm truly sorry."

"For what?"

"For everything. For your past, for your present, for what's to come, whatever's to come. I'm absolutely sorry." The admission came out of nowhere, the byproduct of what the club had pounded out of me. "I'm not sure if I'll see you after all this is done but I want you to know . . . I want you to know . . . I have genuine admiration of you." I'd peered into her world. I knew I had to help her but I was also riding a tidal wave of emotion, channeled entirely toward a bizarre direction that couldn't have been what she wanted to hear from me. "I'm not naive in that . . . uh . . . I'm not naive enough to think . . . that we're . . ."

She kissed me.

Her face met mine with the softest, warmest, most feminine lips imaginable—beyond imaginable. The curvature of her mouth was—I couldn't describe it. The canvas of a masterpiece. I kissed her back, wholly. I held her close despite how painful it'd been to even raise my arm—with so much of the trauma anesthetized by this singular human contact in a rush that drenched each part of me, with her hands slowly sliding across the back of my neck and her kisses becoming additional kisses, until she eventually separated her mouth from mine but only far enough for us to share a breath. My mind surged with both pleasure and a refusal to believe that it was me who would, could, did ignite something in her. Me? Impossible. She'd had such dark days—one after another, thousands—that when she arrived at this night, she merely found something innocent in me. That had to be why. We were two people destined to remain apart. Because this was temporary. This. Here. This bed. This woman. I knew it already. Deep down, with a sinking feeling, I knew I'd soon lose her.

"*T'es ma rêve*," I said to her.

I closed my eyes.

I opened my eyes.

It was morning.

I'd fallen asleep and woken up—several hours elapsing within a blink. The sun rises in this part of the world at 5:30 a.m. I could see a sliver of dawn through the window, but I couldn't tell whether the daylight was new or old. With black-out drapes you never quite know what part of the clock you're on. It was the sting in my shoulder that partially woke me up. The absence of anyone next to me in bed was what fully roused me.

I looked around in the darkness.

"Are you . . .? Are you in here?" I said.

The bed sheets felt damp against my skin. The first sign of the severity of my fever, along with the mental scramble of not quite knowing your own history. Dreams? I'd just dreamed these events, right? No. Was it all just . . .? Was what happened just a . . .? After a strenuous mental effort I began to understand that I'd already woken up once this very same morning, in this exact same bed. Once. Not long ago. An hour ago? I'd woken up in this room. In this bed. After being with Katarina? Maybe it was the middle of the night—when I saw the table lamp on—when I saw Katarina at the table occupied with something in front of her—her hands moving busily. It didn't make sense at the time—the entire episode had been dismissed by my consciousness as I fell back asleep within seconds, drifting off for at least several hours, to wake up now, seeing that her shoes were gone. Shit. I remembered her shoes being on the floor earlier. Right there. Her socks too. Right there. Katarina was gone.

And yet I could hear someone moving inside the darkness of the suite.

"Is that you?" I whispered into the void.

I waited.

I heard someone's breath being drawn in, I swear I did. I'd been in this situation before. The past few days had proven to me that worst-possible scenarios are often quite possible and quite the worst. I heard someone's hand fiddling with a switch—the distinct sound of fingers on metal. I was fresh out of tactics. If someone intended to kill me now, they'd picked the ideal moment. The lamp came on—the entire room flared up with illumination. I sat forward in the bed, now able to see the details of my surroundings, now able to see that Jenn was in here with me.

# CHAPTER 57

"I don't even know where to begin." Those were the first words Jennifer Graham uttered, startling me badly enough to make me cry out.

"JESUS CHRIST!"

She remained leaning against the dresser with her arms folded while I yelled and then began to collect my breath.

"Jesus Christ," I repeated. "Jesus Christ . . . You scared the shit out of me. You . . . uh . . . I . . . I . . . I didn't hear you come in."

She hadn't moved.

"How long . . . have . . . you . . .?" I couldn't finish the thought.

She hadn't moved an inch.

"Right," I said.

"First of all, are you okay?"

My body felt problematically hot, bathed in a cold sweat and swamped in a fog of uncertainty. This was the physiological chaos that began the most surreal morning of my life. "Yeah. I mean, uh . . . uh . . . I mean . . . What do you mean?"

"Are you medically okay? Do you need a doctor?"

"No."

"No."

"Why?"

"Because I'm about to slap the shit out of you and I want to make sure you're okay before I do it."

"You're upset."

I wasn't sure how she could know anything about my situation, about what I'd been through, seen, done, or what happened with Katarina.

"You don't need to be upset, Jenn. There's—"

"You're in here under *my* name, in a room under *my* name, as a fugitive under *my* name!"

"It's really—"

"JUST SO YOU CAN BAG SOME UNDERFED SKANK!"

"No, I—"

"You lied to me!"

"No—"

"You gamed me! You did! So when you say, 'Don't be upset, Jenn, there's no need to be upset, Jenn,' what you really mean is 'My God, this woman in front of me is miraculously calm for someone who has the legal right to castrate me with a hammer.'"

"I'm sorry about the room—"

"I DON'T CARE ABOUT THE ROOM! It's not about the room! Look at you! What is going *on* with you?!" She'd come all the way over to the side of the bed. "Lying there all strung out on some bus wreck of a girl, dragging your career through the sewer while you get yourself sick in a foreign country that you're not even supposed to be in."

I strained to get up, making the monumental effort to do so despite having zero strength to fend off gravity. "Where is she?"

"You have a *real* fever, Adam!"

"Trust me, I can explain everything, but right now—Did you see her leave?" The fever. She was right—felt like a volcano bubbling forth from my torso, through my head, scorching my brain. Sitting upright in bed doubled it. I looked around. I'd dreamed they were both in this room together, Katarina and Jenn. The sight of both of them—it felt tangible. In fact, I had to convince myself I wasn't *still* witnessing it—the fever having gone to work with a slow boil of my cortex. "Last night I updated Katarina on some details I'd seen and then we . . . I think she's heading into a severe situation . . . which I know isn't your . . . You need to understand she's . . . different. She's shown me a reality. It's brutal and powerful. *She's* powerful. She's . . . like . . ."

"Wow."

"Yeah."

"I never thought I'd see it."

"Yeah."

"The day you'd just shit out your dignity in a bowl."

"The—?"

"It's like you're the cliché of the cliché. As far as you having any hope of—Oh my God, your arm!"

The blood had drenched through the pillowcase bandage, which was now hanging halfway off my body so that we both now had a direct look at the infected region of my shoulder. She saw it. I saw it. We were gaping at the crusted yellow and blazing pink of it.

Her tone shifted instantly. "Oh my God . . . Oh God . . . Okay . . . Lie back . . ."

I slumped down onto the bed, feeling the room still move even after I'd arrived at a standstill. The act of sitting up had churned a vortex of liquid vertigo in me and I was pinned back to the mattress as the fatigue renewed itself. My eyes fell shut for what felt like eighteen dreams in three minutes. I saw Jenn rinsing a hand towel in the bathroom. I saw the hotel balcony. I saw illogical events blending together from different days and people, and when I opened those same unreliable eyes of mine,

Jenn was reentering the room carrying a small pharmaceutical bag. She'd exited the hotel and returned before I could comprehend any absence. She made me take the first dose—two pills along with some water.

"Drink," she said.

"What happened to . . . to . . .?"

"Drink. You're dehydrated. If you don't get enough water, you'll slip unconscious. You should be in a hospital but that's not an option for you because, congratulations, you aren't legally allowed to leave France."

"Where's . . .?"

I couldn't think of her name for a moment.

"Katarina?" said Jenn.

"Where is she?"

"She's not here."

"She's . . .? Where is she? What time is it?"

I heard the two of them talking, I swear to God. I witnessed every word they said. I began to see it again, relive it again, their conversation, trying to reassemble the memories in a sequence, like stitching a quilt. It was in the entranceway. Ten minutes ago? Just before I woke up. Katarina returned after Jenn had arrived. Right? Katarina left the room to buy something at a store, then returned with a plastic bag of maybe groceries, maybe something else, and she was set to leave again but she was arguing with Jenn about getting her stuff out of the room. You can imagine how confusing this was. In my state. The two of them arguing near the front door, out of sight from the bed, contesting the practical aspect of whether Katarina was allowed anywhere near me. "It's just to get what is mine," she said, pointing to her tote bag on the table. I could see a black cocktail dress draped over the chair next to a pair of glossy pumps. "No," said Jenn. "The room's in *my* name." Katarina kept asking for it, kept criticizing her: "I don't expect you to understand. You play by their rules." Jenn kept stating her side of it: "That's right, I play by their rules. That's the only way to change the game." I craned my neck to peer down the hall. I couldn't see much except that Katarina had that grocery bag. They argued some more, then finally agreed on something, some kind of compromise, then I heard Jenn approaching me. I was trying as hard as I could to stay coherent. You can't imagine how nauseous this feels—the walls actually bending inward on you. Katarina would be operating on incomplete information to do whatever she was about to do, bad information, from me, from my deliberate omission of what happened in the rape room—regarding the victims, regarding the hatchet.

I had to stop her.

I'd doomed her.

I started to drag myself out of bed, having heard the front door click shut. I only had a matter of seconds before she left the building. "We're following her," I said to Jenn, having mustered the determination.

"Following . . .?"

"C'mon."

"Following who?"

"Before she gets to the elevator."

"Who?"

"We gotta stop her." I was starting to get up. I'd found enough resolve. I pulled my legs across the edge of the bed and planted my feet on the floor, psyching myself up for the upcoming chase.

"Who are you talking about?"

"*Katarina.*"

"What?"

"Let's go—"

"Adam!" My sense of time had been completely eradicated. "Katarina left way before I ever got here. She left *yesterday.*"

# CHAPTER 58

Jenn had come to the side of the mattress to physically block me from getting up. "You need to stay down."

"She left yesterday? How long ago? I have to find her. How long ago was yesterday?" I sat up, tried to get up, then nearly stumbled as I took my first step on the carpet.

"Adam."

"Yeah, I know."

"You need to lie down."

"I know. What do you have on you? You must have an official conference guide." I pointed to her purse. "With keynote speakers."

"Huh?"

"Do you have a brochure for the event?"

She'd blocked me from getting to my feet, which, based on my state, didn't take much. "I know you need me to be supportive and that's what I'm doing but I'm gonna be honest with you and tell you that some random girl whose skill is *to get inside men's heads* has gotten into yours—"

"No."

"And now you're—Let me finish—You're refusing to believe you've lost objectivity."

"Can I see your brochure?" I pointed to her purse. "They have the profile pics. If I can glance through the pics, I can—"

She held her purse away from me.

"Seriously?" I said to her. "Seriously?!"

This wouldn't come cheap.

I was going to have to negotiate with her.

So, I told the entire story, start to finish.

"Okay . . ."

Against my better judgment I told Jennifer Graham everything I could, summarizing from day one, hour one, everything that'd happened, omitting only a handful of tangential details, definitely omitting what happened in this bed earlier, but providing a clear sense of just how convoluted the situation had become, including a description of what I *hadn't* told Katarina—which was how the usher had dealt with me. My whole story took twelve minutes to tell, twelve minutes I hated to waste but Jenn wouldn't budge without it.

"And so now I need a brochure of some sort because if I can identify this tall, red haired, high-pitched forty-ish-year-old man, I can predict where she's going next."

She'd listened patiently. She took a little longer to self-deliberate than I anticipated but that was a credit to how much respect she showed someone else's point of view.

"Look . . ." she said. "I get that she went through a lot at an early age, I get it. It's worse than I can ever imagine, I myself live a privileged life, and I can't imagine how hard hers was. Yes, I get it, but right now you are being *used*. This girl is *using* you."

"I *agree*. Fuck. I'm not saying she's *not* using me. I agree I'm getting played. But I don't think that's a moral lapse on my part. She's in a bad situation and I can get her out."

"She's not being honest with you and you don't even know what that situation is. *She burned a man alive—*"

"We don't know that."

"Oh, we know the cops think *you* did it."

"Are you going to give me the brochure?"

"No."

"You don't believe me?! You really after all these years think I would make this shit up? I mean, if we—"

"He's not listed."

"—can't—What?"

She nodded.

"Who's not listed?"

"The man you're talking about," said Jenn. "His name is Hans Schering. He's not listed."

"The . . .?"

"Hans Schering, whom you described, is not in the banking industry."

"You *know* him?"

"He's a commercial architect who has residence here. Amsterdam. Yes, I know him. I'm the one who coordinates the entire earth, remember? Yes, I can probably find his address in the directory. No, I don't want to because, no, I don't believe our bank sends top executives to some dark, secret dungeon to drink goblets of blood. You spent an *entire day on psychedelic drugs* and now you're fighting an infection and feverish. You're not hot on the trail of some evil mastermind. So, if I help you at all, *if at all*, it's because you're going to *warn* Hans not to touch any psychopath hookers today. For all our sakes, understood? A warning. Understood?"

"A warning. Understood."

# CHAPTER 59

According to the company conference directory, Hans Schering lived in a condo sky-rise at the edge of the main river in the city. How long it might take Katarina to obtain this same address on her own was unknown to me. I downed three glasses of water, threw up once, ate half a banana, then forced—I mean *forced*—myself with excruciating, agonizing, dizzying effort to walk out the door of the suite.

"Tell me what you used my employee card for," said Jenn.

"Why?"

"I'm asking."

"So you can, what, undermine my plan?"

"Maybe."

I could barely see straight. We'd gotten about halfway down the marina walkway. She pointed to the top of a building about three blocks over. "That's his place. Upper left."

The Markermeer Condominiums SkyRise was where we were heading. The top floor had a glass terrace that made the whole thing look even more elitist than it already was. Topiary bushes were visible next to a glass-bottom pool.

"I used your ID card to get my emails and receipts, to download them. I found memos related to deals where our sales team purchased escort girls for clients, notable clients, not just regular seven-figure assholes but name-brand assholes like Bryce Kerney and Sanjay Kraft or that one Brazilian dude with the forehead. When we closed certain large accounts, we closed 'em with prostitution."

"Emails."

"Emails."

"Really?"

"I mean . . . I'm aware it's not . . . formidable. But what if these people don't know that? What if I can bargain with them?"

"You'd need expense reports invoice-cross-referenced to prove anything to anyone who matters. But, back up, you're not trying to *blackmail* the mafia, are you?"

"I downloaded expenses too, but it was always to some vague European Spa, LLC, or whatever."

"You know you had *nothing* to do with our team's bad behavior."

"I was indirectly involved—"

"You were just doing as you were told without being made aware of the extent of the gray area."

"I thought you were gonna undermine my plan."

She kept walking. She looked lost in thought. "I don't have to undermine it. I'm sure whatever you're about to say next will do that for me."

"Okay, then here. Morgan da Vinci uses the vulnerability of the Society to extort his members. That's it. Extortion. The Society isn't some sort of goal. It's simply the rhetoric that he gets everyone to believe in . . . to *cover up* the extortion. You participate and he turns around and holds it against you."

"No."

"Hubris. Yes, watch. Yes, it is. It'll be his own hubris that takes him down. A man with a God complex, right? Sooner or later, he's going to make a mistake."

"No."

"He will."

"Do you hear yourself? No. Even if any of this were true, you don't owe this girl jack shit."

"I gave her limited information. She's now acting on that limited information. I know it's hard to believe but I seriously can't morally walk away from this. She went up there." I pointed to the building up ahead of us. The top floor. The elite perch. "Maybe just now. Maybe in trouble. Maybe expecting me to do my share. Nothing she's experienced with these people has been anything but them trying to destroy her. Do you really imagine Hans is welcoming her in with open arms? I mean look at that place. Balconies. Tinted windows. Tell me that guy's not gonna—"

It exploded.

Right in front of us. Two blocks away. Louder than anything I'd ever heard, ever—Hans Schering's top-floor corner condo unit blasted outward in a thousand pieces.

# CHAPTER 60

Several tons of concussion pressure shattered the upper windows, spraying glass and debris far enough to hit the surrounding buildings in a half-block radius, followed a half second later by the sound of the explosion itself. First sight then sound—which is surreal, the lag time, like an old film playing out of sync—as the top corner of the place became its own gargantuan hole.

I sprinted toward it, right toward the Markermeer Condo tower, with Jenn pursuing me stride for stride, calling out to stop me.

"Adam . . .! Don't!"

My fever became irrelevant—the human body is quite capable of muting its inadequacies—as I ran past a dozen people who heard what we heard but had no idea it emanated fifteen floors directly above them. It was a massive condo complex with a massive lobby, which meant by the time I'd crossed through the interior of the ground floor to get to the elevator, Jenn had caught up to me with a hand outstretched to keep my elevator door from closing.

"I'm . . . I'm . . . going up," I said, panting.

"No." She got right in my face. She wasn't forceful now. She was desperate. "No . . . Right now . . . we leave. We leave the city."

"She could be up there."

"Then she's up there! Where she chose to be! And you!" She had to catch her breath too. "Listen . . . And you . . . you still have a choice." She gestured to the front door, our way back out of the lobby, as in the roof was not an option. "Don't be part of this."

I pressed the button again. Fifteenth floor.

She spoke faster, with more conviction. "There are other ways to handle this. There is a system and we believe in the system. We have friends who participate at the higher levels—lawyers, journalists—Listen—Listen! *God*—You know it works. Don't be irrational. Trust that I care about you and let's fucking go."

I had no intention of her winning this particular debate, but technology was about to win it for her. Right at that moment, the elevator override kicked in, the fluorescent lobby lights went dead, the emergency lights went on, the alarm sounded, and my lift was no longer functional. Its control panel blinked off and on, then went bright red. I pressed my button another twenty times in desperation. I could hear my father's laugh—the guy shaking his head in disdain—with a forecast that his son could never be counted on for anything, at any time, not even for a job as simple as going up an elevator. I punched the thing with my fist, then exited the car, brushing past Jenn, looking up to notice something much worse than any mechanical issue. Behind her on the far side of the lobby, a crowd had started to gather just outside the glass doors—everyone gawking upward as expected, but standing in that crowd, consulting with one of the police officers, and doing so with a disturbing amount of familiarity, was Hugo. The guy from the sedan. The cop was giving him information and in return he—Hugo—was pointing at details and giving the cop information. You could see firemen evacuating the lobby and herding people outside. It'd be a matter of seconds before Jenn and I were flushed out the front door into his view.

"Walk through the café," I said to her quietly.

"What?"

"Don't make eye contact with anyone. Don't look around. Just walk like everyone else is walking except we're gonna walk through the café."

"Why?"

"You win, okay? We leave. We leave very fast."

She saw my face, the seriousness in it. She obviously wouldn't know who Hugo was—never having seen him before—but she sensed a shift in me and immediately cooperated in full. Best friends can sense it—when your internal clock strikes a certain type of midnight. We both walked as inconspicuously as possible toward the café's interior doorway to pass through and exit through the opposite door out to the sidewalk. Hugo had his partner with him. There were two of them. We walked outside. There was a tram that'd stopped a half block away in the midst of unloading and loading passengers. We'd have a chance to catch it if we ran now, right now. I looked back at Hugo without being obvious about it.

These guys would have weapons, that much was guaranteed.

"Jenn?" I said.

He was looking right at us.

"Can you trust me on something?" I said.

Scared, alert, loyal, she nodded yes.

"Okay, this is gonna be hard."

# CHAPTER 61

O
ut came a gun and Hugo fired four excruciatingly quiet gunshots at us.

"Run to it," I yelled to Jenn.

Ffft. Ffft. Ffft. Ffft. She shrieked as the walls crackled around us. We sprinted through the back alley, running as hard as we could, praying the curvature of this bent corridor of concrete would help us disappear. The fire alarm outside was ultra-loud, easily obscuring the sound of the gunfire. Silencers don't actually silence much. They hollow out the sound. You learn that when you're being shot at with one. But there was only one other pedestrian besides us who reacted to it. The rest of the crowd was caught up in the awe of the explosion.

"The tram!" I yelled to Jenn.

We had to make it across the upcoming street to get around the corner of the building and put some serious cement between ourselves and the men behind us. We had to get on that tram. Two more shots came at us—again sounding distressingly innocent. We moved in unison, Jenn and I. I didn't tell her when to turn, we turned together. Then we turned together again, left. She stayed alongside me, matching my pace, mortally freaked out. I could see the anguish in her—her eyes agape, black with shock. My poor, lovely Jenn. Whereas I'd had my gradual introduction to this week's horror, she'd never in her life seen a gun in action, let alone been in the crosshairs of one. We hurried onto a bike path, to make use of the clearance—with Jenn starting to lose speed. I'd only now noticed she'd kicked off her heels. When? Running barefoot. Her purse gone, bag gone, jacket gone. I'd never seen her so scared. Yet there she was, alongside me, doing everything she could to keep up with me, only out here *for* me, *because* of me, literally endangering her own life based on *my* bad choices. It flooded me with that same crippling worst-possible-time emotion I'd had earlier, likely as a result of the fever but also from the physical tension between us, never having told her what I'd rehearsed in my head endlessly—*There's something I've always wanted to tell you, Jenn*—which I knew she'd resent me saying, resent me jeopardizing our friendship. Crack. Another shot. I didn't fear it anymore—the inevitable rejection. I just wanted her to know I loved her. I looked back at the guys chasing us. Behind them came a third guy on a bike, gaining on us rapidly. Here we go, I said to myself, praying they knew who I was at this point, praying they remembered what I'd done thus far.

"Gimme your sunglasses," I said to Jenn.

She didn't ask why. She handed them to me—both of us still sprinting full tilt, all out.

I stopped.

Dead in my tracks. I stopped. I turned around in the middle of the street—stood there, feet planted, holding up no gun whatsoever, pointing that no-gun directly at them. They saw it immediately—that a weapon was held in my hand, aimed confidently at the lead runner, who never considered I had a black pair of glasses in a clenched fist, never believed I was *banking* on him knowing there was no way in hell I'd do this unless I had an actual gun. Nobody's that fucking dumb. Hugo stumbled as soon as he saw it, tumbled and fell, remembering that one hundred percent of the times he'd gone up against me, namely in Paris, I'd intended to kill both him *and myself* in the act. The other guy ducked down clumsily and the third guy on the bike swerved into a parked car.

I turned and ran off.

My reputation bought us, what, an extra ten seconds to make the unseen turn ahead? I caught up with Jenn—who was hardly aware of what just happened—and hurried her into the crowd waiting at the tram stop. We frantically got on board the back, where we shoved our way into the thickest clump of passengers, tucking ourselves onto the far side of the bus. "Go, man," I said to the driver under my breath, Jenn standing in front of me, her face held downward. I could see tears welling up—she never cries. A few of the passengers noticed. Trams here don't have as many tourists as the sidewalks so it's all native Dutch on board and they're incredibly polite, but Jenn looked like she'd just met the devil. I peered through the back window, staring at the spot in the intersection where I expected to see Hugo emerge. Staring. Waiting. Whispering in my head to the driver, Go, man. Nearly fainting with dread.

Jenn's fist tightened on the scruff of my shirt. The traffic light in front of us hadn't turned green for us yet.

"Should I tell him?" I whispered to her.

"Who?"

"The driver."

"Tell him what?" She didn't look up. She didn't want anyone to see her face. "About them? No. *No.* His protocol might say turn off the ignition. Plus, we don't have tickets. No."

One stop. We could ride for one stop—that was all I could risk—which would put us at the edge of town near the marina. If we rode too long, these guys would check the tram route and wait for us at every stop until we got off, or they'd lose patience and board it and accept whatever collateral damage was incurred. I looked at the map above the door. *Think, man.* We needed a place to duck into and call the cops. We needed some area where we could stay out of view. Something. Somewhere. The next mark on the route was C. van Eesterenlaan, which would get us one canal over from the street called Borneokade, which would be down the wharf from—okay, there. There was a possibility—the Decadent Splash. "Okay, we take the first stop," I whispered to Jenn. "We go to a houseboat that might—"

Pchhssshhh. The driver finally released the trolley brake and the tram rolled forward. Out the back window, I could see the three guys just starting to arrive. *Go, man.* They couldn't know for sure we were on board but they definitely glanced at the tram as it started to pull away.

"Okay," whispered Jenn, agreeing.

Going to the Decadent Splash had its disadvantages—severe disadvantages—but we simply had to make it work. We could get in there, take cover, call the police, tell the police we'd seen three suspicious guys near the site of the explosion along with providing detailed descriptions of them. *But, c'mon, the houseboat? Really? Hiding someplace so obvious?* Yes, I told myself. Yes, it wouldn't be the *last* place Hugo would anticipate but it'd be close. We could tell the cops we heard Hugo shout something fanatically religious just before the explosion, just to buy us time. We could find a way.

"This one," I said to Jenn.

It took two minutes to get to the next stop. At twenty-five miles an hour, that netted a half mile, which was a distance that gave us enough time to scramble and hide from anyone chasing us on foot but not enough to stay on the run. We got off the tram and hurried through a park, then a playground, then an alley, then ended up near the wharf area where we could see Astral's address. Whether she was at home or not, I was going to go in—ready to crack the window on the front door with my elbow to undo the lock and find a phone and call the cops and just give up, just give the hell up. I already had my shirt sleeve folded back over my arm, padding my elbow for what was to come—Jenn following me without questioning any of it. We hurried up to the front porch, rang the bell a bunch of times just in case Astral was by the door, then, adrenaline gushing, wham, I kicked the thing open—I could hardly believe it worked—and we entered and hurried to search for a phone, looking through the shelves, the tables, the counters, the nook, the couch, never once seeing the guy who'd entered from the opposite door, who blindsided me with the chair he swung across my forehead.

# CHAPTER 62

Hugo. Within a split second of shattering the wood across me, he started punching my head, hitting me several solid times before reaching behind his jacket to grab a knife. I had my arms up over my face, bracing for the blade to come slicing into me, when Astral came over the back of him. She sprang from nowhere, holding a wool blanket, which she threw over his face, then pulled back to snap the cloth down taut—fiercely—on him, giving me a *fraction* of a second to contort sideways and drive upward at him, discovering that this guy had been reaching for a *gun*, not a knife. Both of his arms came up to fend off Astral's blanket. She already had a bloody nose from whatever happened before we got there, but she kept holding the hood over him like it was her only mission on earth. The rest was up to me—to lurch forward to grab his gun, to secure the upper half of the muzzle so that now he and I were both holding it, so I could bite his finger, my teeth into his bone, which he had no idea was coming.

He roared with pain, "*PUTAIN*," flailing his elbows and forearms and shaking Astral off himself so he could lunge for me.

The rest was a blur.

He and I wrestled for what felt like both an eternity and an instant.

Then we heard it click.

Both of us.

The gun.

Astral had the gun.

That stopped him. She had it aimed directly at his face—directly on his cheek, pushing it deep into him. "Don't move," she said. "Don't, or I change you."

Everything slowed down.

Capitalizing on this, she slowly scooted backward until she could get herself to her feet. "You need to hurry," she said to me, to us, to Jenn. "To the water."

I didn't know what that meant. Weren't we *on* the water? I looked over at Jenn. Jenn was on the floor, shell-shocked, never having seen anything like this and certainly never having seen it from me.

"*Go,*" said Astral, gesturing toward the rear of the houseboat.

I didn't know what she wanted us to do. I'd been sitting there in a daze. The water? I could see out to the street through the main window. The other two guys were on their way, running along the wharf toward us.

"You need to leave!" She had no patience for this hesitation in me. "You need to finish what she started!"

She was pointing to the window but pointing toward the top of it, where we could now see that past the distant rooftops, against the blue sky, there was a pillar of smoke on the horizon—the Markermeer Condo was burning—like a call to arms.

"Leave!" she said.

I swear to God, she had the look of a holy war on her face, now ready to do whatever was necessary to advance the cause. My emotions had me immobile. Astral had to kick my leg to snap me out of it, getting me moving toward the back door. She meant for us to let her take over the standoff. The men outside could be heard storming onto the dock end of the boat. I was in bad shape. I couldn't walk. Jenn stood up and lifted me by getting under my arm.

"Let's go," said Jenn.

Astral was watching the door intently, waiting for the right moment to open it, edging herself closer and closer to it with Hugo as her hostage. She was going to buy our escape as Jenn pulled me by the hand and we hurried out the rear of the houseboat to a deck where there was a small dinghy that had an outboard motor just strong enough to propel the two of us. She dragged my fading body onto it. Something was really wrong with me physically now, not just the fact that my arm wasn't functioning correctly. I was losing coherence. My eyesight was foggy. There was a dull buzz. Numbness. Nausea. Jenn yanked the pull rope and got the engine going. I could see the other two guys entering the far side of the house.

"Stay down," she said to me as she untied the boat. She got us positioned, then revved the motor.

Within seconds she was steering us toward the middle of the marina. We heard gunfire inside the houseboat. Three shots. Then we saw Hugo and his partners emerge onto the rear deck.

"Stay down!" yelled Jenn, trying to keep me out of their sight lines. CRACK, CRACK, CRACK. If we could cross the waterway to the opposite bank, they'd have no chance to track us, but how quickly could this motor get us out of their range? The hail of bullets came splashing across our wake, whizzing by, whizzing near the hull. I strained to see where these men were. I strained against the fever, the lack of blood, the blur, to see what chance we had of evading them, knowing how desperate my overall mission had become, knowing that Astral had just given her life, knowing that, no matter what, I absolutely couldn't let myself lose consciousness again, which was exactly what happened, because when I woke up I was in an entirely different country.

# CHAPTER 63

Belgium. At a speed of 140 kilometers per hour with Amsterdam in the rearview mirror, Jenn's rental car sped us out of the Netherlands, into Belgium, past Antwerp, past Ghent, and toward France with the goal of getting us back into Paris by the end of the day. I didn't know all this yet. I didn't know she'd used back-up credit cards and back-up ID cards that she'd kept in contingency, getting things done as resourcefully as ever. I'd remained sunken down in my seat, inert and feverish, sleeping for most of the ride except for when my eyes would drift open to witness the blur of the passing scenery. By the time I became fully coherent, we'd already hit the outskirts of Lille.

"You need to hydrate," said Jenn, feeling my forehead, then reaching to the backseat to get me a bottle of water.

I forced my eyes to focus on the road, to fend off the glare, so I could process the passing countryside.

"Drink," she said.

I drank. Sipping at first, then taking in half the liter, still feeling nauseous and weak, still beset by a profound unease. I had no idea what to do next. All I could think of was how right Katarina was about the opposition—not just in how relentless they were but their flagrant lack of morality.

"I thought we might've gotten stopped at the border," said Jenn. "I was gonna have you climb in the trunk. Seriously. In the trunk. Which would've been scary. But they were waving every car through, thank God." She pointed to our dashboard clock, calculating the timing. "We should be in Paris in about . . . maybe . . . maybe . . . two and a half hours."

I smiled at her, faintly, the best I could muster, trying to conjure up the energy to express my full gratitude to her, to make sure she knew she'd shown me an undeserved level of compassion. I took another sip of water. My mouth felt horrible—like the inside of someone else's sock.

"There's something I need to tell you," she said.

"Hhhmmhhhhhh."

She continued watching the road. "It won't be easy to hear."

"Hmmmmmh—kay." I could barely get my voice to work.

I waited.

She didn't say anything yet—whatever it was—letting additional scenery pass. I had to wonder if she'd just heard some kind of news report on the radio. She'd been listening to different news stations for most of the drive, mostly French-language stuff.

I worked up the strength to ask her if that's what she heard—some kind of bleak update. "Did any—?"

"You have to turn yourself in."

She sounded like she'd been waiting several hundred miles to say it.

"Okay?" she said.

I wasn't sure I heard her correctly. I had to look over at her.

"You have to turn yourself in," she repeated.

"To the . . .?"

"To the police. The Paris police, yes. There's no other way. I've ana-lyzed every, every, every angle—the laws for the Schengen Zone are inconsistent and highly punitive. We can't go to a hospital, we can't go to the UK, can't get you on a plane, we can't do anything except we have to go straight to Paris BRI."

"Listen—"

"If you don't do it preemptively, Adam, it'll look worse than it already is, and it already looks fucking *dismal*. You walk in, hands held up. I'll be next to you. I'll say fleeing the city was my idea. Paris. You present yourself to the city authority. You act as if you never left the country."

"Jenn, these cops aren't what you think."

"See, I knew you'd say that. No, you can't try to tell me that the entire French law enforcement is corrupt."

"Not corrupt. I'm saying the information given to them is never . . . the . . . They're being fed corrupt information."

"We drive to Paris, you walk into a precinct, you turn yourself in. This is to save your life."

"I have to find da Vinci—"

"*To save your life.* Da Vinci's the worst idea. Find him for what? You want to extort someone who's Russian mafia?"

"I don't know *how* exactly . . . to do it. Maybe I just need to get in front of him, maybe that's how it works. I sit down in front of him and I *feel out* what's next. These guys act like they're immortal behind their wall of PR, but at the end of the day they're human, with a human weakness. I'll find his weakness."

"You're deluded."

"I'm good at people."

"You're talking like a comic book, you and every guy your age, thinking you can be a legend, wanting to show up and battle some monster on a cliff based on unresolved childhood issues—"

"Are you seriously—?"

"How did she know I'd be at the airport?"

"What?"

"Katarina. How did she know?"

"How . . . did . . .?"

"You don't know. How was she able fly to you to Amsterdam?"

"We took a train."

"But how did she *know* about Amsterdam?"

"She was hanging out in a lobby full of drunk, babbling bankers. Our schedule was hardly a secret."

"And she could just *locate* our CEO there?"

"Everyone could *locate* our CEO there. Why're—?"

"How did she know you'd be at the airport?"

"The . . . Me? . . . I don't know."

I didn't know that one. Maybe from what I said at the sex shop? I hated how all this looked. None of it felt right anywhere outside my gut, with my gut telling me there was a chance Katarina had an effective plan and also that there was no way that plan liberated either of us.

"This whole thing doesn't terrify you, Adam? The inconsistency?"

"There's no incons—"

"You got 'let' into a billionaire club? Because you 'wore a mask'?!"

"I snuck in."

"You got *lured* in. They played you. They knew you'd lead to the girl."

"It's one or the other, Jenn. Either you believe I'm up against an ultramanipulative *genius* or you think I'm exaggerating the whole—"

"Neither. I want you to live in reality. Neither. Do the smart thing and turn yourself in and let me call some good-as-fuck lawyers and get you out of this, legally, properly, because your little playmate . . ."

Hi, hello . . . your boo . . . yes, blew up a condo. Blew it up. Hi." She pointed the radio. "They said someone snipped the gas line to his stove. Yes. With pliers. Flour in the air. From inside the unit. Her. 'She was going to his condo, your honor, to be one-on-one with someone she hated, your honor.' What did you *think* she'd do?"

"Talk. I don't know. Find out from him—"

"Talk?! To him?! Just go up and go, 'Hello, Person Who Contributed to My Daily Rape, let's talk.' Talk? No. No, you—No, deep down you *knew* she was on a crusade and you *let* yourself deny—"

"No."

"—that there's—She's hunting, Adam. It's a vendetta."

"I'm onto something. I'm close." I checked my pocket. "And when you get close, they fight back." It was there, my USB flash drive. "They wanna turn against me and accuse me of dirty shit I was never part of? *Fine.* Then I'm using that same dirty shit to prove them wrong in court. And, oh, if I happen to incriminate their asses while I'm at it, oh well."

"Which is it, Adam? Are you defending yourself or do you want a pound of flesh?"

"Great question. I don't know. I'm not the same guy from minute to minute. I'm a wreck. And that's exactly *why* I'm doing this. I'm not much of a man to begin with, Jenn."

"Oh my God, stop with that."

"You don't know how dark that voice is."

"I understand dark. I got a childhood too. Stop it. You're a good person. And now you have a grand total of two options. One, turn yourself in, come clean, take initiative, get exonerated. Two, get caught eventually anyway and be regarded in the eyes of the law as someone who's guilty of, at the very least, obstruction of justice and, at worst, the murder of—"

"I can't betray her—"

"You're not—!"

"I can't betray her!"

"WHY DOES IT MATTER?!"

"BECAUSE IT'S WORKING, JENN! BECAUSE HER MES-SAGE IS WORKING! CAN YOU UNDERSTAND THAT? It's not for revenge! It's in the name of Refusing to Back Down! That's her deal. And that's now my deal. Not anything about my dumbass dad. Not anything other than I look at all the ugly things I've been involved in from a basic happy hour to the corporate expense accounts, every little ugly contribution I made to the ugly machine and I see my role. Because if you can understand that, then you can understand that I owe her morally to help her do what she's doing, because as violent and sick and wrong as she is, she inspired little Astral back there. Did you see that? Little Astral's face? Teenage saving-my-life Astral? That. That meant something. That was the *beginning* of something."

Jenn was silent. We'd been going back and forth at the top of our lungs and ceased fire for a moment. She ceased. She never argued to win. She argued because she thought she was right, which wasn't the same as everyone else. It meant that the moment she thought she was wrong—bless her soul—she backed off. Instantly. Nobody else did that.

I spoke first. "Fine."

"Fine?"

"Fine."

"What is?"

"I'll turn myself in, Jenn. I'll walk into a Paris police station and offer full cooperation with their investigation until either their investigation is concluded or they see fit to do with me what's required by their law."

"You will?"

"Yes."

She looked over at me.

I didn't stutter. "On one condition . . ."

# CHAPTER 64

We were going to see Mathilde. We drove directly toward the north part of Paris to her home, located in what would be the first neighborhood we'd enter as we arrived in town, representing the last chance I had of delivering any kind of message to Katarina. If I were to abandon her cause, Katarina's, I needed to make sure she had fair warning from me. Jenn agreed. My terms were nonnegotiable, but I'd like to note that she understood the importance.

"How long do you think you'd need?" she asked.

"Four minutes, total. To tell her to tell Katarina I'm going to the cops. To tell her to tell Katarina I'm not going to tell anyone details but that Katarina should lay low regardless."

Finding Mathilde at her shop shouldn't have been a problem. Most places in Paris stay open on Saturdays, especially a store for sex toys, but at 5:00 p.m., as we drove past her window, La Radiance, the lights were completely off. I tried to peer through the glass door for signs of activity. None. I banged on the pane. Nothing. We proceeded to try the back-up option. Her apartment. We parked around the corner from it, tucking our rental car on the far side of the street next to a driveway—for extra clearance—across from an alley—for a second escape route if needed. I was being extra careful. I told Jenn to stay in the car and told her we couldn't properly anticipate how Mathilde would react—perhaps violently—perhaps she had hostile friends up there.

"Wrong," said Jenn. "You're not doing more stupid shit on your own. We're in this together." She unbuckled her seatbelt. "Honestly, I'm offended you'd ask."

Our vehicle was a decent little Citroën and had a bag of rudimentary tools in the back—no crowbar but it did contain a Phillips screwdriver. We walked a block to Mathilde's building, which had a big door that required an entry code. We waited for a random neighbor to exit, then rapidly passed him with a congenial *bonjour*, in order to get in without causing commotion, specifically without anyone calling the cops.

"Last thing you want to do on your way to the cops is get caught by the cops," I whispered to Jenn.

The latest pills had done their work—my fever subsided—but with this much medication, I was nearly delirious. We climbed the stairwell cautiously. I didn't want to use the elevator for fear the noise would somehow send Mathilde deeper into her burrow. I knocked on her door several times gently, then tried the bell, then tried a louder fist, then tried calling out her name, then felt slightly defeated, then sat back on the railing to rethink the whole thing. "I don't know. Maybe there's another way to send my message."

That was when Jenn tried the knob. "Uh . . . Adam . . ."

The door slowly swung open.

We looked at each other. I took a half step in. "Mathilde?" I said.

It occurred to me that Mathilde was probably the one who told Katarina that I'd be at the airport and what time I'd be there and that she probably was more integral in all that than I thought.

"Mathilde?" I called out.

Jenn joined me. "Hello?"

I clutched the screwdriver, keeping it held behind me like a dagger, ready to kneel and jab someone in the gut. That was my new tactic. Kneel, jab. Taking corners low. Attacking low. Never being predictable.

"Mathilde?" I whispered into the stillness.

We looked in the bedroom. We looked in the kitchen. The floorboards creaked as we moved.

"*Madame?*" said Jenn, calling out to announce us as a friendly presence. "*On est ici pour vous aider . . . Nous sommes des amies de Katarina . . . Êtes-vous ici? Madame?*"

We searched most of the place and saw nothing until the last room, which would be Mathilde's study. Floor-to-ceiling bookshelves surrounded a floor-to-ceiling window that overlooked the Moulin Rouge. When we opened the door to this room, we found ourselves eye level with her knees. Mathilde was hanging from the rafters.

# CHAPTER 65

I 'd never seen anything like it. Someone hanging from a noose. A suspended, stagnant body, slightly rotating, which was all I could fixate on at first—the nearly imperceptible rotation of her—as I stood there mortified by the implication of it all—with the bent angle of her neck both infuriating and repulsing me. The human body just doesn't deserve to be positioned this way.

Jenn pushed past me, stepping around the middle of the room to get in front of her, face-to-face, to make sure she didn't still have a chance. "*Madame?*"

The full picture wasn't apparent to me right away as I'd been too overwhelmed to catch every detail. Mathilde's hands were tied behind her back.

"*Madame?*" said Jenn again, lightly tapping Mathilde's leg. "*Madame?*"

"What're you doing?" I whispered.

"Just—" Jenn went ghostly pale. "Oh my God."

"What?"

"Oh my God. *Madame!*"

"What?"

"She's not dead."

She'd been roped from the rafters in such a way that her outstretched toes, when fully flexed, could actually contact the table and support her weight—not easily. It was the sick ingenuity of whoever put her here. I rushed over to help Jenn as she took immediate action, sliding a footstool to the center of the room.

"We need to work fast," she said, getting us into the position necessary to hoist her up so one of us could saw the noose off using the first thing we could think of. "A steak knife."

I held her legs while Jenn ran to the kitchen.

"Hold on, Mathilde," I said to her. "*On est ici. Vous êtes en sécurité.*"

We fumbled a bit but managed to help her through an effective descent, after which Jenn got on the phone for an ambulance. "It's one-nine, right?" she said. "For medical?" Then telling the operator as much as she could without telling too much.

Mathilde started to groan, which seemed more like a final spasm of neural activity than an indication she was living but Jenn had hope.

"*Vous allez bien,*" said Jenn, cradling Mathilde's upper half. "*Salut. Vous allez bien. Je m'apelle Jennifer.*"

Mathilde moaned again.

"Stay with us, okay?"

"*Aux . . .*" said Mathilde in a massive exertion of whatever she had left in her, producing the only sound she could.

"Mathilde?"

". . . *rrrmmm.*"

"Mathilde."

There was a last flutter in the eyes and then they went eerily still.

"What?" said Jenn. "What did you say? Stay awake, please!"

That was it.

They'd tortured her—they'd left just enough of a wooden perch for her to struggle to stand tall enough to keep the rope from cinching her neck shut. The toll it took must've been surreal as she fought not only the fatigue of the calf muscles and legs but the sheer erosion of will. The room was in disarray—the table was damp with sweat, marred with nail scratches, books and papers were everywhere on the floor—indicating she'd fought hard.

And yet she was merely a tool.

"They're sending a warning," I said to Jenn.

"Meaning what? That they'll stop at nothing?"

I checked the window to see the local traffic, to see how soon we should expect an ambulance in the Paris rush. "It means they don't know where she is." Their only goal had been to deepen Katarina's despair, for Katarina to read about the hanging in some back page of some trivial obituary.

"*Aux armes.* That's the last thing she said."

The ambulance would not be arriving in time to save her but I kept looking out the window for that help to come anyway, desperate to see either the cops or the paramedics, whichever came faster. What I saw were two passengers in a sedan pull up along alongside two particular pedestrians—making four men total—getting out, checking around, then walking directly toward the courtyard of our building.

They had the look.

"Jenn?"

"Yeah?"

"We've got a real problem."

# CHAPTER 66

"I need to hear you me out before you react to what I'm about to say, okay?" I spoke to my dear friend as quickly and calmly as I could. "There are some guys who arrived just now. Just hear me out. The . . . Look at me . . . I'm going to lure them away from you. I'm going to do this by circling around in a half-mile loop, okay? Half mile. Gimme exactly three minutes to get started. Then you quietly go out the back gate, you keep your face down, you go out—memorize this—you walk uphill north, stay in the thickest part of the tourist crowd, and go to the top of the Sacré-Coeur church to wait on the steps in the middle of it. Middle. In the crowd. Middle. We don't have time to debate this. I'll meet you there as soon as I lose them."

Either they tapped the phone line or the cops themselves were no longer to be trusted. One or the other.

Jenn seemed to understand it. She heard every word I said, processed it admirably, then nodded in somewhat-reluctant-but-dutiful coopera-tion. I went over to the front door. I stopped to listen downward, toward the courtyard, for the men. I had no idea what I'd do if they trapped *both* us up here. I had no gun, no bribe money, nothing potent enough to fend off four people. I turned around. I looked at her, realizing I might never see her again.

"There's . . . uh . . . There's something I need to . . . uh . . ." There was something I needed to tell her but felt ridiculous even thinking of it right now.

She gave me a confident, somber nod. Wide eyed. Willing to hear what I had to say.

"The files . . ." I held up the USB flash drive, backing away from my original thought. "It's better if it's on you."

She accepted it. She didn't hesitate. She's the queen of being practical. "*Aux armes* means 'start the war.'"

I headed down the stairs, got to street level, saw the men, and kept walking—the goal being to lure them away. I made sure they had me in sight, and after I turned the corner I yelled out, "Run! . . . RUN! . . ."

Toward nobody.

I yelled it down the street as if Jenn were two blocks ahead of me.

"Go, Jenn! . . . Run! . . ."

Then I ran ninety degrees away from that direction, taking a hard left, forcing the guys behind me to separate, one group following me, one group following a phantom. I should've taken a head count the moment I saw them split, verifying how many guys chose the ghost over me. I felt the wound in my shoulder opening up—I knew it would—all those hours of progress undone within seconds, but I'd gotten better at the overall game of squaring off against cold killers. After consecutive days of it, you evolve. I processed every detail around me now. I saw storefronts. Upcoming pedestrians crossing. Scooters. Options. Hazards. I ran efficiently. I knew the best recourse if I got captured would be to yell "Thief!" I knew where to find the biggest rock on the ground. I knew the easiest place to get a knife would be in the cooking aisle of a grocery store. I should've taken a head count, though. The whole point was to lure them away from Jenn and, having split them up, I had no idea if I'd cleared her a path. After five blocks I felt I was alone and turned back to look down the empty alley behind me, turning around again to find Hugo charging at me from the corner, making sure that this time I was absolutely blindsided with the solid metal pipe that he swung against my skull, knocking me to the asphalt, unconscious.

# CHAPTER 67

When I woke up, I had a hood over my head. It was translucent against the glare of a naked bulb above me. I could discern shapes moving around. Two males. There was very little being talked about between them. Mostly what I heard was my own breathing. They'd sat me in a chair and roped my hands behind me and were finishing up the knots that kept me anchored to the back strut. Once that binding was tight, they whispered several words to each other, then exited through what sounded like a metal door.

And everything went silent.

I waited a long time.

"Is . . . uh . . . anyone . . . uh . . .?" I spoke into a void.

I waited again.

"Hello?" I said. "Is anyone in this room?"

I had to assess my surroundings based solely on acoustics—my voice serving as a sort of probe. I had no sense of where I was. It smelled like damp dirt. I waited—I had nothing to do *but* wait—but where was Jenn? How badly had I messed this up? Was she in another room just like this one? Could they have hurt her? That's what starts to plague your conscience and it doesn't stop. That's what, without exaggeration, began destroying me from the inside out—the fact that I'd brought her into this, even handed her a hard drive with divisive content on it, and left her to fend for herself. Life gave me so many chances to leave her out of my pathetic trajectory and I'd dragged her downhill, for what? For what?! *What made you think you could take care of her, you selfish prick?* Hugo was alone when he ambushed me and that told me everything I didn't want to know—his crew was too smart for my sad trick and three of them stayed on site to surround Jenn. *How could you be so arrogant as to think you could win?* After what felt like an hour, one of the guys returned. Just one. He didn't say anything. He walked in front of me, eclipsing the light from the bulb for a moment, then went behind me, having only presented a shadow of himself, where he seemed to stay still for nearly an hour, then he came over and suddenly yanked off my hood, which scared the living shit out of me.

Right away I could see I was in a basement. Barren. No furniture. No boxes. Nothing on the walls. He tossed the hood somewhere behind us on what sounded like a workbench, then leaned against that workbench, nothing else happening for a few minutes until he opened a metal toolbox and rummaged through it until finding a moment to say what he had to say to me, which amounted to one sentence, one single sentence, the only three words he'd utter for the next five mind-numbing hours.

"Where is she?"

That was it.

Five hours. Just those words. Said once. I tried to answer him, of course. Over and over, I tried to answer him in various ways, guessing at every permutation of what he wanted. Where was she? I sat there laboring under the unending, self-inflicted, ever-widening avalanche of anguish. For anyone wanting to know how to induce madness in an insecure mind like my own, this is the formula: ask an unanswerable question, keep it short, stand behind your listener with a vague weapon, then let him deconstruct his entire universe until his brain floods itself with idiocies, like calculating the ridiculous physics of flipping his chair backward, up and backward, as if he could miraculously land on the strut and free himself to fight you.

"It's working on me, man," I said to him a half day into it. "I'm telling you, you got me going to dark places inside. If your goal was to fuck me up internally, I'm fucked up internally." I'd begun the downward spiral of unzipping my personal baggage. "Because you know how most people get to a point in life where they can declare admirably impressive shit, like they finally get to stand up to their asshole dad and all that? 'Dad, you can't slap me around anymore'? Took a stand? Well, me, I never had that. And I know you don't want to hear this but a month before I finally found the balls to resist him, he hid himself. You know where? In a coffin . . . In a *coffin* . . . out of reach . . . for all eternity. Guy bailed when I was seventeen. Hahaha, checkmate, son. So I lost. I never got to kick his teeth in. I am what I am today. The cog. Adam the Cog. I wouldn't dare to believe someone like me could outdo someone like you . . . meaning . . . you, sir, you won. You won, Mr. da Vinci. It's you, right? It's you behind me. You won hours ago. Just tell me what to do and I'll do it. You want me to fuck the girl over? I'll fuck the girl over. Just tell me how. Just say how I do it. Tell me how, right? I mean, JUST FUCKING *TELL ME WHAT YOU WANT!*" I was begging him to say something, to shout something—anything—beyond his one sentence—raising my voice loud enough to finally elicit an abrupt sentence from him that would delineate the rest of my natural-born life.

"You have sixty seconds," he said.

"What?"

He didn't repeat himself.

"What?"

I felt the world drop from beneath my feet.

"WAIT! WAIT! WAIT!"

I caved in and began to tell him everything about the young woman known as Katarina Haimovna from start to finish, from start to now, from the hotel fire to Mathilde hanging on the rafter, which left us with where we were now.

He didn't say anything right away. I'd finished my part and he let the whole thing just hover in the dank air between us, then came around to the front of my chair, where I saw his face for the first time.

"And what does she want?" he said.

The usher.

"You've gotten to know her in ways no one else has," he said. "You will have seen what her focus has been."

He was the usher from club. "You're the . . . You're the usher. You pulled me aside in the back room. In Amsterdam."

"What does she want?"

It was at this moment that I knew I was with Morgan da Vinci. Nothing made more sense. He was indeed the most ordinary man imaginable, the random guy you pass on the sidewalk, the man standing next to you in line at a supermarket, five-nine, dirty-blond hair, forty something, forgettable—and completely breaking his own protocol to let me see him, which meant the situation was at an impasse for him since—

"NO MORE GAMES!" he yelled, slamming the wrench across the top of my leg, doing it without warning, bringing it down like an atomic bomb, igniting in me the crescendo of a hundred stringed instruments screeching out the wrong notes. He had to have fractured my femur. He hit it that hard. I almost lost consciousness. And somehow the pain itself kept me alert enough to realize he was raising the wrench *again* and was preparing to hit me across the face.

"She's not hiding!" I rushed to tell him. "She's not hiding! She's not hiding! Katarina—she's here in Paris."

He stopped.

"She's not hiding," I said. "This is what you couldn't anticipate. This is why she's impossible to anticipate. She wants something that we can't calculate in her."

"Which is?"

"You heard me describe all the shit I went through with her, right? So you can believe me when I tell you she was never *actually* trying to hide from you, not lately, because in her world there's something bigger that she's chasing. Something much bigger than survival itself."

He didn't think my answer was enough. He raised the wrench again. I had to sell the rest of it, the entire thing, as fast as I could.

"I didn't think it made sense either until I realized you yourself don't know what she wants because that's just it, that's the entirety of it. Nothing she does makes sense to you, to me, to anyone, to anyone unless . . . *unless* . . . maybe . . . Here it is . . . *maybe* . . . it's not escape she wants. It's not escape. Think about it. She never thought your architect was you but she was going to his condo, why? Because he was your architect? Why? Why go to him?" I had to state the only answer that could work for him. "Because of what you're about to build. Because it's no coincidence that half of Europe is trying to close a multinational deal and she's at her most visible. She's not acting in self-defense. She's trying to undermine you. And I'll prove it. I'll prove it . . ." He had the wrench up. "BECAUSE WHY ARE YOU THE ONE STANDING IN FRONT OF ME?"

He stopped.

This stopped him.

This was his blank spot.

"Why you?" I said. "Why are you standing here doing your own dirty work?"

He didn't have an easy answer.

"You could've had anyone do it, anyone, but you took an unprecedented risk. You took it because, fuck, man, she's *winning*. And she knows it. Your people in your circle know it. They're nervous. Investors are nervous. Gerald Merck. Deutsche. Suisse. They're nervous. To get to her, you now have to compromise literally everything you value. Your own team said it: the scars around her neck—self-inflicted. And I'm now saying *why* would she do that? Because more important to her than anything else, I'm saying more important than her own life, is the *legend* of it."

It was the most desperate sales pitch of my entire existence. Pure bullshit, total speculation, completely grounded in the fact that I actually believed every word of it once I said it.

"Her legend," he said, repeating the words as a trial run on his tongue, and I think it might have had an impact. I think I now had him staring at me, needing a solution.

"So here's the deal . . . I can help you. I can help you lure her. She's dangerous to you because she has no predictable rules but I can get to her. I just need one thing first. I need something from you, okay? I just need you . . . to set Jennifer Graham . . . free. That's it. Jennifer. One life for another. A trade. Nothing else. And I'll help you."

I wasn't sure if he understood me.

"Okay?" I said.

"It is true . . . that you're going to help me."

"Yes."

"But I don't have Jennifer Graham."

"You . . .? You don't?"

"I never had her . . . I have no idea who *would* have her . . . because I don't give a shit about her. And now that this has been clarified, let's get started on the fucking first part of what you said."

# CHAPTER 68

They dragged me into a small rowboat. Maybe an hour later, maybe the same day—it was hard to tell. I'd passed out twice, with my head wound pulsing so bad I'd lost the flow of time entirely. All I knew was I was seated on one end of the hull with da Vinci on the other—facing me—neither of us saying anything as my coherence gradually returned—and we were being rowed by Hugo, who was positioned behind me, quietly paddling us through an underground water canal.

They didn't have Jenn.

Somebody got to her but if it wasn't one of these two or their henchmen, it could only be that the police arrived just as I left, yet I saw the timing of what took place behind me on that street, and any intervention on their part seemed geometrically impossible. My only hope was that she misunderstood what I said, fled the hallway in the wrong direction, and accidentally went out some kind of hidden exit. This was the *one* unlikely scenario I had to cling to because as absurd as it seemed, I needed to believe it happened.

If da Vinci was even telling the truth.

"Quite an extensive passageway," he said to me, breaking the silence about ten minutes after I'd woken up. "We'll soon be entering a network of rooms lined with fine tapestry and marble flooring—a fantastic structure I shall be calling the Theater of Purity. It was built to serve as the gateway to our Swan and, when ready, will be the site of a *very* pleasurable evening." He was talking in that same stilted style of speech he used when I first met him, apparently reinvigorated by his renewed confidence. "Hans Schering, good ol' Hans, found inspiration in the rear section of the Paris Opera House where the artists would enter. Do you know of it? The aesthetics are second to none."

"She won't come."

"Oh, no?"

"Not for me."

"Is that so? You don't think your calling out her name in severe pain will compel her?"

I shook my head.

He smiled. "Then it'll be a useful litmus test of where her little gambit has left us."

I didn't believe places like this existed—an underground river in the heart of Paris. I'd seen random photos of it over the years, but the concept always seemed too mythological, like local lore gone astray, like anything other than the coordinates of my future tomb. Da Vinci never took his eyes off me as he continued to study my predicament. I tried to stay perfectly still, not wanting him to wonder what I was working on mentally, which was using my peripheral vision to gauge the contour and depth of the tunnel.

"You think you know how I function," he said.

"Me?"

"How I operate."

"I-I don't."

"I can see you working it out in your head. You think you understand who I am." He was almost laughing at my uneasiness. "Come, now. A presumptuous individual such as yourself. I'm sure you've formulated your theories."

"Theories?" I didn't know what kind of answer would get me killed and what kind wouldn't, and didn't even know if it'd make any difference. "I think the Society is a tool . . . I think it's your tool . . . It gives you the chance to extort whoever comes through your velvet doorway. A CEO, a CFO, a COO. They begin to participate, thinking they're part of a secret brotherhood until they find out you've been gradually, quietly, going up to each of them, one by one, whispering in their ears the *price* of keeping things secret. Yet . . . if I had to guess . . . what people don't realize is that you *believe* what you preach. All the gender rhetoric you spewed out at me in the club—that wasn't just a commercial. You believed every word of it."

He kept studying me long after I stopped speaking.

"Fifty meters," said Hugo, tracking the distance to the next bend in the canal.

Our path through the water alternated between light and dark patches where the sunlight fell from the ceiling grates. At the far end you could see a posted sign that warned of contamination via contagious disease—obviously a lie printed by da Vinci's crew to deter visitors. They'd fenced off the area as a construction site, then sealed it up, taking no chances with the general public.

"Sir . . ." said Hugo, noticing something.

Da Vinci turned to look.

"The guard."

Hugo got out a shotgun as da Vinci strained to see the subject in question. I couldn't discern anything and neither could the two of them, and that was exactly the issue.

Their guard was missing.

All we could do was slowly float past the area where they apparently thought someone was supposed to be standing watch. It seemed unlikely to me that Katarina could topple a full-grown security guard—not because I doubted her fight-to-the-death mindset, but because the geography of the tunnel offered her no opportunity to surprise anyone. If she'd approached him along the footpath that ran parallel to our route, which was the only path here, she would've had to walk directly at him, at the guard, in plain view for over a hundred yards.

"Up ahead," said Hugo.

We saw a corpse beyond the gate, slumped in the shadows.

"Yes," said da Vinci. "We must be close."

Hugo guided the boat to the edge of a paved walkway that led past a chain-link fence. He had his gun pointed in my direction as he motioned for me to climb out and head for the gate. "Move now, slowly."

If I were going to have a chance to injure him, Hugo, seriously injure him, I'd have to keep him distracted. On a wall-mounted electronic keypad he entered an extensive numeric code while da Vinci looked over at me, apparently wondering if I thought she could've bypassed a series of digits like that.

"She could've," I responded. "She was alone with your architect, torturing him for twenty-four hours before watching him die—if you really think there's anything here she doesn't know."

"So I extort my members," said da Vinci. "That's your theory?"

"That's . . . a guess."

"A bit simplistic, isn't it?"

"Maybe."

"Yet you didn't sound uncertain."

"You didn't say I was wrong."

Hugo led us around the chain-link fence, where the three of us walked past construction scaffolding, then down some steps into what would soon become a lavish theater lobby. Da Vinci's sequel. The Theater of Purity. Surreal. Stunning. Nearly finished. A replication of the rear lobby of the Paris Opera House. There were many random things built in the caves under the city but this one defied every standard. Once we were down to floor level, we could no longer see across the chamber because the furniture had been stacked in a temporary pile in the middle. That's when da Vinci readied his weapon, a hunting rifle, aiming it directly into the vast darkness, as he silently proceeded along the marble.

"You're not wrong," he said to me. He was ready to eviscerate this woman, to punish her, bone by bone, organ by organ, salivating at the prospect of doing so—you could smell the bloodlust. "I very much *enjoy* my work."

"Call to her," Hugo whispered to me.

Call to her, yes. I needed to figure out just how to say it in order—

"*Call to her!*" He grabbed my shoulder with his thumb pressing into my wound, igniting yet another ungodly pain in me for several unending seconds before finally letting go. *"And make it real."*

I swallowed the lump in my throat. I closed my eyes.

"KATARINA!" I called out loudly enough to echo in eight different directions, reverberating along the high ceiling as well as the six smaller tunnels—three on each side—all leading to future rape rooms—plus the staircase we descended behind us, plus the main tunnel up ahead beyond the pile of benches. "KATARINA! . . . IT'S ME! . . . ADAM!"

Both men scrutinized the ensuing stillness while Hugo held his gun against my spine. As much as his boss loathed the female in this equation, I could tell that his private goal—Hugo's—was to kill me as indulgently as possible. I'd been sizing up my odds—how long I could keep him in a fistfight knowing that he was a trained killer. He must've triumphed in at least a dozen mortal confrontations prior to ours, right? If I could somehow engage him for maybe, let's say, four minutes of combat, I'd be giving Katarina a viable chance to do what she could do.

Da Vinci scanned the room.

We waited. Listening.

An eternity.

Just get her the chance, I told myself. Four minutes. My heart was already racing. I doubted she was here, but I also doubted she *wasn't*.

"Call again," whispered Hugo, this time jabbing his gun directly into my wound so that I fell forward. "Tell her you're alone. And make her believe you."

I needed several breaths to recover before I could push myself back up. This was it. Right here. Right now. I was going to shout to her who exactly was in the room along with the fact that they had a shotgun, extra shells, a rifle, possibly knives, where they stood, where they faced, and how they arrived. It'd be my last strategic contribution to her mission.

I reared my head back to yell those final words as loudly as I could. "KA—!"

But before I could complete the first syllable, there was an audible crack of wood on the far side of the pile, which we all three heard. Something deliberate. Not a rodent scampering away, not a young lady's clumsiness—but a loud, authoritative, deliberate crack, followed by a splintering sound, followed by a dim, orange light, followed by what we'd soon understand to be the flames of Katarina Haimovna's final inferno.

# CHAPTER 69

She'd set fire to the walls. We wouldn't know it at first. We'd only see the glow from the opposite side of the chamber once it fully bloomed, once its irreversible reality had been set in motion. Da Vinci moved to the side to try see beyond the pile of furniture.

"Is that . . .?" he said.

"It's . . ." yelled Hugo. "IT'S ON FIRE!"

We looked around, all three of us—the two men frantically advancing forward while I happened, just happened, to glance back in the other direction and see her, Katarina, already behind us. She was carrying one of the buckets from the stack of supplies—paint thinner, maybe—heaving a sloshing quantity onto the area we'd just passed through. Hugo saw that I noticed something, turned around, and immediately aimed his shotgun at her.

"There she is!" He pulled the trigger—bam—just a split second after I'd grabbed his muzzle, making him miss.

I'd shoved the barrel upward just as he fired. Katarina ran as da Vinci then chased her, both of them skirting the edge of the massive room in a footrace—her chance to flee toward the main tunnel while I kept my grip on Hugo's gun, wrangling it with both of my hands fully committed to the act, squaring up with him, getting right up in his face. "Four minutes," I said out loud, battling to gain ground and nearly overtaking him until he pushed me off, shoving me backward. He immediately spun around, trying to bludgeon me but missing because I'd traveled too far backward. He now had enough room between us to get a dominant grip on his weapon and aim it directly at me, point-blank, just as I swung up at him, having lunged forward, to punch him in the throat.

And I took him down with one hit.

I struck him so hard I felt his interior flesh crumple against my fist—larynx, cartilage, whatever was in there—crunching in a way you wouldn't think possible. He never saw it coming—what'd been simmering in me for hours, years, decades, the pent-up rage of an undetonated man. Hugo's head fell forward and his legs buckled.

With the flames from the furniture advancing, I had to duck to get to safety while his body caught fire behind me. I ran for the farthest tunnel, heading to where Katarina disappeared, running as hard as I could, unsure how I'd navigate the corners of da Vinci's demented theater in total darkness, only to arrive and find it fully illuminated by flames and on the verge of collapse.

Still under construction, the gilded ceiling had been braced with wooden beams, which were now crumbling in the heat, falling over in a mangled monstrosity that blocked the main tunnel like a prison gate. I came to a halt at the edge of a passage, where, beyond this barrier, a path sloped up into the darkness. I pulled as hard as I could on the bars of the fallen scaffolding to get in there, not caring how hot the metal was, pulling with everything I had. Crouched. Holding it. Tugging at it. Straining. Crouching lower. Which was when da Vinci came hurtling from the shadowy depths of the tunnel, directly toward my face. He'd lunged at the barrier itself, apparently trying to break through to return to my side, ramming his head through the small gap between bars, gasping for air, colliding with my chin and knocking me on my back. He was different now—his clothes blackened and charred at the fringes—face sweaty and red. He was frantically trying to remove the obstacle between us. Trying. Desperately. Futilely. Quickly realizing his only hope would be to grab my shin and hold me with him, forcing me to assist him just to get myself free.

I didn't struggle against it. I grabbed his shoulders and pulled him *toward* me as hard as I could so that his head, inch by inch, slowly moved farther through the narrow opening between bars, so that his trachea began to mash down on the crossbar farther and farther. I was pinning him with his own momentum. To asphyxiate him. To end him. A boy choking the drunken patriarch. He, of course, fully reversed his effort, understanding what I'd begun to do, while I kept pulling and pulling and pulling, shifting my legs to then leg press against the bars, using every part of what I had in me to choke him, gradually feeling his strength give way, his face growing woozy, until I finally felt his whole body cease to resist anything at all, and just as he was about to pass out completely, he was stolen from me.

Katarina. I never saw her coming. From the opposite side of the barrier, from his side, she'd crawled forth from the darkness like a fiend of the underworld to grab his torso and torque him away from me, pulling him backward until the bastard tumbled to their side of the cage.

She'd won.

She'd taken him from me.

"What're you doing?!" I yelled.

She had her limp trophy. "The . . . stairs . . ."

"I had him. What're you doing?!" I didn't stay down on the ground. "Let's lift the other end to get you out." I got up and rushed to the other end of the scaffolding to move it. "You can slip through. C'mon."

"The stairs . . ." she repeated, totally out of breath. "At the edge . . . You don't have time. You go through the chamber door on the side of the stairs . . . and get to the surface."

I pointed to the tunnel behind her. "That's a dead end behind you. That leads to one of the bedrooms where there *is no exit* . . . built with no . . . no poss . . . no possible . . . way of . . ."

I saw the reality.

I saw it written within her. The flames were swelling. In a matter of seconds the fire would consume the entrance to her passageway, sealing it shut for good.

"I'm where I need to be," she said.

"No."

"You're a good person, Adam."

"No, no, no, I'M NOT LEAVING WITHOUT YOU!"

She pulled da Vinci backward, dragging him into the darkness.

I continued shouting for her to come with me but it was useless. She'd foreseen a choice like this long ago. I tugged on the bars, violently shaking them in a frenzy, yelling her name over and over, refusing to accept that she'd disappeared, then, maniacally determined to save her, I hurried out through the chamber door. If I could make it to street level fast enough, I could get to the outside wall of the bedroom she'd be in, wherever the hell it was, and crack its stupid, special window open. I raced through the burning wreckage, through the Armageddon, through the pieces falling down in flames to find one of the doors on the side of the grand staircase and barge through it, praying it led to whatever place they were calling The Swan. My new tunnel led me upward, east then north, forcing me to return west, then south to recover lost ground, wasting precious seconds I didn't have. Arriving at the exit, I kicked and kicked and kicked at the metal door handle until the door broke open into a nondescript stairwell that fed into a random street. I sprinted up those steps out onto rue de Faubourg du Temple, heading to the massive public square known as Place de la République, the one place where I'd find The Swan. Right in the middle of the heart of Paris.

Bronze. Bold. The size of a city bus. It was a temporary piece of ancient-modern art erected next to the one permanent fixture out here, the statue of Marianne the Goddess of Liberty, who was unwittingly leading the charge for the massive bird behind her—da Vinci's bird—turning her back on the outstretched wings that towered thirty feet over the swarms of people. And there were *a lot* of people.

I ran to the front of the base, where it was immersed in a large fountain, lined with one-way mirrors. This is where I had to attack.

"Break it!" I yelled to anyone within earshot.

I'd torn through the herds of tourists, shoving someone into the water just to get myself through the crowd. Nobody understood. I jumped over the rim of the fountain and into the basin, needing something, anything. The only tool around me was a skateboard, so I yanked it out of a kid's hands and started to swing it at the mirrored walls with all my might, just utterly pounding the glass, wham, wham, wham, wham, one slam after another, trying to shatter the mirror, trying to get even a hint of a dent.

Nothing. It was bulletproof. People were watching me but I was aware of no one. I must've hit the mirror a hundred times before the police finally grabbed me—two roving officers—as I tried to tell them, "*Dans l'intérior!*" Pointing to the interior. "She's inside! You understand? Girl! Inside! Girl! *Elle est là!*" Eliciting only their judgments of lunacy. They pulled me off the wall and forced me to my knees, forcing me down into the fountain water, so that all I would see in front of me was the three of us in the reflection, then they pushed me forward to subdue me, inadvertently pushing me closer to the glass, where I would see nothing but my own face as I called her name, feeling every possible emotion at once. Pain. Regret. Despair. Betrayal. Sorrow. Rage. Adoration. Pride. Shame. Love. Anger. "She's in there!" I yelled. "You get it?!"

And, most of all, admiration.

"Katarina!"

She was admired.

"*Arrête!*" said the cop.

"She's here."

"*ARRÊTE! CALME TOI!*" They pulled me back from the glass, yelling at me to stop struggling, restraining the tantrum of a grown boy punching nothing but shadows.

At the other end of the statue, at the front end, the crowd had started to delight in the aria of the grand bird. A noise had begun. *The* noise. Da Vinci's winged demon was starting to trumpet its song, with every pipe and tube now channeling what were da Vinci's own screams. His alone. I could hear him crying out within the melodic distortion as various people around me smiled. As children giggled. As mothers pointed. It was sickly surreal. On even the most average day in Place de la République, you have street performers and food vendors and music and dancing and street soccer and couples kissing and old folks strolling—hundreds and hundreds of people representing every fragment of the population—and today those fragments were uniting to delight in the bellows of hell itself. Within days of this event, the coroner's report would tell us that Morgan da Vinci died pressed up against the interior pane of a scalding-hot window within the breast of this statue, his face literally having melted off. It'd tell us that Katarina had held him there, that both of them were burned alive, that, based on my own statement, only a male voice was discernible, crying out in pain. Not a female's. Not hers. *Not* hers. She didn't surrender a single tear. Within thirty minutes of his demise, I'd find myself cuffed in front of my dear Detective Élodie Michel. The two patrolmen had summoned her from her office. I'd immediately tell her there was a fire below the entrance of Canal Saint-Martin and that within this fire she'd find exactly what I'd been trying to convince her of—that a number of associates of mine were involved in very bad behavior. I'd tell her how I'd spent the final hour prior to her arrival. I'd give her a minute by minute account: I was in the fountain, the crowd was applauding as The Swan trumpeted its final note, reverberating all the way to the edge of the statue of Marianne the Goddess of Liberty, delivering a crescendo that no one, not even the founding father himself, would've foreseen, and though I continued to search that mirror for any trace of our legendary friend, I saw only my own hand reaching for what was no longer there.

# EPILOGUE

**D**etective Élodie Michel closed a thick manila folder, took off her glasses, rubbed her nose in exasperation, and leaned back in a creaky government chair. She was sitting across from me at an ordinary table in an ordinary room in the most extraordinary of buildings—36 quai des Orfèvres, the former headquarters of Paris's criminal investigation teams—no longer being used by any law enforcement department except for one specific unit.

"This is the report you wish to file?" she said.

BRI. Her unit.

"This is it," I said.

She worked with the Organized Crime division. They'd had me incarcerated for six days and six hours, which felt like two and half lifetimes. Bizarre thoughts visit your mind when you're in a jail cell—everything from self-loathing to self-slaughter to self-aggrandizing to self-improvement—yet one thing became clear to me over that span. I wasn't the revolutionary here. I was the messenger. I was the scribe.

I'd yielded to a strange sense of serenity this week, having witnessed what I witnessed. The volume gets turned down on the minutia in life—that's the good part. The minutia still governs the world around you—that's the sting. My first contact with Jennifer K. Graham, my first indication that she was okay—breathing, alive, that she had, y'know, a pulse—involved the pile of papers now stacked on the table in front of me in that thick folder. Jenn had kept possession of the USB drive, managing to retain it despite being taken into custody by Paris police—that indeed was her fate back in the eighteenth arrondissement. She'd gotten arrested and, days later—thankfully cleared—having collated, organized, annotated, then printed out this massive clump of pages, she handed me my opus.

The detective picked up the top sheet and read it aloud one last time. "I, Adam L. Macias, hereby submit the following receipts, messages, and worksheets as evidence that Euro Mutual Bank, in collaboration with Western Finance Bank in collaboration with Deutsche-Zurich in collaboration with an individual named Morgan da Vinci, also known as Morgan Voltaire, also known as Archimedes, also known as the Eastern Minister, was complicit in illegal prostitution, human trafficking, and possibly extortion."

Numerous people were named with varying degrees of culpability, including Evan Goldman, Gerald Merck, Jordi Carreras, and Hans Schering, none of whom would get splashed across the headlines the way I'd wanted but it was a crack in the dam. Even Trevor's name appeared in my report several times. Nikos never participated, bless his heart—actually having no idea how he "overslept" and missed the party, calling me on the phone several times to apologize for it. Jenn argued with me for hours last night for the right to sign her name on this introductory letter. I'd refused—unwilling to implicate her in my legal whirlpool. She argued. I argued. Her return to my life was all that mattered to me now. Fortunately, her side of the equation was simple enough and she was in and out of jail in a matter of days. For me, it'd take *weeks* for us to find the right loopholes to extricate me from the charges and, at long last, finally, earn the right to go home.

"As of now you would be free to go," said the detective.

I of course decided to throw a monkey wrench in this.

"I understand," I said. I leaned forward to push the folder an inch closer to her. A small gesture. Symbolic.

"You do realize what giving me something like this will lead to?" She knew it was coming. "You would be officially on your way home but in submitting this you're incriminating yourself."

"I understand."

"And that's not the worst part."

With the European economic stimulus package finalized, the amount of people who'd would upset by this had multiplied by a hundred.

"You're about to poke a stick at some very powerful people," she said.

"Those are the best ones to poke, right?"

"They're good at making the world focus on the wrong person."

"We'll see."

She tried one more time to talk me out of it but she was up against the inertia of a man who believed he had a debt to repay. She exhaled like a disappointed aunt, then closed the folder and looked at her watch. "Okay . . . at 14:12 . . . I hereby state that you, Adam Macias, are required to remain in the legal custody of the sovereign nation of France under Article 225-4-9 of the French Penal Code." We stood up and shook hands. She told me the next step was for me to return to jail within twenty-four hours, which was going to be nice timing because I had a chance to do the one thing I really needed to do.

Take Jenn to the airport.

That's how this would go down. Jenn and I agreed that she'd wait for me at the railing of the Saint-Michel bridge.

"Well . . .?" she'd say upon seeing me.

And I'd smile. And I'd stay quiet.

"Well . . .?!" she'd say again, dying to receive the update. "Did you do it?"

I'd keep smiling.

"Wow," she'd say. "You just . . . You . . . Wow."

That's how I imagined it and that's mostly how it went. To whatever degree she'd secretly hoped I'd change my mind, she appreciated why I didn't.

"I made phone calls," she said. "A *lot*. So I have two top international lawyers from DC involved. Greg's one of them. He's the one who's visiting you Wednesday. We talked about that. His fee is astronomical but, again, I keep saying it, I keep hoping you'll change your mind and say yes: Nikos wants to cover it. He likes you. He'd like to be part of this." She stopped walking. "I don't want to leave."

"Jenn."

"I don't want to leave France."

She was facing me directly at this point and there was a lot going on in the silence between us. She looked at her watch as we started walking again. "Although . . . *Although* . . . I mean, I could just let myself be late for the first boarding call so we could stroll the Seine for an hour then . . . y'know . . . accidentally catch a train to Versailles where you buy me lunch . . . and go down on one knee . . . and pull out a five-karat rock and tell me how you've been in love with me for years and years and propose in front of the local staff, who start to applaud but immediately stop when they see me hesitate but immediately re-applaud after I tell you I require a year of mature behavior from you to earn a yes from me, and to celebrate this display of my strength I let you lead us to the far end of the Versailles garden where you take me behind a bush and fuck me senseless. I could just do that."

She didn't want to leave today. She didn't want to leave at all.

"Five karats?" I said.

"I'm a hundred percent kidding. Calm down. About all of that. I can't stay with you today. I get too stressed out if I'm even a split second late for a boarding call. So . . . yeah."

I stopped walking. I looked at her.

"Relax," she said. "Seriously. I was, like, ninety-nine percent kidding."

She hugged me. For a very long time. Behind her was Notre Dame, towering across the river from the Hôtel de Ville just down the street from Place de la République, where The Swan had stood, where local women both young and old had begun to lay flowers for a rumor of the *legend* of what had happened.

"You mean more to me than you know."

"Seriously, relax," she said. "Don't be all weird. I was like seventy percent kidding."

"Can I tell you something?"

"About?"

I kept smiling.

"About what?" she said. "Why are you looking at me like that? About what? About us?"

"Maybe."

"You're *asking* me if you can tell me?"

"I'm . . ."

"Instead of just telling me?!"

"I mean . . ."

"Why don't you actually tell me what you have to tell me and after you tell me, I'll tell you if you should've told me?"

"Okay."

"That's my minimum, Adam Macias who is sometimes aggravating but always sincere. You take ownership."

"Okay."

"Deal?"

"Deal." I cleared my throat.

"Okay, then . . . say what you have to say."

"Okay."

"And be very convincing."

## THE END